VAULT OF GLASS

CANDACE ROBINSON

For Nate and Arwen,

We make up the ultimate Three Musketeers

PROLOGUE

Overwhelmed with boredom, Vale stared down at his fingernails. He could only spend so much time tormenting those he encountered in the afterlife. When his work was complete in making them as miserable as possible, he found himself needing to search for new prey.

The fire beside him flickered and gave off a comforting heat. To Vale, it felt like a warm blanket against his cool skin. He hummed a melody to himself as the fire crackled, accompanied by a chorus of screams that continued to grow more intensely.

Vale should have felt something, yet he was incapable of compassion. It made his torture of others necessary, and with no complete spectrum of true emotion, their agony provided him with a sick sort of pleasure. It was the only real feeling he had ever truly known.

He picked at his nails a little longer with a sharp instrument until they were back to their pristine condition. The one thing he couldn't tolerate was the filth and grime that built up under his nails. One might consider this an oddity. After all, his experiments usually ended up being the cause of his distress.

Studying his nails one more time, Vale set the tool down

next to a row full of other torturous devices—giving him another thrill. When so many of his experiments resulted in such beautiful messes, he could forgive himself the lapse in hygiene.

Rows of cages filled with useless souls lined the walls of his domain. They would help him to crush the mortal lives he needed to flood the earth. After the time he had spent in his dark place, he grew tired of tormenting the ones who "deserved" it—he wanted them all.

The time had finally come to bring down humanity—he wished it could be as simple as a snap of his fingers. Vale didn't like to do things the easy way, though. No, he liked to do things the way that brought him the most pleasure. This time he was going to be known as Quinsey Wolfe. This time he would make sure the world ended in flames while orchestrating its demise and rebirth. There must be a space between his underworld and the human world, where the new souls could become immortal with real power. It would take time, but he would build this place. Then, he could discover the ones he truly wanted. Hearts would surrender, souls would suffer, and at the end of it all—he would watch it burn. From the ashes of its undoing, Vale would recreate it all in his image.

ONE

The mirror was a foggy mess as Perrie stepped out of her, literally, five-minute shower. She'd let her damn alarm continue to go off when she should've woken up right away, so that meant less shower time. With hurried motions, she drew a flower—a weepy-looking daisy, to be exact—on the glass.

Perrie's mom used to do this together with her when she was younger. It was before her mom ran off several years ago with another man, to another state, and never spoke to Perrie's dad or her again. For some strange reason Perrie upheld this so-called mirror-drawing tradition of theirs—possibly to remember something that used to be different.

The one thing her mom left her was her maiden name as Perrie's first name, yet it defeated the whole purpose since she spelled Perrie with an "ie" instead of a "y." Perrie preferred the spelling how it was, that way she was connected to her mom as little as possible.

"Dad!" Perrie yelled.

After throwing on a pair of jeans and an old Queen band tee, Perrie rushed down the hallway. Sometimes she could catch him before he left for work, but he was already gone.

In the center of the table rested a red velvet cupcake and a note beside it. *Have a good day at school! Happy Eighteenth Birthday!* A grin spread across her face.

Since Perrie's mom left, she'd told herself over and over not to care, but she knew her dad still did. There was a picture of them together on his bedside table from when they were maybe sixteen and high school sweethearts. Her mom was looking off to the side laughing, genuinely amused, while her dad was staring at her with such an expression of love and admiration. It used to make Perrie's heart skip, but not anymore.

Perrie knew what that kind of love felt like, and she'd missed it for the past six months. She tossed those feelings of that particular guy into her personal, little trashcan inside her head—almost completely hidden away.

Grabbing a small bowl for her breakfast from the cabinet, she padded over to the pantry where there were at least ten varieties of cereal to choose from. Her dad couldn't get over her cereal-stocking obsession. But she couldn't control how the different sugary shapes on the covers called to her. *What else can I say?*

Biting her lip, she decided to go for the bag containing only colorful marshmallows—no healthiness included.

As she reached for the cereal, feeling like Willy Wonka, a sudden poke came at her shoulder. Releasing a squeak, she flailed in her panic, effectively sweeping her bowl off the countertop. Then she thanked all the fish in the sea that it was plastic as it hit the floor with a *thump-thump.*

Perrie's back smacked hard against the granite countertop when she flipped around to face the intruder. Maisie, her best friend and cousin, stood a few feet away, smirking. Perrie rolled her eyes. Maisie just loved to scare the living daylights out of her when Perrie least anticipated these situations. It wasn't like this hadn't happened before. Odds were, she should've expected this. Maisie lived next door and they'd been playing at carpool for as long as Perrie could remember.

Maisie grinned from ear to ear while Perrie rubbed her stinging arm. Her cousin's one, bright-blue eye twinkled with mischievous intent. The other eye, which Perrie was sure contained a twin expression, was safely hidden behind an eye patch. Maisie usually pulled her long black hair away from her face to highlight that one accessory, but her locks relaxed around her warm brown skin today.

When Perrie's mom left, Aunt Krista offered up the house she owned next door. The tenants had recently moved out, so she'd asked her brother—Perrie's dad—if he wanted to rent the place. Ever since then, Aunt Krista had been more of a mom to Perrie than her birth mother ever was.

"One day, you'll have it coming, Maisie Jaser." Perrie cocked her head and fought a smile. Despite being an adult now, she was still determined to best her cousin at least once in her life. "I do have a key to your house, you know."

"You've been saying this pretty much forever, and I'm still waiting," Maisie said while laughing. She brushed a hand against her latest hot pink eye patch, where yellow stars and a moon were sewn onto its diamond shape.

Perrie motioned at the newest addition to Maisie's two-year-long parade of endless eye patches. "What's going on with this one?"

Maisie scrunched up her nose as if she was thinking incredibly hard about this. "So, I was in the mood for a night sky, but I wanted the sky to be pink because black is, well, you know?"

Perrie arched a brow. "Well, no, I don't know."

"Oh, you know." Maisie shrugged. "It's just such a dark color sometimes."

"You also realize you're still not blind, right?"

Her smile grew even wider. "I know, but I have to show support to those who only have the one eye." She pointed her index finger at the patch like she was actually missing the damn eye.

Ever since she started reading books about characters who wear eye patches, Maisie had been on this kick. She even started an online store where she'd sold quite a few. Perrie wasn't sure if these people legitimately needed an eye patch, or if they were using them for costumes, but either way, the accessories could make any outfit stand out.

If Perrie needed a patch, she would wear the shit out of the ones Maisie created. She still didn't get why Maisie wore an eye patch *all* the time, but whatever—it was her quirk.

"You keep showing that support." Picking up the bowl from the floor, Perrie tossed it in the sink. There wasn't time left to eat cereal, so she grabbed two granola bars out of the pantry and threw one baseball style to Maisie, who easily caught it. Perrie had to admit, her cousin still had remarkable reflexes with only one eye.

At the table, a small green box sitting beside the salt and pepper shakers drew Perrie's attention. Maisie must've set it there before sneaking up on her.

"What's in the box?" As Perrie started toward the table, Maisie flung past her to the gift and lifted it.

"Happy Birthday!" she yelled, thrusting the gift at her.

Perrie plucked it up just before Maisie whipped out a tiny yellow noisemaker from her pocket and blew loudly. The screeching sound caused Perrie to grit her teeth, while Maisie was panting as if she'd run a marathon. Perrie didn't receive a lot of gifts for her birthday, so she always anticipated Maisie's, even if they could be on the strange side.

"Is it another wood chip creation like the lion you made me that one year?" Perrie asked. Several years back, Maisie's parents were going to clear out their flower beds and replace the old with rubber mulch. Maisie objected and found a way to repurpose the mulch for her crafts. The one she'd made for Perrie looked just like a lion and still sat on her bookshelf.

"No, my parents are still all about the rubber mulch."

"Too bad," Perrie said as she inspected the dark green box, wrapped in a delicate, yet vivid green bow of a different hue. She peeled it open slowly, first removing the ribbon then the lid.

Tucked inside was a banana-yellow eye patch. Upon closer examination, there was an image of a roaring lion on the front. She could tell Maisie had stitched it herself using fur-like pieces surrounding the outer edges to create its mane. It was beautiful, and Maisie knew how Perrie had a slight decorating obsession with the fierce beasts.

Gently, she set the patch aside and pulled another gift from the box. It was another lion, though this one smaller. This lion was crafted with twigs, then hand-painted with a miraculous amount of detail, and washed in bright greens, hot pinks, and brilliant blues. Perrie didn't know how Maisie had managed to blend the colors together so artfully.

She envied those skills.

Tears gathered on her lashes, knowing how much time and effort Maisie had put into these gifts for her. Perrie tugged her into an awkward but perfect hug. "Thanks so much. These gifts are everything."

Maisie leaned back and locked her gaze with Perrie, her expression serious. "Are you going to wear the patch now?"

Snorting, Perrie shook her head. "No, but you know what? I'll wear it tonight, just for you."

Suddenly remembering the time, Perrie booked it for her room and shoved a pair of black boots on. She took one last look at herself in the mirror hanging on the back of her door, before pulling her brown hair into a low ponytail. She didn't have time to do anything exciting with it, and it wasn't like she would anyway—that would take effort. Besides appearing a little tired, her chestnut-colored eyes were a little lighter this morning. *It's a step up from a zombie, so it works.*

"Perrie! Hurry the heck up!" Maisie shouted.

Blowing out a breath, she grabbed her backpack and

coveted cello from the floor beside her desk chair. With the combination of a heavy backpack and even heavier cello case, she was guaranteed to have a bad back by the time she reached twenty. A practical person would have dropped the cello, but not her. She'd been obsessively playing the instrument since sixth grade. After her mom left, playing music was her escape, her healing process.

"Come on, Perrie. We need to get going." Maisie was already standing on the porch, holding the door wide open when Perrie came bounding out down the hall.

They piled into Maisie's car, and Perrie relaxed in the seat, munching on the granola bar. Maisie finished chewing hers and ditched the granola wrapper, while Perrie had barely taken one full bite. With that kind of speed, she bet her cousin could win an eating contest … if she didn't choke first.

"So, did you hear there's another person missing?" Maisie asked as she turned down the next road.

Perrie's lips parted as she met her stare. "No. Is it someone we know?"

"No. I don't think so. His name's Ben Johnston. He's a twenty-three-year-old from the University," Maisie answered while chewing on her left thumbnail, flipping her gaze back to the odometer to check her speed.

There were two major things Perrie knew about Maisie, one being that she absolutely had to go the *exact* speed limit. It didn't matter where she was, she kept to one speed at a time. Second, she had the habit of chewing on her nail when there was a riddle she needed to figure out, or a puzzle she wanted to slide the last piece into.

Leaning her arm against the car door, Perrie rested her chin on her hand. She scanned through the people she knew from memory to see if she recognized the name from anywhere. It wasn't a long list of names either. "Yeah, I don't recognize the name, but I don't remember many people who graduated before us besides the ones I was in Orchestra with."

Lately, strange things had been happening in her neck of the woods. Not that Deer Park had many wooded areas... But a few months ago, there had been an increase in disappearances in the city, and even more so over the last few weeks. Ben Johnston was another name and face to add to that list. The local police department had been investigating, but they *claimed* there was no clear answer. No predictable method or motivation, and the victims' ages and genders all varied. Thankfully though, no one she knew personally had gone missing, so it just made it seem less real.

Despite her own calm, her dad, on the other hand, was a worried mess. Perrie's midnight curfew, as well as Maisie's, had been cut back. It wasn't like they had anything to do to stay out that late for anyway, but it was still a blow to their potential social lives. The last time she'd stayed out late was a month ago when her dad and Aunt Krista extended their curfew for prom.

Perrie hadn't been in the mood to go to the dance at first, but Maisie bugged her about it endlessly. Even with offers from a couple of guys and girls, Maisie politely shot them down and convinced Perrie to go with her instead.

Maisie rubbed at her chin, and Perrie could sense her detective skills itching to come out. *Hell, mine are, too.*

"Maybe we could question friends or family who know these missing people?" Maisie asked. "Nothing is getting done here."

"I'm not sure that would go over well, even if you did have a badge. One day you'll have plenty of time to solve any crime you want."

"Yeah, I guess you're right about that." Maisie pulled into the parking lot of the school, managing to find a good spot right away.

Maisie sighed, and Perrie could tell she was still thinking about the missing people. Her cousin had once told her she wanted to pursue a career in fashion design when college started, but these days she seemed to be leaning more toward lead detective.

Perrie was an official adult according to "society," but it didn't feel like much had changed. That was probably because high school still had a few weeks left and she didn't have a good job. Hell, she couldn't even find a part-time job. But she was also still figuring out what college classes to take in the fall, as well as what career she wanted. Apparently, the college she'd been looking at didn't offer miming as a major, which she would be all over. She'd even find it useful wearing one of Maisie's patches while working her hands across an imaginary wall. But seriously, the only thing she had at the moment was an orchestra scholarship.

I have the rest of my life to figure things out though, right?

TWO

Opening the car door, Perrie threw her heavy backpack over her shoulder and grabbed her cello out of the trunk. A wave of mixed emotions flew through her, and she just knew it wasn't going to be a shit day.

As they headed toward the school, with her hands thrashing all over the place, Maisie asked, "Are we going to the horror film festival? It's next month!"

"Hell yeah, I'm all over it. I think the guy who plays Pinhead is supposed to be one of the guests there. If only some of the classic horror greats were still alive."

Maisie's hands continued to thrash ridiculously. "I know, right? Boris Karloff is practically my baby."

Vincent Price would be Perrie's.

When they finally breezed into the school, Perrie made the mistake of turning her head away from Maisie. Her smile and laughter vanished. The first bell hadn't even rang yet and she already spotted the jerk.

Neven Lee. Formerly known as "Nev." Once her Nev. Then he'd ripped her heart into a thousand tiny pieces, cutting those little morsels even smaller before lighting them all on fire—until they were nothing but ashes.

Neven stood off to the side with his black hair overgrown and shaggy, his warm brown eyes catching hers. He tried to give her a close-lipped smile and Perrie turned her head away, but not as quickly as she should've.

Maisie's eye followed the remnants of Perrie's gaze. "Just ignore him. We're almost done with school, and then you won't have to see him again."

Her cousin was being sympathetic, but Perrie knew she still missed him. She never actually told Maisie she couldn't talk to him. But Maisie felt just about as betrayed as Perrie did, and she wanted so badly to scrub that part of her brain clean to forget about him. It had been six months. Six whole months since her heart had been left for dead. She was being overly dramatic, but she didn't care.

"Easier said than done." Perrie turned her head one more time, noticing Neven walking toward them. *Damn.* Maisie scratched the side of her face. Then she looked at the ceiling and off to the side, seeming not to know exactly what to do.

Forget Maisie. Perrie needed to get out of there. Her surroundings offered no escape, and she was completely rooted in place. All her nerve endings lit up, and a slight panic formed in her chest as his large hand delicately enclosed her bicep.

"Happy birthday, Perrie," Neven said hesitantly.

She yanked her arm out of his grasp, as if his touch would melt her skin away. "Don't touch me." Her voice was just a whisper.

Hurt radiated across Neven's face, as it always did when she lashed out at him. For the first two months after she'd stopped speaking to him, he tried every single day to talk to her. Then it turned into every week, then every month, and then he didn't try anymore. *Until today.*

He never stopped looking at Perrie in school, though. It was almost as if he was waiting for her to approach him. That would never happen, and he could stay being an asshole for all she cared. *Yes, I believe asshole is still the correct word at this moment.*

Like always, she had to crane her neck to see his tall hovering form. "Don't give me that look, Nev. It isn't going to do you much good. And don't expect me to feel sorry for you."

He had the nerve to smile a wide grin, displaying each and every annoyingly perfect tooth. "You called me Nev. Not 'Neven' like you have been."

Flexing her fingers at her sides, she brought them to her palms and dug them finger by finger into a fist. She wanted to punch him—*hard*. But she didn't. She couldn't because she still saw a friend in his face, and she shut that thought down fast.

"Neven," she said through gritted teeth. "Leave me alone. I'll never forgive you."

He scowled, frustration written in his expression. He ran his hands through his hair and grabbed it like he wanted to rip it out—most likely to throw the strands at her face. They glared at each other until he calmly lowered his hands to his sides.

"Damn it, Perrie. How many times do I have to tell you that I have no clue what the hell you've been talking about for the past six months? Anyone else would've given up already, but you and me"—he pointed back and forth between them—"we're the real deal. If I have to wait an eternity for you, I will." He tipped his chin at her and walked off.

"Well," Maisie said in awe.

Whirling around to face her, she hissed, "*Well?*"

Maisie shook her head like she had sand or something in her hair and was trying to get it out. "Oh, yeah. Screw that loser!"

Sighing, Perrie nodded. Summer couldn't come soon enough. No more Neven, no more school.

The bell rang then and they headed to their first-period

English class together.

Their teacher, Mr. Carter, was possibly the only instructor who she found to be awesome. Perrie's writing skills were average at best, but he could turn anyone's work into a masterpiece.

After Perrie finished writing a short story on why classic horror movies were an art form, she watched from her desk as Mr. Carter drew a picture resembling the Mona Lisa in Paint. He did this every day after he taught the lessons, and she was always flabbergasted that he could use a computer mouse to do it. She tried once and gave up after attempting the letter P, which was when she realized her handwriting had been much better as a three-year-old.

The rest of her classes before lunch passed way too slowly. During Math, she finished her homework, so she didn't have anything to do besides stare at Mrs. Briggs's seventies-styled hair. It wasn't seventies cool either, it was rough—try Farrah Fawcett with a curling iron and electricity. Perrie wasn't quite sure if her teacher was stuck in an older era or invented one herself. Either way, she had no intention of ever visiting it. Her stomach let out a monstrous rumble. It had been repeating the broken-record process since she walked into class.

Inwardly groaning, she watched as the second hand on the clock slowly forced itself to the number she needed before the bell rang. *Thank fuck!* She practically wanted to do three fist pumps instead of one. That was how much she loved feeding the monster in her belly.

Having already packed up her binder and other belongings, Perrie collected her backpack and started to stand up. Out of habit, she reached for her cello, then she remembered she'd dropped it off after first period in the music room.

As she headed out the doorway, she spotted a familiar face.

August.

Green eyes locked on hers, and in an instant, they both smiled at each other. August was about as relaxed as she'd ever seen him in black Chucks, jeans, and a baseball tee. The sight of him made her heart kick up a notch.

She practically ran into his arms and backed him up against the lockers. Chuckling deeply against her ear, he hugged her back with just as much force.

With her friend August, she didn't have to look up as far as she'd had to with Neven to see his face. She was about to say something when her eyes drifted to the Devil passing them in the hallway. If looks could kill. Neven didn't so much as glance at her—his dagger-throwing gaze was for August alone. They used to talk a little, but not anymore.

"So, I got you something for your birthday," August said against the side of her face. His breath brushed her ear, and her skin absorbed the warmth.

Perrie pulled back, lifting her brows. "You didn't have to get me anything."

He released her to unzip his backpack and fished out a tiny box. "Don't worry. It isn't an engagement ring."

Laughing, she took the box from him and opened it. She gaped, her heart swelling at the sight. Tucked inside was a silver necklace with a cello-bow pendant, encrusted with small, sparkling sapphires.

"You can also read the back." He grinned.

Perrie flipped it over and read the engraved two words: *I'm here*.

Taking a deep swallow, her heart pounding even more, she pulled him to her and kissed his soft cheek. "Thank you!"

She didn't know what it was, but lately she'd been *feeling* something more for August. Unfortunately, she didn't want to have feelings for anyone. After breaking up with Neven, Perrie's goal was to get through high school, do the college thing, and see what happened after that.

August had been making it harder. They may have started out as friends, but something was changing. In the past, Perrie had chosen to ignore it for as long as humanly possible by reminding herself she'd hated him before all of this.

When August moved here and started his senior year at her school, Perrie had never thought she could hate someone so much, so fast. There was no real reason—he hadn't attacked her per se. He just waltzed into Orchestra class and took over first chair, *her* first chair, like his name was written on it. She'd been undeniably *pissed*. That first day of senior year, she was happily sitting in her seat from the prior year. And as class began, their teacher introduced the new student, August, and stated that he had a late audition. It was a surprise to everyone when he took over first chair right then and there, like he was a king or some shit.

Cello was the one thing she excelled at, and she knew it was her one ticket to a scholarship for college. She still got one, but back then she'd thought everything would be wrecked.

Perrie had wanted to rip him apart. She couldn't believe that this guy, with his perfect face and perfect curly blond hair, had taken her spot right out from under her nose. He sat down next to her without so much as a glance, even though she'd been staring multiple daggers at him.

When the bell rang, and the class had emptied except for them, Perrie had waited as far away from the offender as possible.

Neven had been running late after basketball and her teacher had already left for the day. It was just the two of them and that alone made her even more furious.

Finally, he glanced Perrie's way, and the look he gave her held zero emotion. Then the fucker had turned around. It was almost like he couldn't have cared less.

Her brows lowered, her temper rising.

Picking up her expensive bow, that her dad had saved for her last Christmas present, Perrie took it and slowly approached him. As she came upon him, he was completely oblivious, polishing or maybe tuning his instrument—which made her anger pulse harder. When he finally glanced up from his cello, confused by her aggression, she looked him straight in the eye and tapped her bow to his chest.

"So, you think you can just magically come in here like some kind of magician and poof your way into first chair?" She stood so close she could smell his soapy scent. It was an addicting smell, sort of like how gasoline could be, even though it shouldn't.

At that very moment she could tell he didn't think of her as *nothing* anymore.

His lips puckered and his head tilted to the side. "First off, you haven't even heard me play. Not that I'm Mozart or anything, but I earned first chair."

He was fighting a smile at that point, but his words took shape in her head. That was true. She hadn't heard him play a single note of music. Everything inside her was driven by an idiotic amount of jealousy. Tantrum be gone.

"Well then, play for me."

He just stood there, so she said it again as a question, "Will you play for me?"

"Sure. But I can't play if you have that bow jammed into my chest the whole time." His head cocked to the other side, playfully studying her "weapon."

He was right though, so Perrie dropped her hand back to her side, removing her bow. Heat rushed to her cheeks in embarrassment—truth be told, she had been more anxious to hear him play. She shifted from foot to foot, waiting to hear the notes.

As August played, her opinion changed. He was better than her by a landslide. He played with fluidity—everything about the way he moved, from his fingers, to the way the bow went across the strings, was close to Houdini-level magic. Perrie could try and try, and she would never be able to play like he did that day.

When he finished, she knew he had rightly earned his

place.

"Congratulations on first chair," Perrie had said while turning to pack up her things and leave.

"And you are?" he asked.

She slid her bow into its case before responding. "Perrie Madeline."

"Perrie." He tried the sound of it like he was testing a brand-new instrument. "I'm August Hartley."

She couldn't contain her high-pitched laughter as she'd spoken, "Oh, I know. The second Mr. Hamm said we had a new first chair, I made sure I got the name."

August smiled. It was everything a smile should be—real, warm, and welcoming. Perrie knew she was going to like him. When she'd looked back at him from the classroom door, she'd given August one last quick wave.

Who would've thought that glaring daggers at someone for a full class period would gain a new best friend?

Perrie shrugged off the memory, its purpose no longer helping, and accepted August's gift before they met Maisie for lunch.

"Help me put it on?" she asked.

As soon as the cool silver of the necklace rested around her neck, latched at the nape, another crack against what she'd come to think of as her stone heart struck.

THREE

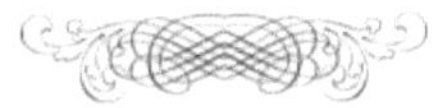

The lunch line in the cafeteria wrapped around the wall but it moved fast. Perrie grabbed a basket of hot fries, and August got his usual variety of pretty much everything.

Perrie spotted Maisie by the flash of her eye patch, consisting of reds, whites, and blacks. She'd already changed into a different one, as she was known to do throughout the day. It resembled a deck of playing cards with hearts, spades, clubs, and diamonds.

"Hey, guys!" Maisie practically yelled.

August and Perrie sat down next to each other, directly across from Maisie.

"Nice patch," he said, pointing his fork at her right eye.

She brushed her hand across it as if in thought, which Perrie guessed she was. "Thanks. This one was getting rather lonely in my backpack, and the other one was tired of working its shift."

"That totally makes sense." Perrie nodded with a smile. *Of course it makes sense, minus the fact that a patch doesn't have feelings.*

"So, have you guys heard about the other missing person?" August asked right before he shoved a piece of pizza into his mouth.

Perrie's stomach sank at the question. "Yeah, Maisie and I were just talking about that this morning. We don't know him, but this is getting pretty sketchy with all these disappearances."

August set down what was left of his pizza. "I thought he looked familiar, but I don't think I've seen him around or anything."

Maisie couldn't contain herself and dove into a list of her theories about the disappearances. "If the missing people were kidnapped, it could be someone like Jeffrey Dahmer, although it isn't only men who have vanished. Or possibly Ed Gein! Maybe the suspect is also digging up bodies from graves. Although, no bodies have been found yet is the problem."

August remained focused on Maisie, clearly intent on hearing every single one of her theories.

"Unless the kidnapper is like Charles Manson and sending people to do his or her dirty work," Perrie piped in, making the mistake of glancing over at Neven's table. At a nearly full table, he sat with some of the other guys from basketball. As if he felt her looking, his gaze met hers, locking.

Perrie glanced down and forced herself to not peer back up in that direction. It wasn't that she missed "them" because she was over that aspect with him. But she missed his friendship.

On the first day of ninth grade, students from the other junior highs in the area came together for high school. Neven, being one of those students, was the first person she'd met that day.

Perrie had no idea where she was going. Feeling completely lost, she'd bumped into Neven who offered to help her find her class. He'd said she looked like a confused tourist in a new country and pulled the schedule from her hand. Neven noticed they had first period together and proceeded to drag her along with him. Even though he'd already known some students in the class, he'd chosen to sit next to Perrie. After that, they'd become friends and he'd gotten along perfectly with Maisie's quirkiness.

The summer before eleventh grade, things began to change between Perrie and Neven. Their friendship grew into something new and different. His dad had passed away from a freak accident at work, and she was there every day with Neven to help him get through it. She'd known from experience how to grieve over a lost parent.

It was July, and Perrie had been leaving his house. When he'd come in to give her a hug, he instead pecked her lips, then instantly pulled away, as if he hadn't meant to do it at all. They'd stared at each other for several long moments before he leaned in to kiss her again. And she'd let him.

Neven Lee was her first kiss and her first everything else to follow. She'd loved him with all of her heart, until he split it in half. Perrie's heart wasn't as broken anymore, and after the bruises and cracks that were left behind, she'd wanted it to remain like stone.

"I think the Manson-esque theory could be possible." August's words knocked Perrie out of her reverie.

It was possible. She met Maisie's gaze and they both nodded in agreement.

"I think it has to be a guy, though," Perrie said.

"That's sexist." Maisie shook her finger at her. "Equality when it comes to kidnapping."

"I'm sorry, but most females can't lift some of these muscular human specimens." Perrie tapped her chin. "Unless there could be more than one."

"Like in the movie *Scream*?" Maisie's eye shone with excitement over the mention of one of her favorite nineties slasher films.

"Precisely." Perrie grinned.

"You two are virtually insane. That movie sucks." August grabbed Perrie's trash and tossed it away. With a horrific remark like that, he may have just destroyed any remaining possibility of them becoming more than friends. But she couldn't help but stare at his backside, the way his muscles flexed, the easy way he carried himself.

"You're ridiculous!" Maisie yelled to his back.

August shrugged without turning around. After he walked back to them, they left the cafeteria and headed to class, discussion about missing people forgotten.

"See you in last period," Perrie called to August as he stopped outside his next class.

"Battle of the cellos, doll face. Me and you!" he shouted back, her heart fluttering in her chest. It always did when he called her that.

Almost every day during their free time in Orchestra, August and Perrie battled it out. Sometimes she won, but only because he secretly let her.

The next period crept by at a sloth's pace. Perrie mainly watched Maisie doodle in her notebook to take up time. The little skeletal drawing looked like a masterpiece, while Perrie's doodles were just a bunch of repetitive circles drawn together that she continuously retraced. Shit-art, Perrie preferred to call it.

Last period finally arrived, and when Perrie walked into class, an unfamiliar face slid into view. A substitute teacher, which meant she would practice whatever the hell she was in the mood for.

August hadn't made it to class yet, so she strolled to the instrument closet, grabbed her cello case, and settled into her chair. As she struggled to pull out the instrument, a blond head passed through the door right as the bell rang. Perrie's chest tightened and she attempted to push the feeling away, but it stood its ground.

She opted to distract herself and focus on messing with her cello, checking to make sure everything was in tune to ignore the butterflies fluttering about inside her stomach. August took his seat next to hers, raking a hand through his hair, and the nervousness subsided.

Perrie's emotions around him were unpredictable, especially when she was trying so hard to fight them. August drew his cello out of its case—the instrument was far more refined compared to hers, not a single scratch or scuff mark on its smooth body.

"What's up with that guy?" He nodded in the direction of the teacher.

Right off the bat, Perrie knew exactly what he was talking about as she focused on the substitute again. How had she not noticed before? The guy looked like he just strolled out of the 1920s, wearing a suit that had to be authentic from the era. His dark brown hair was slicked back, glistening under the light, and far too perfectly shaped around his head.

"I feel like he's going to whip out one of those old bowler hats." She laughed a bit too loud. The substitute examined them and she tried to cover her mouth to muffle her laughter. His eyes narrowed in her direction. Perrie played it off and went back to tuning her cello, still smiling.

Despite her efforts, she couldn't manage to tune it. Even though she could usually get it right away with a tuner.

"Here, let me see what's going on with it." August took the instrument from her, his fingers softly brushing hers. Perrie's cheeks warmed, and she felt like a pubescent teen.

Attempting to tune a cello without a tuner never worked for her. She couldn't ever get the sound right by ear like some people could.

August, however, was a master at this. He plucked at the strings carefully, and she watched how he closed his eyes, noting the focus on his face as he listened to each vibration. Her lips parted in awe as she studied his ease.

He twisted the peg and plucked the string again, releasing a perfectly tuned note that was pure bliss. The sound of it struck her soul in a way only music could. He held the cello out for Perrie to take, pulling her out of her trance.

"There," he said with a smirk.

Perrie took the instrument and cradled it like a newborn baby. "Thank you. You're a god!" she said dramatically, bowing her head in praise of his abilities. August rolled his eyes and chuckled it off.

After what had happened with Neven, Maisie and August had been everything. Perrie liked to think they'd become the Three Musketeers of Deer Park High School. Not the classical musketeers either, but the perfect blend of chocolate and fluffy nougat wrapped up in a flashy wrapper.

For the rest of class, they bickered about musical notes and best horror movies. As soon as the bell rang, Perrie packed everything up and Maisie sauntered into the classroom. The three of them made their way out to the large, empty parking lot, where August's car appeared to be missing.

She whirled to August and frowned. "Where's your car?"

"I woke up with a flat tire this morning." He rubbed his eyes and sighed loudly. "Didn't feel like working on it until after school today. My parents had already left for work, so I walked to school instead."

Maisie straightened, seeming prepared to save the day. "We can give you a ride home!"

"It's all right. It's not that far of a walk." He shrugged nonchalantly.

"Anyway, August—you're coming with us." Perrie rolled her eyes, grabbed his arm, and pulled him with her. He put up absolutely no resistance as they piled into Maisie's car and took off. August only lived a couple of minutes out of the way from their destination.

Maisie took a turn down Oak Street, which Perrie had always found ironic. The street was lined on both sides with tall trees, each one reaching their crooked branches toward the other as if longing for their touch. For a town called Deer Park, Perrie had seen more trees on a street corner than actual deer. *Not* one *single deer, to be exact.*

Out of nowhere, Maisie slammed on the brakes and Perrie's chest struck hard against the seat belt. Then she smashed back into the seat just as hard. *Are my organs still intact?* It was the only thing she could think about in that moment. Seriously, they felt like they were bleeding profusely.

"What the hell?" August and Perrie said at the same time. Maisie didn't reply—she was staring across the street to the left.

"Look!" she exclaimed.

Perrie followed Maisie's pointed finger and stilled. Across from them stood an enormous gray stone building, unbelievably tall, and its walls lined with huge rocks along the base. Among the rocks, it appeared there were absolutely no windows of any kind. A curving archway framed an entrance with one of the tallest wooden doors she'd ever seen. *Creepily unusual.*

"Impossible," Perrie breathed.

"This has never been here before." August's jaw hung open.

He was right. He was beyond right. There was no way in hell this place was magically built overnight. Even if it were possible, the building was obviously old, at least over a hundred years old.

"Maybe we never really noticed it before." Maisie unbuckled herself and opened the car door, completely taken by the sight of the building.

Perrie's eyes widened, and she threw her hands up, waving them like a lunatic. "*Never* noticed it before? This *giant* stone mansion?"

"Perrie has a point, Maisie." August continued to examine the building with his brows up his forehead.

With hesitation, Perrie stepped out of the car, August following behind her. They walked around to stand near Maisie, completely speechless as they prolonged their staring marathon at the place. It really was an unusual structure to be sitting in the middle of her town. How had it not drawn major attention from the locals?

"We should investigate!" Maisie moved before either of them could protest.

"Just a quick look," Perrie said, her interest piqued. She fell into step beside Maisie, and her fingers itched with curiosity.

Perrie walked to the door at a leisurely pace, as if she had all night to see what was going on. They inched closer to the arched doorway, where overgrown grass met a block of cement, and two things popped into her line of sight. First, a golden plaque on the door with words on it written in an elegant, yet outdated black script.

Quinsey Wolfe's Glass Vault

Maisie tilted her head to the side, seeming skeptical of the plaque. "Not sure what a glass vault is."

Perrie motioned at a sign to the right of the door, then shifted closer to see what was written on it.

The illustrious Quinsey Wolfe presents a wonder of the world, a true sight to behold in his infamous glass museum. A forewarning to onlookers and wanderers—beware of your imagination and curiosity. This is not for the faint of heart.

"Not for the faint of heart?" August repeated the line. "Pretty cliché for my taste, but okay."

"I'd have to agree," Perrie said with a quirked eyebrow.

Maisie pushed Perrie to the side so she could get a better look. She lifted her eye patch to rest on her forehead and examined it more thoroughly. "I like the sound of that."

She would.

August reached for the doorknob and jiggled it. "It's locked."

"Oh, look." Maisie tapped a paper sign just below the description. "It also says opening soon and that they're hiring. I can message this Quinsey Wolfe guy at this email address."

Maisie unzipped her purse and pulled out a small notepad and pencil. *Of course* she carried around a pencil and small notepad. How could she not? She always had an idea or something brewing that she needed to write down, so she or *Perrie* didn't forget.

"What's with the notebook?" August asked.

Maisie studied the sign while writing. "Because you never know when you're going to need one."

"You aren't really going to apply, are you?" August pressed his shoulder against the door, his arms crossed over his chest.

Maisie brought her eye patch back over her eye. "Heck yes, I am! I've been looking for a job I would like, but nothing holds my interest. This place sounds awesome."

"Right," Perrie drawled. "So, this place just grows out of the ground overnight? I like strange, but I don't know about this. I say we get the hell out of here."

"Although," August started, "now that I'm looking around, there are a lot of trees that have been cut down. Maybe it's just been hidden all this time?" He stepped in front of them and inspected the ground further.

It was true, obviously there were trees here before and had since been cleared out. Perrie still found it odd that they wouldn't have noticed some old, historical-looking mansion when they'd gone down this street before.

"So, it's settled. I'm going to email this Quinsey Wolfe as soon as I get home!" Maisie bounced in place.

"You do that." Perrie rolled her eyes. She was going to search for a job soon, but this place didn't look like her cup of tea. It did seem to be Maisie's though.

Unease lingered in her chest as they headed back to the car. Perrie glanced back one more time at the aged mansion. The hairs of her arm stood on end as the building seemed to be watching them in return.

Only silence filled the car for the rest of the ride to August's place. When Maisie pulled up in front of his house, he reached around the passenger seat and gave Perrie a hug.

She held onto him longer than necessary as he said, "I hope the rest of your birthday is spectacular, doll face."

After he released her and stepped out of the car, Perrie grasped the necklace at the base of her throat and thoughts of the odd museum vanished from her mind.

FOUR

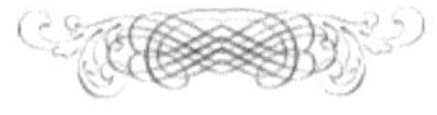

"Are you ready for your birthday dinner?" Maisie asked, turning onto their street.

"My monster is," Perrie said as she patted her stomach.

Every year Perrie's aunt made her a birthday dinner, and it was no small feast. Leftovers would last for almost an entire week—it was more than a two-person household could handle.

"You better get to the red velvet cake before I scarf that entire thing down." Maisie chuckled. She would do it too.

Once Maisie parked in the driveway, Perrie dropped her school things off at her house, then headed back to Maisie's through the freshly cut grass.

Maisie was already somewhere inside her house—most likely eyeballing the cake.

Practically leaping over the steps, Perrie burst inside. Her dad, still wearing his chemical plant uniform, stood by the table with a soda in his hand, obviously surprised by her dramatic entrance. He always took off a little early from work on her birthday so he could make it for this occasion. It almost brought a tear to her eye that he, along with her aunt and uncle, put in so much effort for her. But Perrie's main concern at the moment was the food.

"Hey, sweetie." Her dad walked over to her and gave her shoulders a squeeze, then kissed the top of her head as if she was still his little girl. "Happy birthday. How does it feel to officially be an adult?"

Pulling back from the hug, she laughed. "I feel the same as yesterday."

"Don't worry, you have the rest of your life to feel like an adult and trust me, you younger people have it made."

"Okay, Dad, you're talking like you're seventy. Adulting is fine."

"*Fine?*" Aunt Krista shook her head and waved her hand dismissively. "Not once you get the bills every month."

Since her mom had left, Perrie had wished so hard to have a mom like Krista. She treated her like another daughter, and even though she was great, it wasn't the same.

"You guys ready to cut the cake?" Her dad must've sensed Maisie pining for it.

"Finally!" Maisie sighed dramatically.

"Maisie, please." Aunt Krista glared.

"Yes, Mom?" she asked sweetly.

"Manners?"

"Oh, just give the girl some cake already," Uncle Jaron interrupted, his dark eyes settling on the dessert. "Actually, give me some cake."

Aunt Krista swept her long hair over her shoulder and lit the candles on the cake. Everyone then joined in to sing *Happy Birthday*. Awkwardness washed over Perrie, but it always did when the focus was on her. As soon as the song ended, the feeling left and she grabbed a plate.

Her aunt really outdid herself with the birthday party this year. Any kind of dip Perrie could imagine rested on the table. Aunt Krista knew her so well. Perrie could literally drink the cheese dip and eat the guacamole alone. Every counter and table showcased sandwiches, cupcakes, cookies, cake, and chips. Anyone who saw it would think the food was for a party of fifty instead of the five of them.

As Perrie bit into a cupcake, Uncle Jaron mentioned their summer plans. They would be going to visit Maisie's grandparents in Turkey for their annual trip. She almost wished she could go, but Maisie said it really wasn't that exciting. Perrie's dad agreed to watch the house while they were away, which really meant she'd be the one checking in and doing the chores.

"Hopefully the police will get a solid lead while you're gone," her dad said. All talk of summer vacation was out the window as the conversation took a darker turn. Perrie guessed they were on to disappearing people now. "It just has me worried that no one has turned up." He sighed. She knew what he was more worried about, what he didn't know how to say out loud. *Me.* He was worried about her. He wouldn't know what to do if she disappeared too.

Aunt Krista placed a hand on his shoulder. "Don't worry, James. They'll find the person responsible."

I hope they do, too.

Uncle Jaron nodded in agreement. Aunt Krista was the practical thinker in the family, and Uncle Jaron usually followed her lead. She knew just what to say at the right moment to comfort anyone, but her dad's shoulders remained stiff, his smile gone.

Her dad peered down at his watch. "I think it's time for us to head home."

Perrie helped Aunt Krista pack up the leftovers and gave everyone a hug before leaving. She and her dad moseyed on back to their house to hang out in front of the TV for a little while. He flipped on the news first thing and watched the screen flicker absently with stories about animals dressed like chickens and a woman arrested in a shopping center for "public indecency."

Biting her lip, Perrie could tell he wasn't all there.

"You all right, Dad?" she asked, dragging the blanket

closer to her chest.

"Yeah." His gaze was vacant, still worrying about the missing cases.

Perrie decided not to tell him about her run-in with Neven, August's gift, or the strange mansion on the way home. When he was in this mood, everything stayed a one-word answer. So after about an hour, Perrie kissed him on the cheek and headed down the hall to start on her homework.

Luckily, she didn't have much to do since she finished her math homework in class. All she had left was a paper for English, which she finished in less than an hour. While she waited on her slow ass printer, she checked her email.

Nothing too special ever popped up in her inbox, mostly junk mail. She had a wretched habit of subscribing to pointless websites when they offered discounts on free shipping. Eventually she would unsubscribe from some of them, but for now she started deleting the emails. Except for the one that was a few dollars off admission to the horror film festival next month.

As she scanned the rest, her stomach sank as her gaze settled on a familiar name. Neven. She debated whether or not she should read or delete it, but curiosity always won with her.

Hey Perrie,

I just wanted to tell you that today made me realize just how much I miss you. We've been together on your birthday for the last three years. Could we at least start talking again?
Love Always,
Nev

"What a douche," she muttered, reading it again. *Okay, maybe he isn't being a douche at the moment, but he still is one.* She held the cursor over the delete button, but then an impulse made her change her mind and decide to give him a quick reply.

Short and simple. Perrie hit send and signed out of her email. Shuffling to her dresser, she reached for the clasp of her necklace from August. She took it off and left it to sit neatly on top of her dresser.

Her thoughts rotated back and forth from Neven's email to August's gift, and how she'd lost one friend but gained another.

Perrie had been about two months into her senior year. She didn't want to go to school the next day, but she forced herself to anyway. Her goal that day was to continue to avoid Neven like the Black Plague. Fear and anxiety had taken over her limbs, though, and it felt like they were going to fall off at any point.

Once her first class was over, she'd been fine the rest of the day … for the most part. Well, not *fine*, she just told herself she was going to get through her classes. She was like a stone statue, cold and unfeeling, and that was all she'd wanted to be.

That same day she decided to stay late after Orchestra to practice and to escape, while being alone with music. Perrie remembered walking to the instrument closet to grab a music stand, then becoming frustrated. She couldn't find the stand she'd wanted, the one she *always* used, and suddenly it all felt like too much. It seemed stupid now, but her mind was a jumbled mess back then and her heart ached.

Perrie's legs collapsed and she'd curled into herself. That was when the tears came. It was the first time she'd cried about Neven. She cried like never before. When her mom left, back when she loved her, she didn't cry as hard then as she did that day in the music room. Everything about that day, that time, that place, overwhelmed Perrie from the second she stepped into her first class that morning.

August had barely made a noise when he found her sobbing and huddled up against a wall.

With him standing there so close and her heartbroken, it had made her tears flow even more. Perrie shifted away from him, but he didn't leave. Instead, he sank down beside her on the carpeted floor and pulled her onto his lap. His warmth, his comfort, made her tears slow.

Perrie and August hadn't spoken to each other outside of casual conversation about school or music. He would sometimes talk to Neven after class when he would meet her there. They'd been sort of friends, but more like acquaintances. He was the first person that she'd told everything—before she'd told Maisie.

When her crying ceased, she was holding onto him like she'd known him her entire life. There were questions written all over his face, but he never asked them.

After that day, she and August grew closer and closer. She'd been so sure they could just be friends.

Now, Perrie didn't know. It was so strange how a friendship could begin so fast in a single instant, but it could, and it did. August's thoughtful gift was a reminder of that change.

She shook her head and snapped her fingers. *No more Neven or August tonight.* This wasn't a love triangle or any other weird love-shaped fictional bullshit. It was her moving on from one guy, where the feelings were already dead, to fighting her emotions for someone else.

Tearing off the day's clothes, she threw on her old tattered T-shirt and baggy polka-dot pants before wandering back into the living room. Her dad was already getting up from the couch and heading to bed.

"Good night, sweetheart. I hope you had a great day. Happy birthday one last time." It was the longest sentence he'd said to her that night.

"I did. I love you, Dad." She waved him good night, then flipped on the TV.

"I love you, too." He yawned and disappeared into his bedroom.

Snatching the flowered quilt from the edge of the couch, Perrie pulled it to her chin and turned on *Dracula*. It was the black and white version, and those ones were always the best.

About five minutes after the first woman on screen screamed, a gentle tap sounded at the door. It could only be one person at this late hour. Tossing off the blanket, Perrie padded to the door and looked through the peephole. *Yep, I was right*. Maisie stood there in her pajamas, her fingers tapping her thighs. Perrie whistled a birdy signal like they'd started when they were younger. Maisie released a high-pitched one in return and Perrie threw the door open, tugging her inside.

"What are you doing coming over so late? Is everything all right?"

"I have the most exciting news." Maisie was practically beaming in her bright yellow pajama pants and her long-sleeve banana-print shirt. An eye patch shaped like a banana covered her eye, matching her clothing.

"I have three questions. First, do you sleep in eye patches? Second, couldn't you have just sent me a text or called? And third, can we sit down?"

"My answers are… No, they would get in the way while I sleep. I could have, but for absolute expression, I can't do that over text—emojis aren't a replacement. Last, yes, let's sit down because I see you're watching one of my favorite movies ever."

Maisie plopped down on the couch, snatched the blanket, and covered her legs. Perrie shut the front door, then sat beside her and grabbed the edge of the blanket to cover herself. "Okay, what's this big news?"

She frowned as her gaze settled on Perrie's face. "Hey, where's your new eye patch? Remember, you promised to wear it."

With a huff, Perrie left her comfortable spot and located the patch on the table. She then slid it over her eye, the fabric soft like silk. "There. Happy?"

"Yes! Now, remember the Glass Vault?"

"Of course I remember the old, creepy mansion that appeared out of nowhere! How could I forget?" Perrie rubbed the side of her head and pretended to look lost. Maisie ignored her sarcasm.

"Anyway, as soon as we finished up dinner, I emailed my resume to Quinsey Wolfe. He emailed me back in record time and said I have the job." She paused for effect. "I start this Thursday, nine o'clock sharp!"

Squinting, Perrie nodded in confusion. "Wait a second, so you're starting work at nine in the morning? We have school."

Maisie shook her hand wildly in front of her face. "No! No. He wanted me to start at nine at night."

Her jaw dropped. That seemed like odd hours for a museum to keep on a regular day-to-day. They also hadn't officially opened yet. Maybe they were getting everything in order for whenever they planned to open, though?

"I don't know. That seems pretty late for a school night—or any night—to go into work at a museum. It's not a bar or strip club here, or is it?" Perrie paused. "Did he say what time you would be getting off?"

She shrugged emphatically. "I told him I could work till midnight for now until summer starts, which is almost here anyway."

"What did your parents say? I'm willing to bet they aren't overly thrilled about the late exotic dancer-like hours."

Maisie stayed silent and looked off to the side to try and hide her guilt.

"You didn't tell them, did you?" Perrie wasn't surprised.

Maisie had been looking for a job that met her impossibly high standards for a while now. Besides selling her eye patches, she didn't have any real work experience, and she refused to do anything that involved food. Hell, Perrie refused to do anything that involved food. She supposed working at the possible freak show of a mansion must've meant a great deal to her cousin if she hadn't said anything to her parents yet.

"You can't either. This is like my dream job!" Maisie brought her thumbnail to her teeth and chewed nervously.

"Dream job?" She laughed a little too loudly and she hadn't meant it to sound so harsh. "The whole thing seems sketchy. We don't even know what a glass vault is! A museum grows out of the ground, a guy you haven't even met, no interview, hires you, and he wants you to start right away? It doesn't make sense."

Unfazed by her questioning, Maisie said, "But, Perrie, he sounded so desperate in the email! It's so new to the area, barely anyone has applied. He wants to open soon and needs the help. It's perfect timing!"

Of course no one else had applied. She'd had no idea the Glass Vault even existed until this afternoon.

"Fine." Perrie relented. "I won't say anything, but you have to get August and me in for free once it opens. I want to see what this place looks like."

"Deal." She grinned widely and drew an exaggerated cross over her heart with her finger.

They stayed up a little longer and finished watching the rest of the bloodsucking goodness. When it was over, Perrie walked Maisie to the door and waited until she made it home safely. After her cousin had crawled through her bedroom window, Perrie waved good night and shut the door.

Once she locked the door behind her, she yawned and removed the lion eye patch from her face. She turned it over and over in her hand, thinking about the Glass Vault and what kind of things waited inside.

FIVE

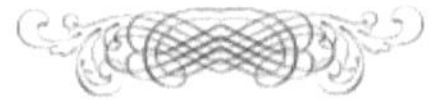

School that day was as mundane as it could get. Maisie had a group project she needed to work on with a few people in her class, so Perrie caught a ride home with August since he'd fixed his tire.

"Do you want to come inside and hang out for a bit?" Perrie turned to August as he pulled into her driveway.

He was rocking the wind-blown look, his blond hair a curly mess and sticking up all over the place. A smile spread across his face and her cheeks warmed *again*.

Enough of that shit already.

"Yeah, sure, I don't have to be at work until later." August was a janitor at his dad's law firm and cleaned the building a few times during the week.

The house would be empty since her dad was working overtime, so he wouldn't be home until later this evening. Not that she planned on doing anything besides them hanging out. *Or do I?*

She couldn't help the image coming to her of her straddling August in the driver seat, her hips rocking against his as he gripped her waist. Their mouths coasting over one another, his tongue dancing with hers.

Perrie didn't look at him as she stepped out of the car, a heat spreading through her, lower and lower. She cleared her throat and told herself to calm the hell down.

"Do you want something to drink?" Perrie asked as she opened the door and entered the foyer.

He shrugged out of his jacket. "I'll take some water."

Perrie grabbed them each a room-temperature bottled water from the pantry. She then chugged hers almost all the way down as she went back into the living room to where August was waiting.

"Thanks," he said when she handed a bottle over to him.

"Sorry if it's too warm. Cold water just rubs me the wrong way."

"Yeah? We're in sync then." He nervously fiddled with the cap. "So, Perrie, I've wanted to ask you something."

"Oh, yeah? What's up?" His rambling had gotten her full attention. He was totally focused on her face and she could practically feel the intensity of his stare. Did he *know* what she'd been thinking earlier?

"I was wondering if you wanted to hang out sometime?"

She frowned, a little unsure of what he was trying to get at. "Sure, but we hang out all the time. We're hanging out now."

He raked a hand through his hair and took a deep breath. "I mean like go *out* out."

"Do you mean like an actual date?" She bit the inside of her cheek, feeling like a deer caught in headlights.

He inspected the floor as though he was searching for something. She hoped she didn't just embarrass herself by asking if it wasn't what he'd even meant.

"Yes, doll face, like you and me. An actual date." Her heart slammed against her rib cage as he continued, "I like you. I have for a while now, but I wasn't sure when would be a good time. If you don't want to, if this is too soon, I understand. I don't want anything to get weird, but I had to try."

Perrie's heart pounded harder as her gaze locked onto his green irises. The stone in her chest cracked even more. Perspiration pressed against her shirt as she swallowed her remaining sip of water. She'd told herself she wouldn't get in this position again for a long time, but the truth was she liked him. This was her chance to tell him she'd give it a shot. Perrie had been hiding under the surface of her feelings for too long. She needed air, and August was oxygen.

But then the fucking doorbell rang.

"Hold that thought, okay?" Ragged breaths escaped her as she rushed to answer the door. She was prepared to tell whomever it was to get lost when she pulled the door open to Neven. The words were knocked right out of her, and her stomach plummeted to the earth. She should've checked the damn peephole first.

Anger coursed through her veins, and her words were trapped in her throat for a moment. "What the hell are you doing here?"

"We need to talk."

"Sorry, pass." Perrie motioned to the living room where August stood. "I have company. This will have to wait." She began to shut the door, but Neven stuck his foot in to stop it from closing.

Perrie clenched her jaw and was about two seconds from pulling the door back open to slam it on his foot, when he reached out to touch her. "It's important. Please?"

The worried look on his face made her halt, think. "Fifteen minutes." Maybe the sight of him wasn't bothering her as much anymore, so she decided to let him in.

Neven stopped dead in his tracks when he spotted August. "Alone?"

"Anything you have to say you can say in front of him," Perrie said and crossed her arms. August rocked back and forth on his heels, clearly uncomfortable.

"It's fine, Perrie. You can call me later." August started to collect his things.

Perrie rushed over and tried to stop him, not wanting him to leave. "August, you don't have to go."

"Don't worry about it. Just call me later, all right?" He threw his jacket over his shoulder and she walked with him to the door. Neven remained in the background watching them quietly.

"Okay. Talk to you later." She smiled, trying to ignore the awkward situation.

Closing the door behind her, Perrie pressed her back to it and took a deep breath.

"This better be good." When she looked at Neven, she couldn't control the past from coming to her in a rush.

The day everything went downhill with Neven was six months ago. Everything in Perrie's life had felt perfect. She wasn't as worried about the future and college because life at that moment was great.

It only took one mistake to ruin everything. Neven had called her one morning to say he wasn't feeling well and wouldn't be at school. She'd told him she would check on him after.

Perrie remembered every minute detail about that day. She could recall the crisp smell of the fall air, the caress of the light breeze, the sound of the leaves and branches brushing together, and even the crackle of Nev's neighbor grilling meat outside.

Maisie had dropped Perrie off at his house on the way home, and she should've told her cousin to wait, but she'd never needed to before.

Nev's car had been the only one in the driveway, and the door to his house unlocked. He'd always left it unlocked for her when he knew she was coming over, so she didn't think anything of it at the time.

After grabbing a bottled water from the cabinet in his kitchen, she'd headed upstairs. Loud music echoed from his room, the way it always had when he was home alone. As she inched closer, *noises* came from inside the open door. Perrie had known what the sounds were from the second they struck her ears, but still she persisted. She needed to confirm her worst nightmares and torture herself further.

When she reached the doorway, her gaze first landed on male and *female* clothes scattered about the room. Perrie swallowed her anxiety. Nev was right there in his bed with a redheaded woman who she'd never seen before. Then again, she couldn't see her face, but she would've recognized that hair anywhere—it was the color of fire. She was on top of him rolling her hips against Neven's naked body, his fingers digging into her waist, his eyes closed, his lips parted. Neven's hands drifted up to cradle her breasts as he groaned, the redhead arching in pleasure.

It hit Perrie all at once and she couldn't take it anymore. She hightailed it out of there. Thinking back now, she should've done or said something. She should've pulled the redhead off him and slapped Neven hard across the face. There was always the should've, would've, could've, but instead, she'd chosen to leave.

Perrie had walked all the way home, dazed and disoriented, the tears never coming.

Neven called several times that evening, but she refused to answer the phone. The whole night and the following day numbness consumed her. She robotically went through the motions of brushing her teeth, showering, dressing, and so on. It wasn't until later in the orchestra room she'd let go and allowed herself to feel everything—the hurt, the betrayal, and the brokenness.

When Neven had called that evening, she told him it was over, to leave her the fuck alone, and never speak to her again.

The sound of Neven rambling on about something interrupted her thoughts, but she couldn't focus on what he'd said.

"Well?" Neven blurted, instead of explaining himself, shifting from one foot to the other.

"Well, what?" she snapped, even though it was her fault for not listening.

He slid his hands into his pockets, seeming hesitant to say anything else. "Have you been down Oak Street lately?"

Perrie's heart lodged in her throat, her voice coming out in a rasp. "You saw the Glass Vault?"

His eyes widened at the mention of it. "Yes! I went down the street this morning on the way to school and noticed it. When I asked the guys at basketball, they had no idea what I was talking about."

"Why didn't you just send me another email? Or a text? I do have a phone. You didn't have to show up here."

"Would you have responded?" He shrugged and pursed his lips.

"I did email you back the last time, didn't I?" she bit back.

He waved it off, as if that detail wasn't important. "So you saw the Glass Vault?"

Perrie rubbed her chin with her thumb and forefinger. "I was with Maisie and August yesterday when we stumbled on it. Maisie already has a job there."

"She's gone inside the place? When I stopped there this morning it was locked up tight." He sighed.

"No, she emailed the owner, Quinsey Wolfe. He hired her right on the *internet* spot. It's incredibly odd."

His eyebrows shot up. "This creepy building appears out of nowhere, and Maisie gets a job there, even though she has no idea what's inside or what she'll be doing?" Neven shook his head. "It sounds just like her."

"It so does." Perrie snickered.

Their conversation was at least about the Glass Vault, but then the silence became tangible.

Neven let out a long breath. "Is there something going on between you and August?"

Fucking great. She crossed her arms. "No. Not at the moment. There could be, but I don't think that's any of your business."

Neven laced his fingers at the back of his neck and released a frustrated groan before throwing his hands into the air.

"Come on, Perrie! I still don't understand what I did wrong. You said I cheated on you, but I don't know when or how I could have if I was throwing up all day."

"But you went for a run? Who the hell goes running after vomiting?"

"Apparently, I do."

"I saw you, Neven. You were fucking some redhead." Perrie tried to keep her voice as even as possible. If she worked herself up, she would explode and break everything in the house.

"What girl?" he shouted.

"I don't know! She was naked, you were naked"—Perrie pointed at her brown hair—"and there was red hair with both your clothes on the floor!" she screamed. How could he keep lying about this?

He gritted his teeth, and she didn't think she'd ever seen him so mad. "Either you've been making this shit up for the past six months to mess with my head, or there's something seriously wrong with you if you think I would've ever cheated on you. I don't even like red hair!"

"Well, apparently, you did that day!" She was anxious to meet his fury with her own.

"I told you I was sick that morning and then about an hour later I felt fine. It was already too late, so I stayed home. You know how antsy I get, so I decided to go for a run before you came over. When I got home, you never showed up, so I called you several times. I didn't come to school the next morning because I was sick again." Leaning against the wall, he appeared to try and cool himself down by once again explaining what had happened. She had heard this story too many times already.

Her head pounded from having the same conversation again.

Neven went on, "It doesn't make sense, but what if that wasn't me? What if that was someone who *looked* like me?"

Perrie couldn't keep from rolling her eyes.

"That's the dumbest thing I've ever heard! So, you mean to tell me that two people broke into your house to have sex on your bed? Not to mention one of them happened to have your face?" She waved her hand in front of her own face for emphasis. "Come on, Nev."

"I get it. There's something strange going on here and I'm going to figure this shit out. Please trust me this one time, Perrie. I'll prove it to you. I just want my best friend back."

"Damn it. Fine." It might've been foolish, but anyone could hear the sincerity and frustration in his plea. She wasn't foolish enough to doubt what she'd seen though, but she would let him do his thing and see what he came up with.

His head drooped, seeming heavy with the weight of this mystery. "You know you're not the only one who's pissed. I wish you could have trusted me. I loved you then, and I still do, Perrie."

She was confident she could burn a hole straight through his heart if she stared hard enough. *Why can't he move on already*?

As he turned to leave, Neven glanced over his shoulder one final time. "See you tomorrow, Perrie."

He was wrong, though. A strange feeling poured over her, making her think that she wouldn't see him the following day.

SIX

The phone rang and Perrie struggled to open her eyes. With a tired yawn, she reached to answer it.

"Hello?" she said groggily as she glanced at the time. It was only 6 a.m.

"Perrie?" a voice rushed out.

She blinked, trying to adjust her eyes to the darkness. "Yes?"

"Hello, dear. It's Julia, Neven's mom." Her words were blended together and Perrie could barely hear her name.

Neven's mom never called her, and Perrie had no earthly idea why she would be. But she was wide awake now. With the phone already pressed hard to her ear, Perrie sat up and leaned back against the headboard.

"Hello, Mrs. Lee."

"I'm sorry to disturb you, but it's important. I know you and Neven haven't been around each other for some time, but have you talked to him recently? I tried calling his friend David, but he didn't answer."

It was as if she'd dumped a full bucket of cold water over Perrie. She was asking her about Neven?

"As a matter of fact, Neven stopped by for a little bit after school yesterday."

"What time was that?" Mrs. Lee asked anxiously.

"I don't remember the time exactly, but it was sometime in the afternoon. Why? What's going on?"

She waited a few seconds before answering. "He never came home yesterday."

Perrie's heart practically froze in place. That didn't sound like him at all. He wouldn't just disappear. Neven and his mom always had a great relationship, more so after his dad died. He would've called her and let her know if he was going to be late.

"Are you sure he didn't stay the night somewhere and forget to call?" she asked, keeping her voice calm, but her stomach churned with apprehension.

"I don't know. If that's what happened, then he's in a lot of trouble for making me worry like this. Can you call me if you see him at school, or better yet, tell him to call me?"

Her hands shook. "Of course I will. I promise."

"Thank you, Perrie. I hope to see you soon too. The house just isn't the same without you."

Perrie missed Mrs. Lee, but she couldn't face being in that house after everything. So she lied and told her she would come over soon before hanging up.

Hands still shaking, Perrie shot Neven a text.

Perrie: Call your mom.

Perrie: And text me back to let me know you did!

Her thoughts flew in every direction. The worst-case scenario being that he was part of the growing list of missing victims, but that was the last thing she wanted to consider. She hadn't prayed in a long time, but she was praying now that she would see him at school. Perrie would take anger over this nervousness and worry any day of the week if it meant Neven was safe.

Sleep wasn't a possibility any longer, so she flicked on the lights and tossed on the first clothes she found in her closet.

Maisie needed to know, so she reached for her phone and called her.

"Hello!" Maisie sang, already wide awake and in a good mood.

"Maisie!" Perrie practically screamed into the phone.

"Perrie? What's going on?" The bounciness left her voice.

She rushed to tell her the story of what had happened on the phone call between Neven's mom and her, and how he'd stopped by yesterday.

"Hold on. Neven stopped by yesterday and you didn't *tell* me?" Maisie said with exasperation before switching to detective mode. "He probably stayed at one of the guys' houses from basketball. Didn't you say Mrs. Lee couldn't get a hold of David?"

He would stay at David's sometimes during the school week, but something about how he'd forgotten to call his mom rubbed her the wrong way.

"All right, Perrie. Let me finish getting dressed and we can leave for school now and see if he's there."

"Yeah, okay. See you in a few," she said and ended the call.

Neven still hadn't texted her back, so she messaged him again.

Perrie: Neven, quit being a jerk and text me back already!

She ran a brush through her hair, threw on a pair of shoes, and hit the steps as fast as she could. Maisie was already waiting for her in the driveway when Perrie hurried to meet her. Throwing open the door, she flung her stuff in, sat down, and buckled up as quickly as she could.

"Let's go!" Perrie said, chest heaving.

Maisie hit the gas, all safety protocol tossed to the wind. Normally her cousin would've finished buckling before the car moved, as she always drove the *exact* speed limit. However, she avoided the snail-pace routine and booked it. Perrie would give her a proper thank you later for her massive sacrifice. Squinting her right eye, Maisie stayed focused on the road. Her left eye was comfortably hidden beneath a doughnut-shaped patch, with little sprinkle jewels glued on it. A nude piece of colored cloth rested where the doughnut hole should've been. *Yes, the patch did distract me for about ten seconds from our current dilemma.*

Perrie noticed then that they were some of the first students pulling into the parking lot. As soon as Maisie threw the car in park, Perrie leapt out of the passenger side with her cousin hot on her heels.

"Gym first!" Maisie called out.

Twin minds. Sometimes Neven practiced basketball before school started.

Inside the gym, several guys were bouncing basketballs around, but not one of them was Neven.

"Look, it's David." Maisie tapped Perrie's shoulder and pointed toward a guy wearing a blue jersey.

"Hey, David! Can you come here for a second?" Perrie called.

David halted his dribbling and glanced up at the pair of them like they were lost. He then jogged over and stopped just short of bumping Maisie. "What's going on?"

Maisie was already prepared. Somehow, in their mad dash to get to the gym, she'd managed to fish out her small notebook and pen.

"Have you seen Neven?" She scribbled down the question and peered back up, awaiting his answer.

David exchanged a confused look with Perrie, skeptical now of the notebook and their business with him.

"Well," he started, "I saw him at school yesterday."

"And what about after school?" Perrie asked before Maisie could write his first answer down.

Worry lines appeared on David's forehead. "Is there something wrong, Perrie? You've been ignoring Nev. Why are you asking me where he is?"

"That doesn't matter right now!" Perrie shouted.

His eyes grew wider as he seemed to come to his own conclusion. "Wait. Don't tell me he's missing?"

"No!" Perrie's hands flew up to her face. "I mean, I don't know. His mom called me and said he never came home from school yesterday. You know Nev—he always checks in with his mom if he's going to be late."

He nodded in agreement, then shifted his focus to Maisie. So far, she'd been writing everything down.

"What's the deal with the notebook?" he asked her.

She just smiled and winked. "Wouldn't you like to know?"

A crooked, flirtatious smile spread across his face. He seemed to be mistaking Maisie for another girl. Knowing her, she winked at him because she thought he wanted to see her written notes. Perrie had been around her long enough to know when to pull out.

"Okay! So, let us know if you see Neven." She grabbed Maisie's arm and tugged her to leave.

"See you in class, Maisie," David called.

Before parting separate ways, Perrie returned with Maisie to her car for their things. Perrie spent the first half of the day searching for Neven between classes and asking some other students if they'd seen him. She even went to the bathroom during her first-period class to purposely pass by his classroom to see if he was there. No such luck.

When the bell rang for lunch, Perrie found August waiting for her.

"August, you really need a cell phone. Have you heard the news about Neven?" She then spilled everything to him. From the conversation with Neven, to the crazy shenanigans this morning—she didn't leave out a single detail. "I'm really worried."

"Don't worry, we'll find him." He pulled her into his arms and rested his head on top of hers.

She inhaled his comforting soapy scent. "We don't know that. What about all those other missing people?"

He drew back and cupped her chin with a warm hand. "Perrie, relax. We have to try to be positive here."

Positivity, smositivity! she wanted to shout.

"Do you want me to come over after school?" he asked.

Perrie wanted him to, but she really should go and see Neven's mom. "How about I call you at home later?"

August gave her one last squeeze and they walked to lunch, but her appetite was nonexistent. The day remained a perpetual blur, and Perrie found herself repeating a cycle of self-pity. At first, she was mad at herself for yelling at Neven the previous day. Then, she was angry with Neven for making her mad at herself. Then, she was back to being mad at him for making her angry in the first place. It was a vicious cycle.

After school, Maisie drove them to Neven's in record time, but Perrie was surprised to see they weren't the only ones visiting. Parked right at the edge of the driveway was a police cruiser.

Maisie slowed to a stop in the street, and they were both a little unsure of what to do.

"Should we turn around and go home?" Maisie asked.

Perrie mulled it over yet decided against it. They were already here anyway.

"Let me go alone." Maisie opened her mouth to protest, but Perrie shook her head. "I don't want it to look like an ambush."

"Wave at me if you need me. I'll be right here waiting for you." She ducked down low in her seat, trying to become invisible.

Climbing out of the car, Perrie slowly made her way up the long drive. Her heart was pounding and she could hear the rush of blood in her ears. She didn't think she could take any more heartache if anything truly awful had happened to Neven. Regret poked at her, for her earlier words and calling him a jerk all the time.

Perrie flexed and unflexed her fingers before ringing the doorbell and patiently waiting. Mrs. Lee answered within seconds and Perrie wasn't sure what to expect. She'd never seen her so disheveled. Her blonde hair was an untamed mess, and her brown eyes—which were the exact shade of Neven's—were bloodshot.

Neven was a perfect mix of both his parents. He had the balanced combination between his mom and the Chinese on his dad's side.

"Hi, Perrie. Have you heard from Neven?" she asked anxiously, still wearing her pajamas. Even in her sadness and exhaustion, Mrs. Lee was incredibly beautiful. The small amount of hope glimmering in her eyes was killing Perrie.

"No, Mrs. Lee. I was hoping you had better news for me." She wished she could tell her he was all right, but she wasn't so certain. He still hadn't answered any of her texts.

Mrs. Lee's shoulders slumped and the hope she'd held was gone. "No. I was just answering Officer Rodriguez's questions."

Peeking around Mrs. Lee and the door, Perrie tried to get a better look at her guest. A petite female officer stood in the living room, her black hair pulled up in a high ponytail. She looked as if she would be able to hold her own, despite her small stature. The officer whipped her head around and caught Perrie staring.

"Are you Perrie Madeline? I heard Mrs. Lee call you Perrie." *Damn. So much for going alone.*

Perrie's muscles went taut, and the hairs on her neck stood on end. "Yes, ma'am. I am."

"Can you answer a few questions for me?" Officer Rodriguez stalked toward them with her notepad and pen at the ready. The whole thing reminded her of Maisie this afternoon—only this was an actual officer in a real investigation.

"Yes," Perrie squeaked, then cleared her throat. "Yes," she said again.

"Julia here tells me you saw Neven Lee after school yesterday. It appears you're the last person to have seen him."

Oh, God. Panic rushed through her veins. *Does she think I did something to him?*

Beads of sweat formed on her back, and her shirt was starting to cling to her skin.

"Yes, I did," she sputtered. "But I have no idea what happened to him after he left."

"Relax. I'm only trying to figure out where he might have gone so we can try and locate him. Can you tell me about yesterday?" Officer Rodriguez's tone was gentler this time, less intimidating.

Perrie took a deep breath and told her how he'd stopped by for a few minutes, then how a conversation about a new museum turned into them fighting about their past relationship. She didn't seem surprised by any of it. People argued all the time and didn't murder them. Although, some did…

Officer Rodriguez finished up her notes and handed them both her card before she left. Heavy tension remained between Perrie and Mrs. Lee, palpable and stifling.

"Would you like to come in? I was just about to put on some tea," Mrs. Lee asked, unable to muster a smile.

Perrie probably could, but she just couldn't.

"Actually, Maisie is in the car waiting for me. I just wanted to stop by and see how you were doing." She pointed toward Maisie's parked car across the street.

"If you hear anything, please let me know," Mrs. Lee begged.

Perrie nodded. "I promise. If I hear anything at all, I'll call you right away."

The walk back to Maisie's car felt longer, heavier, because there were zero answers.

"Finally!" Maisie said after Perrie opened the car door. "I was going out of my mind with worry. When I saw that officer walk out, I ducked down again as fast as I could. I wasn't sure what the heck to do."

Perrie smiled at Maisie's craziness, even though her eyes were filling up with tears. She tried to push them away as she attempted to forget the rest of this damn day.

"You always know just what to say, Maisie."

SEVEN

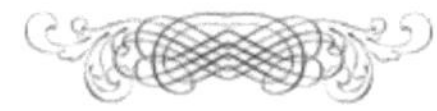

After going over the talk with the officer and Mrs. Lee on the way home with Maisie, Perrie had called August on his landline for him to come over.

"Ladies, I'm at your service," August greeted her and Maisie with a sack full of chips and candy bars.

Perrie sifted through the plastic bag. "Sorry, Maisie. No cheese Doritos, but there are these." She whipped out the ranch style and Maisie wrinkled her nose.

"All mine then." Perrie's sudden enthusiasm deflated as she took a seat beside Maisie on the couch.

August lowered himself on the floor in front of her and leaned against the table, his curls falling across an eyebrow. "So, no news about Neven?" he asked, stealing a handful of chips from Perrie's bag.

"No," she started. "The cop doesn't know much yet, either." If Neven didn't show up that day, who knew how long it would take the police department to find real answers.

"Any theories?" Maisie sipped on a can of soda.

"I'm leaning more toward the *Scream* factor now," August said. "Neven's pretty big and I don't think one person could take him down."

56

"Unless they knocked him out with chloroform," Perrie pointed out.

"I can actually see that."

"I don't want to see that." Neven was no André the Giant, but she wouldn't deny he could hold his own. If it really was more than one person, though, then it was possible he'd been overpowered. Perrie didn't want to dwell on that aspect too much.

"Do you think it might be someone we know?" Maisie asked with the question already written on her notepad.

Perrie shook her head. "If he's part of the group who has gone missing, I'm going to say no. Especially since we don't even know any of the previous people. There's just no connection."

The conversation veered off into stupid territory when they started relating circumstances to Jigsaw, and so she was done. Maisie turned on the first *Saw* movie just in case they could get some ideas from it. But Perrie couldn't focus on the film.

Halfway through the movie her dad walked through the door. Maisie and August then picked up their things and left.

"Are you hungry?" Perrie started for the kitchen. "I can make us something to eat. Spaghetti?" It wouldn't take long to cook, but her mind would stay occupied. She didn't wait for him to respond, so she gathered everything she would need.

Her dad set his lunchbox on the counter. "That sounds good."

"So, Mrs. Lee called this morning." Perrie wanted to lay this on him gently.

"Neven's mom? I didn't know you two were talking again." He unpacked his lunchbox, quirking a brow.

"We're not, technically." She blew out a breath. "Neven's gone missing."

Her dad's hands stopped their methodical chore and dropped to the counter. He squeezed his eyes shut and frowned. Perrie needed her dad to say something, to make her feel better—the same as he had when she'd gotten a scrape in her younger years, when he would say it was all okay. But things weren't really okay.

"Neven? Missing? Are you sure?" He pursed his lips and removed his work badge, resting it beside the lunchbox. Another hard thing about her breakup with Neven was that her dad really liked him.

"Yeah, I went over to see his mom and we talked for a bit. I spoke with a police officer investigating the case, too." She turned back to her task and filled one of the cooking pots with water. The sound of running water was strangely soothing.

"Is he part of the other missing people?" His question was the same as her own.

"I—I don't know." Tears stung the corners of her eyes. She hated doing this in front of her dad.

"Oh, Perrie." He sighed and wrapped his arms around her. "It'll be okay."

She peered up at his face, seeing his apprehension. He knew the same as she did—that it wasn't okay and most likely the same as the other cases. But he squeezed her one more time before releasing her.

"Let's get dinner going. I'm starving!" He clapped his hands together and the edges of her lips tugged up a fraction.

After dinner, stuffed from two servings of spaghetti, Perrie headed to bed early. Once in bed, she cried to herself, trying to muffle the sounds out with her pillow and blankets pulled up, covering her whole face. She didn't want her dad to hear her, to worry more.

She barely slept a wink, tossing and turning all night, reliving those last moments with Neven. What more could she have done? Should she have invited him to stay longer? Asked where he was going? With a groan, she threw one arm over her face in frustration.

Perrie rolled over and stretched for her phone. She attempted to text Neven a few more times but to no avail. All she wanted was to stay in bed, so she shot Maisie a text too.

Perrie: No school for me today.

Maisie: Try to hold your head up, jellybean. I'll talk to you later.

The last thing she wanted to do was go back to school. Around the time her dad woke up, she told him she wasn't feeling well and she would probably stay home. He didn't question, only wanted her to get some rest.

But she didn't. She stared at her ceiling for hours until her phone ringing drew her out of her nightmare of a reverie.

Maisie.

"Hey," Perrie answered.

"It's August. Maisie let me use her phone. I just wanted to check in on you. The school works in mysterious ways when your face isn't here."

"I know, I know, my face deserves the attention. But I'm fine, I'll see you tomorrow." She just needed one full day to be alone, even though it wouldn't have been the worst thing to have him in bed beside her with his arms folded around her.

"If you need anything, I'm here. Maybe I'll eventually become part of the social circle and get a cell phone." He paused. "Nah, I like the freedom. But for you, anything."

"I agree. It's too overrated." All she had was a basic phone from her dad without a camera, and honestly, she didn't even care.

"See you tomorrow, doll face." He understood. He always did.

A knock sounded at the door around four in the afternoon. Perrie forced herself out of bed to see who it was. She spied Maisie through the peephole and swung open the door.

Crimson stained Maisie's cheeks, and her hair was all over the place. Her cousin must've gotten home and rushed over—not that the run over here took more than a few seconds.

"How are you doing?" she blurted.

"Oh, you know. A day full of nothing is like a day at the circus."

Maisie grunted, slid in past her, and booked it for the fridge. Before Perrie knew it, Maisie pulled out several slices of cheese and a juice box. "Compared to my day, it very well could've been."

Perrie's brows shot all the way up. "Is that negativity I hear? Coming from the queen of all things positive?"

"Yeah, whatever. You weren't there to deal with David all day. He's worried, I'm worried, we're all worried, but I had to comfort *him* throughout third period. Then August left early during lunch, so David came and sat with me. That human specimen has drained all things positive from my very soul."

"Wow. So, I take it you aren't into David then?"

Maisie offered her a slice of cheese, but Perrie dismissed it with a flick of her hand. She shrugged and plopped onto one of the barstools at the breakfast bar.

Her cousin seemed to contemplate Perrie's question further, sipping quietly from her juice box. "Um, no thanks. Anyway, David talked to Neven's mom and she's even more panicked. There's still no sign of him and everyone's on edge."

Perrie took a seat next to Maisie on the other wooden barstool, where she was unfolding another piece of plastic from a cheese slice. She removed the slices and folded them both into smaller squares before sticking the entire thing into her mouth.

"I get it. I've been replaying the whole day over in my head and I still don't understand what could've happened."

Maisie patted Perrie's shoulder. "We have to breathe and take a step back. We can't overthink how we're feeling until we know something solid."

That was exactly what she was going to do.

"Speaking of circuses, you don't think it's possible Neven could've joined one, do you?" Perrie asked, her shoulders slumping forward.

"If only we could all join the circus, Perrie. If only." Maisie shook her head, chewing on her thumbnail. She stayed a little while longer to chat and finished her snack, which included two more slices of cheese. Then she stood from the stool and stretched before leaving.

Perrie attempted to keep herself occupied after Maisie had gone, opting to snack on something while watching TV. She could barely focus on the screen, which was sad considering the movie was *Dr. Jekyll and Mr. Hyde.*

A couple hours later, another knock sounded at the door. Perrie peeked into the kitchen and looked at the clock as the pendulum swayed. It was just a few minutes before eight and her dad was working until nine tonight.

"It's just me!" Maisie shouted through the door, then birdy whistled.

Perrie's shoulders relaxed. She birdy whistled back as she unlocked and opened the door for her. "Back already?"

"Yes!" She squeezed past her again.

Perrie got a good look at her, noticing she was wearing black from head to toe. Black leggings tucked into boots and a lacy baby-doll dress. Dark, little felt buttons were dotted down the center of the dress for decoration. It was a *very* Wednesday Addams look.

She'd completed her ensemble with a matching black eye patch lined in lace and silk trimming. The patch was calm in comparison to her other eye, which had been made up with black eyeshadow, bringing out the blue in her iris. Perrie supposed black wasn't a dark color for Maisie this time.

"Are we going to rob a bank tonight?"

Maisie snorted. "No, silly. I start my job at the Glass Vault, remember?"

Perrie totally let that slip her mind and had forgotten all about the new job. Worry stirred within her.

"Are you sure you don't want to skip it tonight?"

She scrunched up her nose. "If you don't want me to go, Perrie, I won't go."

There was a distinct sadness in her cousin's offer and she could tell Maisie wanted this job. Maybe it would be a good distraction for her. Personally, Perrie wished she'd applied with her and had the diversion right now.

"No, it's okay. I know you want to go." Perrie sighed. "But you have to promise me you'll be *extra* careful. Seriously, don't stop for anyone. Drive straight there and straight home."

"Deal. Now, I'll need your help getting the car backed out of the driveway," she said. "I'll put the car in neutral and then we can roll it onto the street. We'll have to take it a few houses down before I can start the engine again."

"Wait, what?" Perrie jumped upright. "You still haven't told your parents?"

Resting her hands together, she batted her eye innocently. "No, but I promise I'll tell them tomorrow. I just want to get a feel for the place first. I don't want to get my hopes up if it's not going to work out. It's not like I'm going out partying—I just want a job."

"Damn it, fine," Perrie grumbled. "Just a heads up, if they come over here asking me where you are, I'm going to tell them. Aunt Krista can see through my lies, no matter how hard I try to tell them. She's like a human lie detector."

"I know! I don't know how she does it." Maisie giggled.

"All right. Let's get that car ready. The sooner you go, the earlier you can get back and let me know what really isn't for the "faint of heart" in there."

They snuck as quietly as they could next door and managed to get the car on the street. There were a few times they almost gave themselves away with laughter. But success came as they rolled it down the drive without a problem. Perrie helped Maisie walk the car a few houses down before her cousin got in and started it up.

"Good luck." Perrie reached through the window and high-fived Maisie. She watched the car roll away, her stomach in tight knots. A gut feeling told her this was a bad idea.

A light pulsing throbbed at Perrie's head, waking her up. The beeping of the alarm buzzed a few seconds later, and it wasn't making her head feel any better. She took some Excedrin, washed it down with water, and got dressed.

Grabbing her things for school and a quick bite to eat, she made her way over to Maisie's. She couldn't wait to ask her all about her first night on the job and find out exactly what was inside the Glass Vault. Knowing Maisie, she would have plenty to spill, not one detail spared.

Perrie stopped short of the front door and noticed Maisie's car wasn't in the driveway. She looked toward the street to see if maybe she parked against the curb. Maisie hadn't.

Did she leave for school without me? Impossible.

Uncle Jaron's truck was still parked in the driveway, and she knew her aunt's car was in the garage. As she raced to the door, Perrie tried not to overthink. She rang the bell several times and banged on the hard wood in between, her nerves bouncing like crazy.

Aunt Krista answered the door in her pajamas with a scowl crinkling her forehead. It was obvious she'd woken her aunt up. "Perrie? What's going on? Is your dad okay?"

"Where's Maisie?" Her heart was pounding ferociously, seconds from jumping out of her chest.

"She probably just overslept. Let me check on her," Uncle

Jaron said, appearing behind Aunt Krista, looking crisp in a pressed suit with his dark hair slicked back. As he walked away, her aunt peered out toward the driveway and scrunched her nose when she noticed the missing car.

"Did she already leave for school?"

Perrie cupped her mouth and shook her head frantically. "No, I don't think she came home last night."

Uncle Jaron returned frowning. "She isn't in her room."

"What do you mean she didn't come home last night? She came home, did her homework, and went to bed early," Aunt Krista noted aloud.

No. No. No. Fear and worry consumed Perrie in that moment. She ran her hands through her hair, gripping hard as she tried to make sense of this. Uncle Jaron and Aunt Krista were talking, but she couldn't hear what they were saying. It was all noise. She needed to tell them.

"Maisie started a new job last night at this place called Quinsey Wolfe's Glass Vault over on Oak Street." Perrie laid her confession before them like a neck exposed to the guillotine, waiting for the blade to come down.

"What are you talking about?" Aunt Krista barked.

Perrie hadn't seen Aunt Krista this mad in a long time. The last time she'd been this angry was when she and Maisie accidentally broke her aunt's three-piece set of unicorn figurines. They'd been playing with a ball in the house and had gotten a little too reckless, then blamed it on the dog, of course. But she'd known in a split second they were lying. Now Perrie just wanted to crawl into a dark hole and find a way to reverse time.

"Perrie, tell us exactly what happened." Uncle Jaron's tone came out calm.

Perrie started with telling them about Monday, the day they'd found the new glass museum and how they were hiring. She then confessed to them how Maisie emailed the owner, Quinsey Wolfe, and how he'd hired her right away.

Taking a breath, she also spilled the beans about last night being Maisie's first day. She purposely left out the fact she'd helped her move the car for her cousin's grand escape plan.

"Thank you," Jaron said for her honesty, as if she'd just performed a miraculous deed. She turned to Aunt Krista, who studied Perrie with narrowed eyes. *No pat on the back from her*.

"Let me try to call her, okay? Just relax." Uncle Jaron produced his cell and raised it to his ear. Perrie took hers out and shot Maisie a text.

Perrie: Maisie, call me now!

When no answer came, Uncle Jaron left a short message and hung up.

"This is what we're going to do first"—he placed a comforting hand on Aunt Krista's shoulder—"we're going to go to the school to see if Maisie's car is there. Maybe she went to school early and forgot to tell Perrie. If she isn't at the school, then we'll stop by this Glass Vault and look for her there. Okay?"

Perrie and Aunt Krista nodded in unison. Uncle Jaron grabbed his keys and Aunt Krista slipped on a pair of sandals. They all hurried out the door to his truck and climbed in.

Before Perrie could buckle, Aunt Krista rattled off a hundred questions. "Why didn't you tell us Maisie started a new job? Who is Quinsey Wolfe? When was she supposed to be back? Why didn't she tell us about this?"

"I don't know the first two. I think she should've been back around midnight. She knew you guys would say no."

Aunt Krista gave her "the look" and Perrie wished she would just stop for a minute. "That's right—we would have said no," she shouted. "There are people missing, your friend is missing, and not to mention it was a school night. There's no way we would let her work a job that late at night with everything going on. I don't care how close she is to turning eighteen."

Silence filled the truck for the rest of the ride to school. Perrie slumped in her seat, unable to stop the miserable emotion consuming her. Her phone hadn't buzzed once from Neven and now Maisie wouldn't answer. Uncle Jaron kept his cool, but she knew he was as disappointed as Aunt Krista. No telling when they would get her dad involved, but she was sure it wouldn't end well.

Uncle Jaron pulled into the school parking lot a few minutes later. He circled it twice, and Maisie's car was nowhere in sight.

"Where is this place? You said on Oak Street?" Aunt Krista peered around the front seat.

Perrie could barely find air to breathe as she said, "Yes. It's right off Oak Street."

Her uncle was already leaving the school parking lot when Aunt Krista asked, "Are you sure? That doesn't seem like a place for a museum."

"That's what we said, but it's there."

With Uncle Jaron speeding down the road, it didn't take long to arrive at Oak Street.

"Slow down so we don't pass it up." Perrie leaned forward in her seat to focus. "Stop! This is it." She pointed.

Uncle Jaron slammed on the brakes and they all lurched forward.

"Where?" Uncle Jaron asked while Perrie jabbed her finger at the air.

When her eyes finally refocused, her hand faltered. Quinsey Wolfe's Glass Vault was nowhere to be seen. There wasn't a trace of a building—it was as if nothing had ever been there at all.

EIGHT

How could the Glass Vault be gone? There was no way. Perrie knew she hadn't imagined it being here. Swinging open the car door, she ran to the edge of the curb and stared at the cut-down trees. Aunt Krista jogged up beside her and placed both hands on Perrie's shoulders. Those two hands did nothing except weigh her down.

"Are you sure this is the right place?"

Wriggling out of her grasp, Perrie spun to face Aunt Krista and her uncle—who now stood directly beside her.

"Yes, I'm sure! We were here Monday after school and there was an old stone building right there." Perrie pointed at the empty space. "Neven saw it too. There was a big wooden door with a plaque that said Quinsey Wolfe's Glass Vault." She trudged through the grass. "See, there are trees that have even been cut down."

"Who knows when those trees were cut down. And if it was here, it's gone now," Uncle Jaron said skeptically.

"It wasn't a traveling carnival on wheels!" Perrie yelled, her breathing ragged.

Aunt Krista tried to rest her hand on her arm again, but Perrie pulled away before she could.

"Well, maybe it was"—she shrugged—"or maybe you're just confused. Either way, we need to go to the police. We have to find out where Maisie is."

Perrie didn't respond. There was nothing she could say that would make them believe her, not when her proof had vanished into thin air. She knew the Glass Vault had been there and she knew what she'd damn well seen. A mixture of anger and confusion stormed through her veins, and in that moment, she couldn't even begin to imagine how Maisie must be feeling.

"Come on, let's go to the police station." Uncle Jaron sighed. He ran a hand across his forehead, his expression grim, as if someone just died. Maisie wasn't dead. Neven wasn't dead. Even with all these people gone missing, there hadn't been any bodies found.

With a heavy heart, Perrie followed them back to the truck. Her panic had subsided for the time being, but she'd been left with an incredible feeling of doubt.

First Neven, and now Maisie. Who's next? What's next? Nothing was adding up.

Aunt Krista couldn't keep it together and cried all the way to the police station. Perrie wanted to comfort her, but she couldn't even keep herself from rocking anxiously in her seat. Uncle Jaron looked as confused as he was hopeful, which was an odd expression. At least he was holding it together better than Aunt Krista and her.

Again, Monday played over and over in Perrie's head until she'd exhausted her brain. She couldn't let her imagination play tricks on her. *Maybe I'm crazy.*

When they finally pulled up to the station, the three of them hurried inside and approached the lady at the front desk. She wasn't the type of person Perrie would expect to be manning the front end of the station. Hot-pink lipstick stained her lips, and she loudly smacked her gum. Uncle Jaron explained the situation and she lazily handed him a missing person's report to fill out. After the report was completed, they were pulled back to speak to Officer Rodriguez in her office. She seemed to recognize Perrie immediately.

"Hello, Perrie. I would ask how you're doing, but I know these circumstances have a way of turning that question into a disaster," she said as she ushered them inside her office.

Perrie couldn't argue with her.

Officer Rodriguez's brows lowered as she read over the missing person's report. She took a quick sip from a navy-blue coffee mug with little white birds on it before making eye contact with any of them.

"Have you heard anything about Neven?" Perrie was too antsy to hold back her impatience.

"No, not yet," she answered. "We may have some promising leads, though."

Shifting her gaze toward Aunt Krista and Uncle Jaron, she asked, "What exactly is going on?"

They explained to her everything they knew, which wasn't much. Aunt Krista told her about this morning. She started with Perrie's frantic visit, Maisie's new job, and ended with their realization that Maisie wasn't in her room when Uncle Jaron went to check on her.

"It appears you're the last person to have seen Maisie. Can you tell me exactly what occurred last night?" Officer Rodriguez fixed her dark eyes to Perrie, searching her face for a hint of understanding. She tried incredibly hard to maintain eye contact, even though it was a struggle.

Something in her brain clicked and she wanted to curse herself for not thinking about it sooner. In both cases, Perrie was the last person who had seen Maisie and Neven before their disappearances. Nausea bubbled up her throat with the notion of being a suspect in her own cousin's missing person's case.

Sweat formed on Perrie's palms, and she rubbed them against her jeans nervously, but they started to perspire again.

So, that was pointless. "Yes, let me start from the beginning."

Before speaking, Perrie inhaled deeply, then began with the trip down Oak Street on Monday, how she'd seen this building that seemed to have come out of nowhere. She told her about Quinsey Wolfe's Glass Vault, the strange description, and job listing. Then, how Maisie emailed the owner about the position on the same night, and a man named Quinsey replied back, letting her know she could start working that Thursday night. After that, she mentioned how the Glass Vault was the same new museum that Perrie had talked about with Neven. She ended it with the last time she'd seen Maisie, which had been at her house the night she'd disappeared.

The tale was becoming a shitty walk down memory lane because everyone in the room was staring at her. Perrie's hands shook and she didn't know what to do with them. So she tightly folded her arms across her chest, wishing she were back at home in bed and this was all a damn nightmare.

Aunt Krista voiced her disappointment in Maisie for not telling them about the job, but Uncle Jaron calmed her before that anger could take root again.

"You said you saw this building going down Oak Street?" Officer Rodriguez asked, seeming to be her best attempt to ease the growing tension.

"Yes, ma'am."

She leaned back in her chair. "I just went down Oak Street this morning and I didn't see a building. In fact, I go down Oak Street every day and I've never once seen anything except for trees. Maybe you're mistaken about the street?"

"What about the freshly cut-down trees?" Perrie tapped her fingers against her knee in anticipation.

"Yes, I did see those, but there isn't a building there."

This shit storm was going nowhere. "I know. We just drove down Oak Street before coming here. There was no building, but I swear to you I saw it."

Officer Rodriguez tilted her head to the side. She rubbed

her index finger against her temple as her thumb rested on her chin. "Are you sure it wasn't some type of trailer?"

"That's what I was thinking!" Aunt Krista blurted. "It would make sense! Maybe it was a lure and when Maisie went in, someone took her."

Perrie knew what she'd seen and it was an actual building. A building with a stone structure like that would've been impossible to move, even if it was on wheels. Unfortunately, she had no proof and nothing to say. She'd told them her story and that was all she could do. No one was going to believe her unless this place reappeared from whatever hell it had come from. She should've thought to take a picture of it Monday with Maisie's phone.

"I'm going to look into this. I'll search around Oak Street this morning, but for now, keep your eyes and ears open. There's always a chance she ran away. I've seen so many cases where the family thinks their child has gone missing, but it turns out they've made the choice to leave."

"Perrie, do you know if Maisie was talking to anyone?" Uncle Jaron turned to her suddenly.

"You would know better than anyone," Aunt Krista piped in.

The gears in her brain started to turn, first clockwise, then counterclockwise. She tried to think about this objectively. Maisie didn't date. She'd never shown interest in anyone, at least no one Perrie knew about.

"No, not that I know of."

Officer Rodriguez studied her with curiosity. "I know we've had a lot of missing persons lately, but I was thinking about how close Neven and Maisie's disappearances are. Is it possible that they were romantically involved? Could they have run away together?"

Her jaw dropped. She hadn't even thought about that. *Why would she even think about that? There was no way. I would have known, right?*

"No." Perrie shook her head. "I mean, they used to be friends, and I dated Neven for a long time, but they aren't like that."

"She's right," Aunt Krista snapped. "Besides, Maisie would have never run away." She also knew Maisie would never have done that to Perrie, even if she wasn't with Neven anymore.

"We have to look at all the possibilities." Officer Rodriguez reached for her business cards and handed one to each of them. Perrie pocketed the card again, even though the officer had already given her one at Neven's. "Like I said, keep your eyes and ears open. I'll check things out on Oak Street this morning. I'll even track down the company that cut down the trees. We're going to do our best to find out exactly what's going on."

On the way home, Aunt Krista sobbed uncontrollably. Uncle Jaron was a worried mess and Perrie was freaking out. It didn't help that she was already worried over Neven's disappearance, but now she was a key player in her own cousin's missing case. Her aunt and uncle would never say it aloud, but she was sure they blamed her for not telling them sooner. She was the last line of defense and she could've stopped Maisie from leaving.

Once outside her aunt and uncle's home, Perrie's shoulders hunched forward as she walked inside and plopped down in the living room. For the first time in a long time, it was awkward to be around each other. She assumed they were all wondering on some personal level about what could have been done differently. The silence was overwhelming, so Perrie escaped by giving her dad a quick call.

He rushed home from work and came right over, then they revealed everything to him.

"You should've told us Maisie was going out last night," Perrie's dad pointed out.

Groaning, she slid her hands down her face. "I know. I

even told her if Aunt Krista or Uncle Jaron found out she had left that I was going to tell them. I didn't think she was truly in any danger. It wasn't like she was going off to a club or a party. She was going to work, so I wasn't worried."

That was only partially true. She'd had that gut feeling about something bad happening, but she didn't think it truly would. Especially nothing like this. She never dreamed Maisie would go missing, not once.

The rest of the afternoon and evening was spent with Aunt Krista and Uncle Jaron. Her dad tackled dinner and sent Perrie to the house to get ingredients. She believed he did it to give her a breather and a moment to herself, which she was silently thankful for.

They tried to sit down for a meal, but no one could eat. Perrie picked at her food until her dad said, "I think we'll go home for the night."

With very few words, Perrie left with her dad and headed up to her room. She flopped onto her bed and stared up at the ceiling once again.

All day Perrie had been thinking about Neven and Maisie, about what more she could do, and then it finally came to her. She had a plan. With a grin, and a stirring of fresh determination, she jerked forward. She grasped her phone and called August's home number, praying he was there.

"August!" she shouted as soon as he answered.

"Perrie, are you all right?"

She scooted to the edge of her bed and rested one arm on her leg. "No, I'm a fucking mess."

"I knew you probably weren't up to coming to school again today, but where was Maisie?" Worry flooded his voice.

And then, she finally broke down. A helplessness enveloping her—she couldn't manage to get one single word out. August patiently waited until she'd relaxed a little.

"Do you need me to come over?" he asked once she was finished sobbing.

Wiping her eyes, Perrie shook her head and realized how fucking stupid that was because she was on the phone. "I do, but I need you to wait until my dad falls asleep."

"Oh? So, it's going to be *that* kind of hanging out," he teased, lightening the mood.

A hint of a smile played across her lips, the first one she'd had all day. It quickly faded as she told him everything. For the fourth time that day, she relayed her story about Maisie and the disappearance of the Glass Vault. She could hear the shock in his breathing, same as hers had been, then he launched into a series of questions for which she had no damn answer.

"Maisie's gone? What do you mean the Glass Vault disappeared? And what the hell is this about the building being on wheels? Didn't you tell them it was huge and had *stone* surrounding it? I'm not sure any wheels could carry that entire building off in less than twelve hours! Are you sure you told them *everything*?" he exclaimed.

"Of course I did! No one believes me, August. They heard me out, but everyone thinks it's a trailer or something that can be moved." Perrie fell back onto the bed, her body lightly bouncing. "It doesn't really matter what they believe. We need to find Maisie and Neven ourselves."

He paused for a few seconds. "Then that's what we'll do."

Curling herself around a pillow, she squeezed it tightly. "Maisie means everything to me. She's practically my sister. Neven used to mean so much to me, too." She supposed her feelings of friendship with him never truly disappeared. "We can't sit here and do nothing."

"It won't hurt to take a look around where the Glass Vault was. I'll pick you up around eleven."

"That works for me. My dad is a sound sleeper, but I'll still meet you outside."

Living with her dad didn't give her too many options. Perrie couldn't just go out, so that really only left her with the sneaking out option. She understood the situation from his point of view, but going after Maisie was the right thing to do—she knew it.

The rest of the night, she kept to herself, basically twiddling her thumbs while watching the pendulum on the clock swing. Right at nine, her dad's door closed, and she counted the minutes until it was five to eleven. She was suddenly grateful to all that was holy that her dad's bedroom was at the opposite end of the house, because sneaking from her room to the front door was easy.

Wind ruffled the end of Perrie's ponytail as she stepped out into the night. She peered up at the dark sky while crossing the damp grass into the street. The few stars she could see shone brightly, seeming to watch her every step.

As she crept closer to the end of the street, Perrie spotted a flash of silver. August was already there waiting for her, so she picked up the pace until she reached his car. He'd left it unlocked and she slid easily into the front seat. August looked like he was on edge, as if his day had been just as stressful as hers. His blond curls were everywhere, and his eyes were dull with heavy bags beneath them. He might not be as close to Maisie as she was, but he cared about her, too.

"Are you all right?" she asked.

"Yeah, it's a lot to take in, you know?" he replied.

Perrie knew exactly how he felt. She leaned her head against the back of the seat and buckled up. "Let's just go and hope Quinsey Wolfe's Glass Vault isn't really gone."

NINE

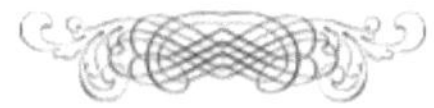

Perrie and August sat in silence the whole drive over to Oak Street. The silence helped her to refocus her thoughts and concentrate on Maisie. She didn't realize it before, but she was beyond exhausted. If she could look into a mirror right then, she was certain she wouldn't recognize the zombie-looking person staring back at her. If Maisie were there, she would know just what to say to lighten the mood.

When Oak Street came into sight, Perrie shoved aside her fears and worries. It was so frustratingly dark and not a single street lamp lit either side of the road. Farther up ahead, though, a flicker of bobbing light caught her attention.

"Wait! Look down there. What is that?" Perrie squinted her eyes to try and see better.

August leaned closer to the wheel to get a better look. "I have no idea. Let me get near it." As he inched forward, her eyes grew into saucers.

"Holy Mother." *Yes*, there was a light, but not only that—the looming silhouette of the Glass Vault. It appeared the same as she remembered. Large stone siding, big door, and windowless walls—it was all there.

August parked near the curb. "Okay? It's still here."

"Apparently, it is," she said sarcastically.

He barely acknowledged her. His eyes were trained on the stone building and the single light radiating from the porch. On the other side of that door, there was no telling what was inside.

August drummed on the steering wheel. "What do we do now?"

"I don't know. I didn't think that far," she whispered.

"Why are you whispering?" August whispered back.

Clearing her voice, Perrie spoke in her semi-normal voice. "I don't have an answer to that either."

He relaxed his head against the seat for a minute, then straightened. "Do you want to go home or take a look at the door *again*?"

"Is that sarcasm?" She smiled. "This is the one time I wish my phone had a camera. Honestly, I hate photographs." Her dad had gotten her a basic phone a few years back because of all the "nudes" teens sent of themselves. She could've had an upgrade this year, but hadn't cared enough to get one.

"You're in luck, doll face. Look what I picked up this afternoon." August produced a sleek smartphone from his jeans pocket.

"So you gave in to society's demands?"

"Sometimes you have to." He held the new white phone up and snapped a picture.

Perrie leaned across her seat, pressing her chin against August's shoulder. His clean soapy scent struck her nose and she wanted to shift even closer.

The photo of the building on his phone darkened. "Why's it black?" she asked.

He squinted at the screen, as if it would make the picture turn out this time. When it didn't, he snapped another photo. And another. And another. Black. Black. *Black*. The images were there for a nanosecond and then *gone*. Even if she'd taken a picture on Monday with Maisie's phone, it would've been pointless.

With a frustrated sound, August placed the phone back into his pocket. "Are we even sure this place was gone this morning?"

"Yes, I'm sure of it."

His lips twitched, like he was trying to hide a smile.

"Spit it out, August."

He pressed his head against the window. "This isn't the time or place, but I was just thinking that there's no way this building could have wheels hidden underneath."

She snorted loudly. "Seriously, and obviously, there's no way this is a trailer."

Silence surrounded them for a few seconds longer, but Perrie was itching to let the damn cat out of the bag. "I have a plan."

"Oh? Let's hear it, then."

"For the record," she said, clasping her hands together, "this may be the stupidest thing I've ever done. It's like we're in a horror movie and the audience knows we're about to rush right into danger. But we have to go inside regardless, right? Most people would just leave and go home, back to where it's safe. I would be that person calling out how stupid they were, too.

"Maybe the Glass Vault has nothing to do with Maisie and Neven's disappearances, but I have to know for sure. I want to go inside and investigate. If we don't find them, if there aren't any clues, then we leave it up to the police. I'll understand if you want to wait in the car or go home. I won't be mad, August."

August reached over and gently pried her hands apart. He moved his other hand up to tenderly stroke the right side of her cheek. Her body heated, and her heart accelerated. Even though she couldn't make out all the details of his face, she could see the sincerity in his smile plain as day.

"Perrie, you're an idiot." Her shoulders slumped at his

words, and she started to move back from his touch, but he pulled her closer, refusing to let her look away. "But, I'm an idiot, too. I'm with you every step of the way. So, if you want to get out of the car, I'll follow you. However, I must warn you that I'm no knight in shining armor. I don't have any of those skills."

She let out a loud laugh and dragged August to her, folding her arms around him. "Neither do I, August. Neither do I."

Before releasing him, she stared at his face a moment longer than she should've, his lips mere inches from hers. Then she drew back because they needed to get inside the museum.

As quietly as she could, she stepped out of the car, except when they shut the doors. Even though they tried to close them as softly as possible, it sounded like a gunshot echoing down the entire street.

"Shit," August said at the same time Perrie ducked to the ground. "Did you just crash to the cement and leave me in the open?"

With nonchalance, she popped back up from the hard ground, as if it had never happened. "I have no idea what you're talking about." She smiled, meeting him on the other side. "Let's do this."

Clenching the back of August's shirt, Perrie followed him to the door while damp grass brushed against her ankles. Besides the sounds of their footsteps, they were surrounded by the uncanny melody of chirping crickets and croaking frogs.

Except for the small ball of light illuminating the porch, she couldn't see anything. The tall wooden door came into view, daunting as ever. The same words were scrawled across the front:

Quinsey Wolfe's Glass Vault

The job posting was no longer listed. In its place, it now

read one word: *Open*. Yet, there were no hours of operation written anywhere.

She and August exchanged glances, giving each other a similar look of surprise. "So, I guess they're open?" Perrie asked.

"Only one way to find out." He shrugged.

The golden knob flashed under the light and Perrie reached to turn it. She gasped. *Unlocked*.

As she pushed the door open, no squeaky hinges greeted them, which wasn't what she'd expected. She thought there would be darkness, but they were instead met with a row of lit lanterns hanging on the wall in a long and narrow hallway.

Perrie stilled, swallowing hard. "Should we keep going?"

"Yeah, or we can stand here all night and admire the hallway."

"Good point," she replied, rolling her eyes. "Guess I'll go first."

Quietly, she stepped inside. August followed suit and softly closed the door behind them. There was nowhere to go but forward. A musty smell filled her nostrils as she took stock of their surroundings. The walls on either side of them were decorated with red-and-gold leafy-patterned wallpaper, highlighted even more by the lanterns attached. The lanterns guiding their way seemed to float and move with the eerie shadows they cast around them.

Perrie listened for the echo of footsteps or distant voices, anything that would point them in Maisie's direction. Nothing … only the soft padding of their own footsteps against the flat blue carpet.

She and August walked side by side, like equal partners. At the end of the hallway, there was only one way to turn, a sharp left. August went first, gripping her hand and bringing them down the next hall covered in solid-gold tile.

This place was beginning to feel like a miniature maze because of the narrow halls leading them in a certain direction.

She suppressed the urge to turn around and run away—back to August's car.

I am not a coward. Maisie needs me. Ignore the voices in your head telling you otherwise.

Refocusing her thoughts, Perrie noticed the hallway had changed. These walls were blue with a gold trim dividing them. Instead of lanterns casting light, expensive-looking crystal chandeliers hung above them. The smell was beginning to remind her of an old library, except no books lingered.

"I'm starting to feel like this place is all hallways and no rooms," August mumbled as he looked ahead. There was obviously going to be only one way to turn again.

"I just hope we run into someone soon," she said.

Maybe, if they could find the owner, he would tell them how his building could vanish into thin air, or why their photos wouldn't appear. Then again, she wasn't entirely sure she wanted to know any of those details.

"If we ever get out of these hallways." August ran the tip of his fingers along the wall, barely touching the surface. Bits of dust floated off into the air.

They reached the end and their only option was to turn right. The flooring transitioned from tile to another flat carpet, but with a strangely unique Victorian pattern, containing threads of browns, golds, and oranges. Again, she noticed the walls had changed their pattern. The blue-and-gold wallpaper had become green, the deepest, most luscious shade of it she'd ever seen. It almost reminded her of the wrapping paper Maisie had used on her birthday present.

"Look!" she whisper-shouted. Up ahead, at the end of the hall, was an opening.

Perrie latched onto August's arm and gripped it so hard she feared she might break it in half. He picked up the pace and she stayed attached like a baby sloth. As they got closer, she took a long, deep breath. The hallway spilled into a large room, and the first thing her gaze landed on was the shimmer of a thousand colorful glass statues. They were *everywhere.*

The room itself formed a complete circle and different displays were placed next to each other, one after another in the same fashion.

Perrie didn't know what August was thinking, but she was both disturbed and enchanted. Everything in the room was made of glass or made to appear like it. She wanted to get a closer look, but she was planted in place by the warning signals going off in her mind. *Ignore them.* There was no one here, and unless they were hiding in the displays, then they were completely alone. Perrie's hands shook when she noticed there was no other door, window, or way out besides the way they'd come in.

"August." She hesitated.

"Yeah?" He attempted to move forward, but she grabbed his arm and yanked him back.

"Did you not notice the, um, lack of exits?" Her gaze continued to search for another way out, maybe even a trapdoor on the marble floor. There wasn't one. Tilting his head, he scrunched his eyes, seeming to try to recall each one of their steps from the moment they'd come through the door.

"Well, now I do," he said finally.

"This is too strange."

He gripped his curls and scratched his head. "I couldn't agree more. There also appears to be no one here."

"Let's take a look around then." She took a cautious step to her left and August followed.

Maybe they were missing something—a secret door or clue that would tell them where to go next. Perrie was ready to believe anything, even the possibility there might be an invisible door. Maybe they would find someone. Maybe they could find this Quinsey person, if he even existed, so they could ask him about Maisie. Unfortunately, that was one too many maybes for her.

This museum was unlike anything she'd ever seen. The

displays each contained frighteningly life-size glass statues with realistic, human-like characteristics. Perrie would never have known that glass could be molded to reflect life, both physically and in color. They were all made that much more unique by the precise coloration of the scene they were playing out. It was like they'd been caught in the moment, as if a photographer had captured them as the action occurred.

They were undoubtedly beautiful, but spine-chilling in the stories they were trying to tell. The displays were from some of the best horror films to date, historical events, and gruesome fairy tales.

Perrie came upon the display of a creature with long, distorted nails standing over the bed of his dreaming victim. The victim's eyes were pressed tightly together and her mouth was crafted into a frown. She must've been having a nightmare and didn't even realize the worst of it was about to come true.

Moving onto the next one, she studied a display with a wolf that was equal parts man, in shredded clothing, howling at the moon. Beneath him, Little Red Riding Hood was sprawled out on the ground with her red cape twisted and mangled like her body. Her eyes were left wide open. Unpleasant chills tingled down her spine and the hairs on the back of her neck rose.

What is this place? She shuddered.

Perrie and August walked in continued silence, his hand clasping hers. Neither of them could bring themselves to speak to each other, so she kept her eyes busy.

There were many, *many* more. They passed a display of kids with white hair and glowing eyes, a cemetery surrounded by ghostly figures, the witches of Salem ready for revenge, and then she halted. Frankenstein's Monster was hard to miss in the menagerie. He faced the wall, back to her, so she was unable to see his expression. She maneuvered around for a better look at his kneeling figure. Stitches covered his glass body, mended wounds that would surely leave behind scars if he were a real person. The way he held himself told her he'd lost everything.

Perrie didn't know why, but she felt sorry for him.

August led her away and onto the next display. These particular scenes she was familiar with, as they were all fairy tales, twisted to be obscure and obscene. Mother Goose ripping the feathers from her beloved goose, Alice setting fire to Wonderland, Hansel and Gretel eating the witch they'd cooked, Ariel halfway finished cutting off her own fin to become human, Pinocchio had sewn a suit of what appeared to be skin to wear over his wooden body, and plenty others that she couldn't find the right words for.

A large sign in her peripheral vision caught her immediate attention.

Welcome to Sleepy Hollow

A glass girl knelt beside it with her hands over her face, as though she was crying. Behind the girl was the Headless Horseman mounted atop his horse, a long blade in his hand. Perrie looked to the right of her, finding the next display to be Jack the Ripper.

Perrie was about to walk toward it to get a better look at what was inside, when something tugged on the front of her shirt. She inhaled sharply and peered down. Nothing was there.

"August, I felt—" She tried to catch his attention, but he was focused on the Sleepy Hollow sign.

A strong force pulled her right leg and Perrie crashed to the floor, landing hard on her side. She quickly rolled to her stomach to get back up, but she couldn't.

"Perrie!" August stooped down and grabbed her hands, but before she knew it, they were being dragged forward. He tried to yank her back, but the force tugging at them was too strong. It was almost as though an invisible wind was drawing them toward the Sleepy Hollow display.

"Please don't let me go!" Perrie screamed at August. She didn't know what was happening, but she did know she didn't want him to leave her there.

His face was flushed red from attempting to haul them in the opposite direction. "I'm not letting you go! Just keep holding on to me."

Perrie squeezed as hard as she could, but then another powerful rush of wind sent them crashing into the Sleepy Hollow exhibit. She was sure they would have to pay for whatever they broke inside this vanishing death trap. Closing her eyes, she prepared for the impact of body against glass. She'd been expecting to hit it hard, so when the wind ceased and she collided with soft grass, a gasp escaped her mouth. August fell on top of her, knocking her sideways.

"What the hell was that?" Perrie shouted and scrambled to her feet.

"No idea." August shook his head and pushed himself up.

"We have to leave. *Now!*" Panic seeped its way through her, down to her bones.

"I'm with you"—he grasped her hand—"but how do we leave?"

His words caught her off guard. *The exit of course!* Except … there was no exit. When she looked around them, they were no longer in the exhibit. In fact, they weren't in the museum at all, and she had no idea where they were.

TEN

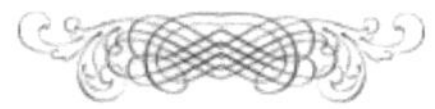

Perrie and August now stood in a forest, surrounded by a fog so heavy she couldn't see anything past the trees directly in front of them.

How are we not in the museum?

"You okay?" August poked her hand with his pinky, waking her out of her staring spell.

"Yeah, I'm fine." Chest heaving, heart pounding, she walked back in the direction they'd come from. Something thrust her backward before she could go any further. She shot August a confused look.

"What the hell?" August tightened his fists and took a few steps back, then jolted forward, hitting the wall of invisibility. As he bounced back, he caught himself before falling to the ground. It was as though there was a wall made of rubber in place of their exit.

Feeling dazed, Perrie shook her head to clear it before her gaze settled on August. "Hold on. What are you wearing?"

Forget the wall, what is with his ridiculous getup? He wasn't dressed in the same clothing as before. August wore black trousers with a button-up black vest and a white collared shirt underneath. A long black coat swept around him, ending where a pair of tall black boots began. Besides the eye-catching quality of his ensemble, she had no clue what era it was even from. But it was old.

August eyeballed her and pointed at himself. "What do you mean *me*? What are *you* wearing?" Shuffling forward, he lifted a lock of her hair. "And when did you get curls?"

Inhaling sharply, Perrie snatched the strands from him and examined it. One long, curly hair twisted in her fingers. Dropping it, she quickly ran her hands over the top of her head and felt the newness of it.

What is going on? Seriously, she was in full-on panic mode as her hands trembled. She took a look at her clothing next, shocked to see August was right.

Perrie wore a long black dress with a big skirt and sleeves that came to her elbow. A layer of lace flared out at the ends and brushed the skin above her elbows. The bodice was cinched tight with decorative buttons trailing down her middle. She skimmed her hands up from her stomach to her neck where she could feel the collar squeezing her throat.

Never in her life had she been claustrophobic, *but she was now* with all these buttons. The dress almost dragged on the ground and she lifted it away to see her shoes. *These shoes!* They were charcoal gray, with pointed toes and skinny heels. Perrie had never worn real heels in her life! Actually, the last time was her princess dress-up shoes back in preschool—they didn't count.

Even when Perrie had gone to the prom with August, she'd chosen flats over heels. Using caution, she took a couple steps and, thankfully, they weren't as uncomfortable as they appeared. Shaking her head, she dropped the skirt to cover her feet. They needed to find Maisie and the last thing she needed to worry about were shoes.

"I don't know why I'm wearing this, honestly. I sure didn't have time to change or magically find these clothes in the one-second transition from where we were—to wherever we are now," she snapped more to herself than August.

"I need a picture of this." August reached for his pants pocket but realized he didn't have any. He patted his hips and backside down. Nothing.

Their cell phones were *gone*. Her dad wanted her to have a phone for emergencies. Well, where was the damn thing when she needed it? Even the necklace August had given her had vanished. She was at a loss for words and it seemed August was, too. Perrie's legs slowly carried her back to the barrier, while she held her arm out with her palm up and fingers spread apart, until her hand contacted the invisible wall. It was like rubber mixed with gel. There was no breaking through it. She pushed, clawed, and scratched as hard as she could.

Using her miming skills around the barrier, she first went to the left, then again to the right. August copied her movements until they realized they were practically surrounded. Their only option was to go in the other direction, toward the forest in front of them. She hesitated.

"I really don't want to just sit here." August sighed.

Perrie had no intention of sitting there and waiting for who knew what. This whole week had been a fucking mess, and this place was about to put her over the edge. She didn't know where she was or what the hell was going on.

Is this a nightmare? Perrie pinched herself on the arm like they did in the movies to wake up. *What a waste of time.* All that did was make her arm hurt.

"We're not going to sit here," she said. "Let's try going forward, since that appears to be the only direction to go." There was little to see except bushes and trees, so she let nature lead the way.

August motioned her forward. "Ladies first."

"Why thank you, August. Aren't you just a gentleman? I'll let you know if I see a werewolf in the forest so you can, you know, run first." She smiled, lifting her skirt and trudging ahead.

Surprise washed over Perrie by the level of comfort in her pointy *hiking* shoes. Still, she wished she had on something more practical. Climbing over tree limbs wasn't exactly a tea party.

"Let me go ahead of you then. Wouldn't want anyone to mess up that pretty face of yours," August said, reaching to move a tree limb so she could pass through. The long limbs were covered in green leaves, dotted in between with shriveled red berries that she was sure were poisonous.

August's jacket snagged on a branch, but he didn't seem too worried. He was looking ahead, far too focused on that than disentangling himself.

"No way," she breathed.

Before her, on the other side of this forest, stood another large wooden sign. This one was different—it curved and was secured on either side by tall, round wooden posts. The sign was so old, rotted and worn from harsh weather. She was impressed that it had any life left in it at all.

Even though she could see the large letters, Perrie squinted hard to read what was written across it to make sure she wasn't dreaming.

Welcome to Sleepy Hollow

"That's the same sign we saw in the exhibit on display." She cupped her mouth and clenched August's shoulder.

"I realized that when I saw the sign," he said sarcastically with a grin.

She slapped his arm. "Stop trying to be funny."

Swallowing, she stepped closer to get a better view when, rising out of the fog, two rows of houses appeared beyond the sign. Straight ahead, past an ordinary field, the houses continued to stretch to the left with its twin set on the right, becoming a village.

They looked like old cottages, practically falling apart with crooked roofs and leaning structures. She had no clue how they were still even standing.

Perrie threw her hands in the air. "Where are we? I mean, *seriously*, what's going on?"

August glanced up at the sign again. "I feel like we already have our answer."

He was right. This was the exact sign from the display. It didn't seem possible, but somehow, they'd been transported to Sleepy Hollow. And nothing here was made of glass.

Just to be sure, Perrie brushed her hand across the grass and picked one small, single blade, then rolled it between her forefinger and thumb. Its smooth texture grazing against her skin was as real as it got. Satisfied enough, she threw the blade of grass on the ground.

"Maybe we'll find someone here who can help?" Perrie suggested.

"As you wish, milady." August bowed.

She rolled her eyes and smiled. "I'm pretty sure that's a different era."

"Are you sure?" He chuckled, flicking his gaze back to the houses.

"No, not exactly."

August walked ahead and Perrie followed, taking one last glance at the sign above their heads. The world was as silent and intimidating as the thick fog encasing them. Finding it hard to see very far in front of her feet, she kept her eyes trained on the back of August's head.

As they approached the first set of houses, they decided to go left and knock on the doors. Maybe *someone* would be inside.

They walked up the couple of wooden steps of the first house and managed not to fall through the stairs in their dilapidated state. No one answered when she knocked, so August tried turning the knob, only to find it locked.

After about ten houses, Perrie was starting to believe no one was home. They trekked to the next house, her fist in midair and ready to knock when a male voice shouted from inside, "Leave now!"

Startled, Perrie jumped back. Thankfully, August caught her before she fell down the stairs.

"Please, can you open up? We're lost," she said.

A man's voice shouted again, even louder than the last time. "I said, leave!"

"Look, we need help, and we're lost. My friend here is injured and needs somewhere to rest," August lied.

Perrie shook her head. "Injured? What am I going to say I have, a fucking stomach ache?"

"Just go with it."

After a pause, the man responded. "No. Go find someone else. If you don't get off my property, I'm going to have to shoot you and your friend. Do you hear me?"

That did it. Perrie scrambled down the stairs with August—imaginary injury be damned. She wasn't ready to take a bullet for something like that.

"What now?" she asked as she leapt down the last step.

August cocked his head. "I guess we can try a few more houses? Investigate more. I mean, there has to be a way out of here."

The word 'investigate' reminded her of Maisie and her notepad. Had she gotten magically sucked into this hellhole too? If she had, then there was a chance she was hiding somewhere in one of these houses. Maybe she was too afraid to come out, but no, that wouldn't be Maisie. Perrie could feel the hope in her heart building to a catastrophic letdown.

She placed her arm in front of August. "Do you think Maisie might be here? She did go to the museum that night."

"Honestly, I hope not, Perrie. But it's a possibility." August's gaze shifted up ahead past the field. "Do you hear that?"

"Hear what?" Perrie tilted her head, trying to listen.

"Exactly, I'm not hearing *anything*. No birds, insects, nothing."

"I haven't been paying attention to sounds since we've been, you know, a little busy trying to find people." She thought about it a little harder. "But the wind doesn't seem to be blowing anymore."

August tensed, his eyes scanning the landscape. "Something's off, even more than it already is."

They moved on to the next house and like the others, no one answered. There had to be someone inside one of these homes. Especially since they'd encountered some crazy down the cottage strip who'd threatened them already. She wondered if locals weren't answering the door because they were frightened of them.

It dawned on her then when she remembered what she'd seen in the display. Gasping, she whirled to the side and grabbed onto August's coat and stopped him.

"What do you know about Sleepy Hollow?" she rushed out.

"Ichabod Crane"—his eyes widened—"The Headless Horseman."

"I think we're inside the story. I've never actually read it, only seen the movie, but I know the basics." Perrie's thoughts ran wild and suddenly the locals' behavior made sense, or … the one local they'd encountered.

The Headless Horseman wasn't real—she didn't think—but who was she to say what was real and what wasn't anymore.

A strong sense of urgency flowed through her veins as they walked up to the last house. August rapped gently against the door, while she wanted to pound it like a madman. Same as with the others, nothing happened. Perrie was almost tempted to run back up the field to the first cottage and take her chances with the other guy. If he hadn't threatened to shoot them, that was, she would've kept bugging the piss out of him until he'd let them the hell in.

"You have to hide now," whispered a meek female voice.

Perrie's head jerked up. Did she imagine it? There wasn't anyone here. "Is someone there?" she asked. When no one answered, she turned around.

The door creaked, and Perrie whipped her head around so fast that lightning wouldn't have been quick enough to strike. A small hole opened up in the middle of the door. The lone eye of a local peeked out at August and her, unblinking.

"What do you mean hide?" Perrie said. "Can you let us in? We're sort of lost." They were more than lost, but she didn't doubt this stranger would believe them if they told her the truth.

"It is only I here," the woman said. "If I let you in, you must promise to do as I say."

August shared Perrie's skepticism, like he didn't know what kind of creature this woman was, yet they both agreed to her terms.

The tiny opening closed and at least a dozen bolts ground together on the other side as the stranger unlocked the door.

"Uh, maybe we should go back to that guy with the gun," August muttered.

Perrie glared daggers at him, and he just smiled wide at her dirty look with that maddening grin she loved so much.

The door slid open and they were greeted by a young woman in a gown that was once fashionable, but now moth-eaten. Perrie peered down at the stranger's bare feet. She was not what she'd expected—not at all. Beautiful, golden hair fell in waves around her cherubic face. If it weren't for the fact she shared Perrie's height, she would have mistaken her for a child.

The young woman waved them inside, and they hurried into a small living room. With a practiced hand, the stranger locked each one of the bolts, then turned around to face them.

"Thank God!" Perrie exclaimed, relieved by the fact they were no longer alone. "I'm Perrie"—she motioned from herself to beside her—"and this is August."

"Pleased to make your acquaintance." The young woman slowly nodded. "My name is Katrina Van Tassel."

ELEVEN

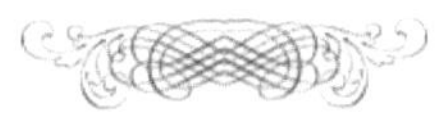

Katrina Van Tassel.

Perrie might not have read the Sleepy Hollow story, but she recognized that name from the movie. Even her face looked familiar, like she'd seen her before, but maybe Katrina just had one of those faces. Either Katrina was mad, Perrie was mad, or they were all entirely crazy here. She wanted to hysterically laugh at this circumstance, but then she remembered Maisie and Neven were missing.

"Hi, Katrina, it's a pleasure to meet you, too." Perrie was unsure if she should bow or what, so she stood awkwardly beside August.

Strolling over to a circle of wooden chairs, Katrina sat and motioned for them to do the same. "I would offer you a refreshment, but we need to wait until it passes."

"Until what passes?" Perrie asked, just as confused as August looked.

Katrina's face paled. "The Headless Horseman."

She has to be joking.

"You've got to be shitting me." August clasped the back of his neck.

Swaying, Katrina gazed dreamily at the ceiling. "Yes. He

95

has taken everything from me—my father, mother, my love, and everyone else I have ever cared about. The taunts continue one by one, until he decides it is my time."

The hairs on Perrie's arms rose like needles. The way Katrina talked—it was dazed and absent-minded, as if she wasn't all there. She believed in something that wasn't even real. Perrie wanted to ask her if she knew about the Glass Vault, or if she'd seen Maisie, but this wasn't the right time or place.

August gradually leaned forward, as if he was approaching a frightened kitten. "What year is it?"

"Seventeen-ninety. Why?"

Perrie sucked in a sharp breath and her eyes widened. Seventeen-ninety? They couldn't have traveled through time. *The Legend of Sleepy Hollow* was just a story.

August shifted back, his expression blank. "Excuse us, we have been on the road a long time and have lost count of the days. We were unsure if the New Year had already passed."

A much better answer than she would've thought to give. She didn't have the mind for coming up with lies on the spot. It was why Aunt Krista could always call her out when she'd lied.

When Perrie scanned the inside of the cottage, there wasn't much to the living room—four chairs, a large rug, and a kitchenette, complete with a wood-burning stove and dated cookware. They really weren't in Deer Park anymore—that was for sure.

"Where do you hail from?" Katrina asked.

"Well, we uh, come from the East?" It came out more like a question than an actual answer. Katrina tensed and dropped to the wooden floor and flattened herself against the dust.

"Lie down on the floor. Don't make a sound until I tell you to," she said anxiously.

"Is there something wrong with the East?" Perrie furrowed her brow.

"Shh! Get down!" she whisper-shouted.

August laid down flat on his stomach, and Perrie followed right next to him, inching closer until their shoulders were pressed together. She didn't want to find out what would happen if they didn't follow her instructions. Straining her ears, she listened for anything out of the ordinary. It wasn't hard to pick out the strange noises when this whole world had been silent. Outside, the noises grew louder, and louder, until she could almost make out the source of it. The sound of a horse's hooves beat upon the ground in a steady cadence.

The ground quaked around them as the horse drew nearer. Perrie's heart was pounding so rapidly that she worried whatever was outside could hear it. August must've sensed her growing fear and looped an arm around her waist, tugging her even closer to his warm body. It calmed her enough.

Perrie glanced at Katrina, who watched the door like a bird of prey. A sheen layer of sweat dotted her forehead and rose-red lips. Katrina knew exactly what waited outside her home, as if it was her daily ritual.

Then the noise outside came to an abrupt stop. The horse and its rider had to be in front of Katrina's house. It whinnied loudly enough that it reverberated in Perrie's ears like a powerful musical note. The sound was so deafening that she cringed into August's side in an effort to shield herself, while he didn't so much as flinch.

Someone jumped to the ground from the horse with a heavy thud. Hefty footsteps followed.

Thump, thump, thump.

Perrie clenched her jaw so tightly she was afraid her teeth would break. She wasn't sure how much time went by, but it must've only been several seconds before the rider turned around. The boots hit the steps as they walked back to their horse.

The horse let out another loud whinny before galloping away. Perrie didn't even twitch. August lifted his arm from around her and started to move, but Katrina was faster and whipped out her hand to catch his wrist.

"Not yet!" she said in a desperate whisper.

August's lips parted like he was ready to argue, then seemed to see the seriousness on her face, and relented.

BOOM!

Perrie's fingers dug into the wood at the sound of the gunshot, and she snapped her eyes back to the door, hoping they were not under fire.

BOOM!

Another sounded, but it was different this time. The echo of the gunshot was nearly drowned out by a man's deep, aching scream. Perrie trembled, holding her breath until her chest burned and she thought she would pass out. She'd never in her life heard the strangled sounds of someone suffering.

She wanted to run to the door and help whoever was in need, but she had no weapon or combat training, and didn't even know what the hell was out there.

Only hushed silence filled the air, followed by the hard stomping of hooves as they drew nearer and nearer. They passed by their hideout, then drifted farther into the distance. The beat of the wind whispered once more as it blew against the house and the three of them were alone.

Katrina rested her head against the floor and breathed deeply. "We can move now."

"So what's going on? Who was that?" Standing took some time from how rigid she was, but Perrie lifted herself upward, albeit shakily. She was beginning to believe Katrina wasn't so crazy after all.

August pulled up beside Perrie and stretched his arms to the ceiling. "It can't be who we think it is, is it?"

Gnawing on her lip, Perrie turned to him. "It has to be the Headless Horseman, but how is that possible?"

"Think about it, Perrie. We're in a place that makes no sense—the impossible could be possible."

Katrina lifted herself up and quickly tidied the messy strands of her hair. "The tales of the Headless Horseman are most certainly true. There is no certain time he arrives, but when he does, he continues to take us one by one. Mr. Roberts, God rest his soul, and I were the last ones left. Now it is only the three of us."

"Mr. Roberts? I think he may've been the man who wouldn't open the door for us earlier," Perrie said.

Katrina sighed. "He has not opened his door in quite some time, not since his wife and two children were taken."

"I'm confused." August stumbled back to the chairs and sat. "Why don't you just pack up your things and leave?"

Perrie wondered that too as she plopped down on a chair. If a headless psychopath was going around taking people, she sure wouldn't have stuck around.

"I can't leave. I have tried" —Katrina took the seat across from August—"but the both of you can."

"We didn't—" Katrina interrupted her before she could explain.

"I know the two of you are not from here, or the East as you say. There have been others like you who have come and gone. When I have tried to follow them, something always keeps me here."

Perrie rested her hands on the arms of the chair and gripped the edges. "What do you mean?"

The young woman before her withered, as though she'd resigned herself to remain in Sleepy Hollow for eternity. "If you continue following the field and pass through the graveyard, I believe you can cross somewhere else. When I have tried to do the same, a force pushes against me, and I am unable to pass."

August hunched forward, hands on his knees, seeming to anticipate her next words. "What about the Headless Horseman? Have you seen him?"

"I have. It is true he is without a head, but I have never

seen him take anyone's," Katrina said, not meeting their eyes as she busied herself with the lace cuffs of her sleeves. "My true love, Ichabod, was the first to be captured. I was with him that night and taken by surprise. The Headless Horseman emerged from nowhere. Ichabod told me to run, and so I did, deserting him. That was the last I ever saw of him. After that night, the Headless Horseman has come when it pleases him, picking us off one by one."

Her eyes grew distant, and Perrie shuddered at the idea of being taken by this *thing*. Maybe there was a way to save Katrina and themselves.

"Could you show us the way to the crossing?"

"Perhaps in the morning. It is too late and he will have returned to the graveyard by now. It will be safest to go at dawn."

Perrie's eyes fluttered wildly. "We have to pass where he lives?"

Katrina pursed her lips and nodded. "I am afraid so, but that is your best chance. When he returns for me, I pray the two of you will be far from the danger."

"Will you come with us?" August asked.

"I will try."

The whole point of them going into the Glass Vault was to find Maisie and possibly Neven. She was still unsure if Neven even came to the Glass Vault. "You said others have passed through. Was there a girl named Maisie or a guy named Neven? The girl possibly wearing an eye patch?"

"No." Katrina touched her cheek. "No, I cannot recall those names. I am certain."

The little bit of hope Perrie had evaporated from her chest. But she couldn't give up. She wouldn't.

Katrina sagged her shoulders tiredly. "In the meantime, I will feed you and grant you the spare bedroom tonight for some rest."

Exhaustion hit Perrie at that moment, and she had no idea

when they would eat next, so she agreed. Katrina heated up some food that she already had prepared in a large pot. While the meal was cooking, Perrie decided to confess the truth to her.

She and August alternated explaining to Katrina where they were from, the date, and the glass museum. Katrina took it all in stride and didn't seem that surprised. In a place where a man with no head kidnapped people, it didn't appear that far-fetched to be able to believe something seeming out of the ordinary.

Katrina handed them steaming bowls filled with a warm meat and vegetable stew. Perrie took a small bite and was surprised by how delicious the flavor was.

After dinner, Katrina led them to the spare room. Based on the time frame, Perrie wondered what Katrina thought about them staying together, but the young woman obviously didn't seem to care.

"Rest easy," Katrina said softly.

"Thank you." Perrie smiled.

She felt like they'd hit a dead end. If Maisie wasn't here, then where was she?

TWELVE

The spare bedroom that Katrina gave to Perrie and August was cramped and only held a few things in it. On one side of the room, a chair and small writing desk, with several blank sheets of paper sprawled across its surface, took up a corner. Then on the other side of the area stood a dresser and a decently sized bed, complete with a handmade quilt to keep warm.

August lowered himself to the floor.

"What are you doing?" Perrie asked.

His lips pulled up to one side. "I was going to let you have the bed."

Perrie drew the covers back. "August, just because we're in a different century doesn't mean you have to act like the perfect gentleman and sleep on the floor. Just get in the bed and be quiet."

He didn't think twice about it and removed his jacket and boots before sliding right into bed. She repeated his motions with her shoes and settled beside August. Surprisingly, her dress wasn't as uncomfortable as she'd first thought. Maybe she would be able to sleep.

August laid on his back, staring at the ceiling with his

hands tucked behind his head.

"What are you thinking about?"

He rolled over to face her. "I'm thinking about tomorrow and hoping I can get us out of here and back home."

"Where do you think Maisie and Neven are? Katrina hasn't seen them."

"I honestly don't know," he said. "I don't think they're here. Katrina has been here longer, so I'm sure she would have noticed someone like Maisie passing through."

"Maybe Maisie didn't stop here?"

"If that's the case then she could've found her way back home already."

"What about Neven? People go missing every single day, so what if something terrible happened to him? What if he isn't here?"

August reached over and pulled her to him and she rested her head against his chest. "One day at a time, okay? Let's stay positive and start fresh tomorrow. Once we get the hell out of here, that's when we can worry about everyone else."

He was right. She would do it for Maisie and Neven. If she could stay positive about this then she could remain focused. Although, she wondered if her dad, Aunt Krista, and Uncle Jaron had discovered she'd gone missing too.

Perrie placed her hand on August's cheek, turning his face to meet hers. "Thanks for coming with me tonight, August. I'm glad you're here. This would be a messed-up place to be alone."

"I wouldn't want you to be alone here, either. Hell, I wouldn't even want to be alone here." His lips brushed her forehead, and Perrie nuzzled into the crook of his neck, drawing in his soapy scent. For the time being, she felt safe.

"Good," Perrie said, breaking into a wide smile. She looked up one more time to find him grinning, too. As she lay back onto his firm chest, she was unable to stop smiling.

"Good night, Perrie."

"Good night, August."

As she shut her eyes, she waited for exhaustion to creep in and slip her into a deep sleep.

Someone was chasing her. Perrie was back at her house running from someone, something, and there were no lights to guide her. She hurried to her room and attempted to turn on the light there. But as she flicked it up and down, no light came, so she ran into her closet to hide.

The door banged open and the shape of a person now stood in the doorway. Nothing was visible, not even when she squinted her eyes to try and see. This darkness was different— it had a life of its own that swirled and twirled around her, enveloping her until she was a part of it.

He found her. The person in the doorway grabbed Perrie and she still couldn't see him. Pulling her from behind, he dragged her while she bucked and kicked at the floor to lessen his hold. Even her scream was weak, barely any sound escaping, the volume so minimal that no one would be able to hear it except for him.

By the touch of his strong hands and the feel of his large body, Perrie knew it was a man. His hands smelled of something putrid and decomposing. She gagged, but nothing came up.

Screaming was getting her nowhere. When they reached her front door, outside stood a horse on a road lit up from the beams of street lamps.

He hauled her onto the horse with him while Perrie continued to scratch and claw. Then she finally got a look at her captor. Swathed all in black and cocooned in a cloak of obscurity, but where his head should've been, there was nothing—only a void.

Her body froze, locked in place, but then a cold brush of metal rubbed against her neck. She was on her side, and he raised his arm to pull back what looked like a long sword. Closing her eyes tightly, she hoped and prayed she wouldn't be able to feel this. The wind roared against the blade as it fell.

Something brushed across Perrie's face, and she was barely coherent, bringing her hand up to swat it away. A few seconds later, the same something tickled her cheek, and her eyes flew open when she remembered the nightmare.

A soft sigh escaped her when she found August holding one of her long, brown curls caught between his fingers. He went to brush her face with it again, but she knocked his hand away before he could.

His laughter rumbled deeply, and she shoved his shoulder, which only made him laugh even more.

"I heard Katrina moving around, so I thought I should wake you up to get ready." He yawned. "Although, I wouldn't mind watching you sleep some more."

"You were just sitting here watching me sleep?"

"Well, no, I was actually sleeping until your snoring woke me up."

Perrie kicked his leg softly, her cheeks heating. "I do not snore!"

He leaned his head into her shoulder and chuckled. "Sure you don't, *Snoring* Beauty."

The fact that he'd called her beauty took away all the embarrassment.

"Whatever." She smiled.

They lay there for a little while longer as reality soaked in and then they forced themselves to get up. Perrie didn't know why but she'd thought she would wake up in her own room, as if this had all been a nightmare. August slipped on his boots while she laced up her pointed shoes. He waited for her at the door and opened it after she finished.

Katrina sat at the kitchen table, wearing the same tattered dress. They joined her for breakfast, which consisted of stale bread and half an apple each.

"It's all I have left," Katrina said.

"It's perfect," Perrie replied.

"I agree." August shoved a piece of bread into his mouth. The three of them ate their share in silence. Perrie tried to savor the taste of the apple, to make the stale bread last, but it was hard to do that when the monster in her belly demanded its fill.

"Are we ready to go?" Perrie was the first to stand, anxious to get moving before they were no longer alone. She hoped they would make it out and find Maisie.

Katrina folded her arms and nodded. "There is nothing left for me here. I only hope I can follow."

Perrie hoped so, too. The key word was *hope*.

As Katrina led them out the front door and onto the porch, the day appeared the same as it had yesterday. Trees rustled, and fog covered the ground, making it hard to see anything that wasn't immediately in front of her.

Perrie flinched as the stairs creaked and moaned with the weight of their footfalls. They stepped into the early morning dew blanketing the grass, and waited for Katrina to continue leading the way. They hadn't walked for long when a graveyard formed in the distance, the headstones seeming to go on for miles. The land appeared dead with only leafless trees and blackened dirt.

As they drew closer, the shapes of the headstones became clearer and a chill raced down her spine. She was beginning to get a shitty feeling about this.

Then the scent of decay struck her nose.

"Oh damn," August groaned, wrinkling his forehead.

Katrina came to a horrified stop and dropped to her knees. Large black beetles scattered across the dirt ground as she covered her mouth. Perrie could tell there was a scream anxiously trying to dig its way out from Katrina.

It wasn't only headstones covering the graveyard, but severed heads sprinkled everywhere, like seeds waiting to be planted. There were no bodies, just a never-ending graveyard of scattered bloody heads and grave markers.

Perrie closed her eyes and counted to five, foolishly hoping they would be gone when she opened her lids. *Nope.* They were all still there. Her gaze darted to Katrina who remained on her knees, rocking back and forth. August bent down beside her and said the words Perrie wished she could get out. "There's nothing we can do, Katrina. They're all gone. We have to be strong and get out of here."

Perrie crept closer, kneeling in front of her. "He's right. We're going to have to run through there. As hard as it is, avoid looking down and don't focus too much on anything except what's ahead."

"Okay," Katrina said breathlessly. "We are going to have to run."

That was a start. Now Perrie just needed to get her own nerves in check.

They sprinted through the graveyard and avoided the heads the best they could. She spied more of the color red, pooling where the severed heads lay. The headstones appeared mostly old, broken, and cracked, but she didn't have time to admire them—she brushed past everything.

The trees' rustling slowed to a stop—frozen in time. Perrie made the mistake of staring toward a spot where a tree had quit moving, causing Katrina to do the same.

Shifting her gaze to the ground, Katrina screamed in despair. "Ichabod!" She lunged to a fallen head, resting on its side under the tree. The dark-skinned head wore a hollowed-out expression, charcoal-colored hair, and eyes the color of ebony. Katrina reached out to grab it, but August dragged her back.

"We can't stay here," Perrie said. "Let's go. Now."

Tears rained down Katrina's cheeks, but her strength managed to take over.

From behind them, sounds came alive. The same hoofbeats from the day before approached. Perrie couldn't see through the fog, and she wasn't going to linger there either. They didn't look back. They ran.

The beats drew closer and closer, and there was no way in hell that all three of them were going to be able to outrun a horse.

August stayed ahead and Katrina was in the middle. Perrie glanced back, gasping. To her horror, a headless rider pushed out from the fog. It wasn't that she was shocked by the fact the Headless Horseman did exist, it was how he looked exactly as he had in her nightmare. A demon swathed in black.

She pumped her legs even faster, but she had never been a good runner. The horse's hooves pummeled the earth, taking its rider beside them, the headless creature holding the same shining blade from her dream. August looked back for the briefest second and saw how the Horseman was trying to cut them off. The blade was coming for her. She knew it.

Her legs were growing tired, heavy. The Headless Horseman wouldn't let up his speed when he neared, and he lowered his blade to her neck level as he pursued. Perrie should've dove to the ground, but she wouldn't be fast enough. Katrina gave her a hard shove to the side, just in time to keep Perrie's head on her shoulders.

Somehow, between Perrie hitting the ground and looking back, Katrina was in his grasp, her excruciating wails reverberating through the fog. Perrie grabbed for her, but missed.

"Run! Get out of here before it is too late," Katrina yelled.

Two arms snatched Perrie from behind, and she shrieked. All she could think about was her nightmare. She was next, this was it for her, and now she would never find Maisie or Neven. With a brutal twist of her shoulders, she tried to break free but couldn't.

"It's just me," August whispered, and she relaxed slightly.

The Headless Horseman held Katrina with one hand, and with the other, he raised his blade.

Perrie didn't see what happened next because August drew her forward, urging her to run even faster than before. The path where they were headed was unclear, but then she didn't have to wonder too hard. Just like before, back in the museum, a strong force pulled her toward it. The wind yanked at her entire body, then August shoved her from behind.

Their fingers brushed as she reached for him, but it was too late.

There was no going back.

THIRTEEN

As Perrie pried open her eyes, the whole world spun.

She lay on the floor of an unfamiliar room. A bed rested beside her, covered in silky sheets, and a small dresser stood across from it.

The graveyard was gone. Katrina was gone.

"August?" She forced herself to stand, but she didn't see him anywhere. Lifting the bed skirt, she looked under it, but found nothing.

Groaning miserably, Perrie fell to the bed. Her dress made a loud crunching noise as she sat and peered down at her lap. She inhaled sharply. It wasn't the same dress as before, but an entirely new one. The black material had become a vibrant green, like the color of the purest emerald.

As Dorothy would've said, *There's no place like home.* And she still wasn't there. *Where are those damn red ruby slippers when you need them?*

Perrie kicked the skirt of her dress out in front of her and the gown seemed to weigh her down. Layers upon layers of shiny green fabric made up the skirt. Even the bodice was finely crafted with little buttons and ruffles.

What the fuck is happening here?

On the wall, a single oval mirror hung, and she hurried over to it to take a better look at herself. A ton of skin and cleavage were on display, more than she'd ever shown in her life—aside from a bathing suit, which the last time she even wore one of those was in junior high before she developed.

She pulled the skirts aside and a heeled shoe protruded. *Heels again?* This time ankle length and laced up at the front. Her hair was still curled, but instead of hanging at her waist, it was now just below her shoulders.

Her hands flexed—she thought she would've been back at home, and now she was somewhere else. She needed to get the fuck out of this room and find August and hopefully Maisie if she was here.

Perrie's gaze fell to a door by the dresser, and she opened it wide enough to peek out. No one was there.

Breathing a sigh of relief, she opened the door wider.

"Not so fast, Mary," said a gruff male voice.

She whipped her head to the left and took a deep swallow. A tall man, dressed in a black suit and gloves, with a wooden cane in one hand, loomed above her like a gothic tower. He was an older man—maybe in his late fifties—with peppered gray hair and an impressive mustache. The man was physically fit, yet she wasn't going to be intimidated.

"Sorry, you have the wrong person. I'm not Mary. Maybe you could try another room down the hall?" Taking a measured step back, Perrie looked into his dark-brown eyes. She didn't like the way he was looking at her, as if she was his next meal and he was starving.

When she spoke, she realized her voice wasn't her own. Apparently, she'd adopted an English accent in favor of hers. It wasn't any stranger than anything she'd experienced so far, but it was still startling.

He studied her as if *she* was the crazy one. Mary might rhyme with Perrie, but there was no way the two could be confused. She'd never seen this man before in her life. He stepped forward, and she took another step back. He waggled his gloved index finger in front of her face, scolding her like he would a naughty little child.

"Oh, Mary, Mary, Mary. I didn't know tonight is to be our role-playing night. I believe we only do that on Fridays."

What is this asshole talking about?

"I told you my name isn't Mary, so I think you need to leave, or better yet, *I* need to leave." Perrie attempted to take a step around him, but he grabbed her by the arm, pushing her back toward the bed, and she stumbled.

His expression turned predatory. She was about to vomit on this bastard's face if he put his hand on her one more time.

"What should I call you then? How about *Helen*?" His head fell to the right. "Or *Margaret*?" He rubbed his right hand over his left that was squeezing the top of his cane. "Or maybe *Rose*?"

Anger blossomed inside her and she was sick of this fucker already. He needed to back off.

"Look, man, I don't know who you are or what's going on, but I'm not going to sit here and play this sick game of yours. I'm out of here, so find someone who actually wants to play and get you off," Perrie snapped.

There wasn't time to think, so she attempted one more time to dart around him. He jabbed his cane forward and hit the middle of her chest, stopping her in place.

Who does this guy think he is? Perrie threw her hand up to shove the cane away, but he was too fast. He bumped it harder against her chest and she fell back onto the bed. A deep throbbing came against her sternum, making her want to cry. She held her chest and a ragged breath escaped her.

"Tonight, Mary, I am going to call you *Victoria*." He smiled, showcasing a crooked incisor that was single-handedly laughing at her.

Screw this guy. Perrie pretended like she was still grabbing at her chest in pain, then rolled to the side, but the stupid big dress slowed her down. He shot his cane to the side to block her path.

Perrie's instincts kicked in and told her to try again, so she attempted to maneuver around his cane, but he was there, his arms slamming around her shoulders. He was even stronger than he looked.

"Naughty, naughty, Victoria. The fun hasn't even begun yet. Remove your dress, then I'll fuck you slowly before getting rougher. Maybe."

Perrie couldn't breathe as he tossed her back on the bed, waggling that damn finger at her again.

"No way in hell. For the last time, I'm not the person you're looking for!" she shouted.

"I *said* remove your dress"—his voice became harder—"or I will do it myself."

Perrie needed to come up with a plan to get away from this beast. So, she one more time went to dive around him, when he grabbed her by the throat, thrusting her backward once more onto the bed.

"You smell like honeysuckle on a sweet spring day." He caged her in with his arms on both sides, so she couldn't stop him from leaning forward to sniff her neck.

His body smelled strongly of odor and alcohol. "You reek of piss," she spat.

"Sweet, Victoria"—he laughed as if she'd told him the most hilarious quip in the world—"I wonder if you taste as good as you smell."

He leaned forward and skimmed his lips along her neckline. His tongue slid over her flesh, licking from the base of her throat to her left ear in a long, slow stroke. And then she felt his hardened length pressing into her. Perrie kicked, thrust, and screamed, but he was too heavy for her to knock away.

The edge of Perrie's skirt inched up her thigh as his hand traveled against her leg. Her stomach twisted into never-ending knots. A true feeling of terror washed over her at what he was going to try to do next, when the door burst open.

"This room is already taken."

"August!" she cried.

August stepped in, wearing gray slacks, a black jacket with only a few buttons at the front fastened. The jacket was longer in the back and concealed a high-collared white dress shirt with a gray tie. A black top hat covered his blond hair. "Sir, I am sorry I didn't catch your name? I believe this is the room I am supposed to be in."

"This room is mine for the evening." The man pushed himself off Perrie and her body relaxed immediately. I really don't think my name is any of your business."

August stroked his chin, as if what the crazy said was worth thinking about. "You seem to be mistaken, sir. I have already paid for her services for the entire week. Therefore, I believe it is time you take your leave. There are many other ladies here to fulfill your needs."

What is August talking about? Where are we? She could take a couple guesses herself, but she was sure that none of them would be what she wanted to hear.

"Mary?" The man whipped his head back to her so fast he might have pulled something in his neck—his eyes were bulging. "Is this true? This can't be true, can it? We always have Mondays and Fridays together."

Swallowing, Perrie mustered the most apologetic smile she could and casually shrugged. "It is true. I'm so sorry, but he offered to pay a better price and I accepted it for the entire week."

"Mary, you are nothing but a filthy, lying whore—like the rest of them." His eyes narrowed and he clenched his fists tightly to his sides.

"Hey, let's not call the lady names." Slowly, August walked forward with his hands spread before him, as if trying to calm a wild beast.

The frown left the crazy fucker's face the instant he turned to August. The way he behaved, spoke to him, it was like they were old friends out strolling in the park.

"No hard feelings, just watch your back with this one. That whore"—he pointed at her—"will feed you lies, and then throw you away like trash for the next person who will offer her something better."

The man sneered at her with disgust in his voice. "Mary, don't expect me to come back, even when you are begging on the ground for me to help you again. I am going to Irene. That is a woman who can help me feel like a real man."

While nodding, she attempted a solemn expression. "Good evening, then." *You crazy asshole.* "Truly, I am sorry."

He went without saying another word but still reached out to shake August's hand, as if they'd made a business deal together. *I guess they kind of did.*

Once he was out in the hallway, August shut the door after him and closed the distance between them in three long strides. He gently took her face in his hands and scanned her up and down.

"Are you all right? He didn't hurt you, did he?" Worry lines etched his forehead.

"I'm fine, but I'm most likely going to bruise here where he thrust his cane." Perrie's hand drifted to her chest and rubbed the spot where she was hit. Despite that, she already felt so much safer with that lunatic out of the room.

"He *what*?" August shouted.

She covered his mouth with her hand. "Shh! I don't want anyone to hear us."

August sat beside her and placed her hand into his lap, holding it there. "If I see that guy again, I'm going to beat the shit out of him, just so you know."

"That makes two of us." She really wished it would've been three. "I wish Katrina could've escaped with us." Perrie knew the Headless Horseman had Katrina in his grasp, but she didn't know what happened next. She could only assume the woman suffered the same fate as the others.

August straightened. "Katrina saved your life, Perrie. She wanted us safe. *You* safe. So what she did for us back there, for you, don't beat yourself up about it."

"Okay," she murmured, wishing there was something more they could've done.

"That's better." August squeezed her hand with an encouraging smile.

"On another note, where are we this time? How did we get separated?" Perrie asked as she reached to remove his top hat. Like her dress, it was finely made.

August took it back and ran his finger across the edge before setting it down beside him, deep in thought. "I think it may have been because we weren't touching," he said finally. "I mean we were, but then I lost hold of your hand and ended up in another room. Oh, and by the way, I like you with or without an accent."

She bumped his shoulder with hers. "The unexpected is to be expected, I guess. But this place isn't what I think it is, is it?"

"Oh, it is. It's a brothel." He waggled his eyebrows, followed by a semi-expression of apology.

Her body tightened at his words. "*What?*"

FOURTEEN

"What are you talking about, August?" Did he say *brothel*?

"I landed in a room further down the hall in a lady's bedroom." He arched a brow. "I had a front-row view. Kind of hard to misinterpret that."

Perrie's pulse quickened. "And?"

"And, she had on a lot less clothing than you're wearing. She kept asking me for her money up front. I told her I had no idea what she was talking about, and then she told me I only had an hour to 'get on with it.' I told her I was sorry, that I had the wrong room, and I left."

Jealousy pricked at her, but she pushed it aside. "How were you able to find me?"

His lips twitched with the slightest hint of amusement. "I didn't know if you were in here or outside somewhere. I started checking all the rooms, which was a big mistake. People do some acts in those rooms that can't be unseen.

"Then I heard a scream, and I recognized the sound of your voice, following it until I was led to this room. Made it just in time, right?"

"That you did." Leaning in, she wrapped her arms around his waist and held him tight. "And I guess you didn't see

Maisie?"

"No." He shook his head sadly. "I wouldn't—" A blood-curdling scream coming from outside their door interrupted August. They both jumped to their feet, startled.

"What do we do?" she asked.

"Check it out?" His answer came out more like a question.

Perrie led him out the door and into the empty hallway, where he followed her down it to a flight of stairs that took them to a large area.

The front room of the brothel served as a pub, and several glasses filled with alcohol were spread across the counter. The thick stench of cigar smoke and alcohol burned her nose. A group of people stood scattered in a circle around a hysterical middle-aged woman.

Perrie cautiously approached the group, careful to keep her distance.

"He got her! He got her!" cried the woman. "I saw a figure hovering over her and then she dropped dead."

August broke through the crowd. "Did you see who it was?"

Everyone in the circle turned around and stared at them. Perrie wanted to pull him back and smack his arm for putting all this attention on them.

"It's Jack, of course." A young woman, maybe in her early twenties, pushed her way through. Her red hair was pulled up in a once fashionable bun where it poofed in the front. "He isn't stopping, and he won't stop unless we get him before he gets us. He is bringing us down one by one."

The realization hit Perrie like a speeding train. "You're not talking about Jack the Ripper, are you?"

A tall, broad-shouldered man stepped beside the young woman. "Who else do you know of going around murdering whores?"

August stiffened beside her and ground out, "There's no need to call them that. For most of these women this is their only option to make a living."

"Call them what you want, but a whore is a whore, and you are no better than me, *sir*," answered the broad man. He glared at the both of them and then stepped around the group, leaving.

The red-haired woman rubbed Perrie's shoulder in sympathy. "Watch your back. I know out there they say not to trust anyone, but it's hard for our type to do that when what we do is part of our survival. This is the only way to get food in our mouth."

All right… Perrie needed a minute of silence so her brain could catch up. She'd left Sleepy Hollow and wound up with Jack the Ripper. Thinking back to the museum, she remembered seeing the Jack the Ripper display set up beside Sleepy Hollow. When she crossed out of Sleepy Hollow, instead of jumping back into the museum, she jumped to the next display. They had to be traveling between them then, so the next question was, how do they instead jump back into the museum? Still, as much as she wanted to go home, she wanted to find her cousin more.

As the woman started to turn away, Perrie asked, "Have you seen a girl named Maisie? Dark hair, brown skin, blue eyes with an eye patch covering one?"

"Does she work here?"

"No, I'm not sure if maybe she passed through here, though." Perrie scanned the room and no one here looked anything close to Maisie.

"No, I haven't heard that name. A lot of these girls are faces without names."

"Thanks," Perrie said as the woman moved to sit at a nearby table.

She should feel relieved that Maisie most likely wasn't in the Jack the Ripper display, but she still wasn't close to finding her.

At least she knew quite a few facts about Jack the Ripper. Maybe not the minor details, but she and Maisie had once done a research paper on him for English class. His true identity was never discovered. And for the most part, Perrie remembered the names of the women he'd murdered. Doing her best Detective Maisie impression, she approached the woman once again.

"So, who was it that Jack got this time? What was her name?" Perrie grabbed the stranger's sleeve, hoping to get some answers.

The other lady, the witness to the murder, had stopped crying long enough to be led toward the stairs. She looked like she could use an escape. The redhead waited until the woman was removed from the room to speak.

"Elizabeth. Elizabeth Stride. He managed to hold her still long enough to slit her throat, and the bleedin' was enough to do her in." Her voice was low, solemn.

Perrie wasn't sure what to do, but unlike Sleepy Hollow, this wasn't a work of fiction. *True crime section at the bookstore all the way.* Ripper was a real dark creature of the night. She knew the history, and it was her own personal key she could use to at least warn the next victim and avoid another murder.

"I'm so sorry." Perrie frowned.

The young woman held her hands gently. "Just be careful, Mary, it's all I ask. I don't want anything to happen to you."

Mary again?

"So you know who I am?" she asked, a little more delighted than she should be.

"Are you well?" Her brows drew together, and she brought a hand to her forehead. "Of course I know who you are. You're Mary Kelly, and my name is Fannie Caldwell."

Mary Kelly. It almost felt as though the pressure building in her head could push her eyeballs right out of their sockets.

"Yes, I'm sorry, Fannie. This whole situation is playing with my head." Perrie scrambled for the words she needed to pull herself together.

"Just go on back to your room and get whatever rest you can." Fannie nodded in understanding and shooed her off.

"Thank you and be careful yourself. Good night." Perrie gripped August's hand and gave him a hard tug. He'd been watching them the entire time, probably unsure of what was going on.

"What was that about? What's with that look on your face?" he asked in a hushed tone.

"I'll tell you as soon as we get back to the room."

Once they were back where they'd started, Perrie ushered him into the room and locked it up tight behind them. She collapsed onto the satin-covered bed, joined seconds later by an anxious August.

"Spit it out," he said as he searched her face for a clue.

"You know who Jack the Ripper is, right?" Perrie folded her hands in her lap and squeezed them together until her knuckles turned white. She then gazed into his green eyes.

"Of course I know who Jack the Ripper is. Who doesn't? His case is one of the most famous in history."

"What do you know about his victims?" She questioned, ready to burst with her answer.

"Not much. I know they were all ladies of the night, though."

She shook her head, almost smiling. *Almost.* "Nice way of putting it, August."

"Well, they were."

Sighing, Perrie brought her hands to her forehead. "Anyway, the point is Mary Kelly was one of his victims, and I *am* Mary Kelly. I'm one of Jack's victims—he's going to fillet me like a fucking fish!"

August's eyebrows shot up. "First off, that's not going to happen, and second, you're not food—no slicing and dicing for you."

She puckered her lips. "August, I'm serious."

"So am I, doll face."

Perrie fell backward onto the bed with a great sigh. August did the same, his top hat falling off his head and bumping hers. She rolled over and propped her head up on one arm, tossing his hat to the floor.

"Elizabeth Stride was murdered tonight."

"Right?"

She ticked off the murders in her head. Martha Tabram, who might or might not have been a Ripper victim, Mary Nichols, Annie Chapman, Elizabeth Stride, Catherine Eddowes, and Mary Kelly. That meant there was one left before her. In the real world, Elizabeth and Catherine were murdered the same night.

She went over the list of victims with August, then said, "We have no clue if the time frame is going to work the same here. There was no mention of Catherine Eddowes, only Elizabeth Stride."

"I don't know, Perrie. Maybe the people down there just haven't heard about Catherine yet, and how do you know this, anyway?" August rubbed his temples, whether from a developing headache, thinking, or both.

"I had to do a research paper on it with Maisie." Her heart stuttered at the sound of her cousin's name, and she hoped Maisie was somewhere safe, being her usual quirky self. "When Maisie does a research paper, she has to know every single detail, right down to the nitty-gritty. Therefore, *I* have to know every single detail."

August was about to open his mouth when she stopped him. "Wait!" Perrie told him her theory about how she'd seen the Jack the Ripper display next to the Sleepy Hollow one, and how they must be jumping from one display to the next.

"I don't know if we're going back in time, or if we're somehow stuck in a world inside of the displays. Whatever it is, is fucked up," August said as he raked a hand through his hair.

"I don't know, but the events in Sleepy Hollow weren't

accurate from what I know. Well, from the movie, anyway. And you know just how well Hollywood matches film to book. *Poorly*. However, I know the entire town wasn't missing in it, so I don't think we're going back to a true time."

August sat up. "Agreed. So, you said you fell in this room, right? Did you search around for a portal?"

"No, I didn't. I just looked for you, and then that asshole came in." Perrie leaned forward and pushed up from the bed.

August patted around the walls. "Let's look in here. I already searched in the room where I fell in with that woman and didn't find anything there."

Perrie moved to the opposite side of the room and knocked on the walls. Finding no exit, she headed toward the bed and tapped the floor underneath, slapping it several times with her hand just to be sure, but she felt nothing.

This wasn't like last time. When they'd appeared in Sleepy Hollow, the barrier was right where they'd been standing. This time it was like they were spat out and then it completely vanished. *Is our escape somewhere outside of the brothel?*

August halted his search and brushed his partially gelled hair back from his eyebrow. "I say for now we just get some rest since it's still dark. In the morning, we can go search around the city and try to find a way out of here."

"Then what? Are we going to go home, or are we just going to end up in the next display from the museum exhibit?"

Perrie wanted to get out of this one. When she thought of what had happened to Mary Kelly, her entire body shuddered. What happened to her was only something that the sickest of individuals could've done. Mary was pretty much skinned and dismembered.

Even if they ended up in another place that wasn't home, she would prefer it to having a meet and greet with Jack the Ripper. Especially since she *became* Mary this time—*however the hell that happened.* And if Maisie was in a different display, then how would they find her? There was no way they could go home without her.

August placed his hands behind his head and looked up at the ceiling. "Perrie, I know as much as you do, but we're going to find a way out of this. If I have to tear this city apart bit by bit to find that damn portal, I'm going to get you out of here."

She let herself smile. Even during the hardest times, he knew just what to do or say. August was . . . she couldn't even put into words what she felt for him anymore. "No, we're going to find a way *together*, and we're going to get out of here *together*."

FIFTEEN

Exhaustion consumed Perrie from head to toe. A crazy asshole and an unsolved murder were enough excitement for one day. She didn't fight the need for sleep, so she lay down next to August and closed her eyes. They forfeited warmth and chose to sleep on top of the blankets. Who knew where these sheets had been and what horrors they'd seen anyway.

August pulled her close and wrapped his arm around her stomach. Taking hold of his arm, Perrie tugged it up to her chest and shut her eyes. It felt nice to be held again. It felt even better knowing that August was the one keeping her close. Her body heated at the thought.

Perrie didn't want to think about murder or Jack the Ripper right now. She wanted to think about a time when everything, mostly everything, was fine, and possibilities were endless. Yet something terrifyingly good could happen. So she chose to think about that night at the prom when her feelings had started to change for August.

After everything that had happened with Neven, she hadn't wanted to go to the prom. She was never big into dances or anything like that, yet Maisie was, and her cousin hadn't wanted to miss the prom. Perrie insisted she take someone, but

Maisie told her she wanted to go and hang out with her. Perrie had been extremely reluctant to cave to her begging. Then, when Perrie wouldn't budge, Maisie made a desperate play at lunch one day.

"August, will you go to prom with us?" Maisie asked.

Perrie had been sitting beside him at the time and was totally caught off guard. He was in the middle of swallowing a french fry and choked from surprise. She started patting his back and he grabbed his water bottle and started chugging. "You guys are going to prom?"

Maisie leaned forward with her strawberry eye patch and said, "Yes, if you'll take us?" She hadn't even given Perrie a chance to answer.

Perrie looked at both of them. "There's no way I'm going. If you two want to go, then more power to you. I'll be at home in my pajamas, most likely having a personal movie marathon."

"If Perrie doesn't go, then my duty will be joining her at this movie marathon." Grabbing Perrie, August hauled her to him in a side hug. He stroked her hair with his other hand while shrugging at Maisie.

Maisie threw up her hands, squeezing her fists in front of her, and begged, "Please!"

"Fine." Perrie sighed in defeat, wiggling out of August's arms. "I refuse to wear heels, though."

"Yes!" Maisie pulled her arm in a downward fist pump.

Perrie rolled her eyes and laughed.

August had picked them up for the prom that weekend. Perrie hadn't gone too fancy with her attire, opting for a relaxed curl in favor of an expensive updo. Her dress was red and strapless, tight on top with a wicked flared skirt right above her knees. Like she'd told Maisie, Perrie would not be wearing heels and had chosen a pair of black flats instead.

Maisie, on the other hand, stole the show. She wore a similar style dress of sapphire blue with one shoulder strap.

Peacock feathers lined the strap, and across the bottom of the dress, were more feathers woven in, hanging from the front, all the way to the back.

Her hair was curled and tied in the back into a loose bun. Maisie's eye patch was the same blue shade as the dress, except around the edges of the patch were miniature peacock feathers. She'd looked beautiful.

Once they'd arrived at the dance, they took prom pictures together. It was the first and only time she'd ever felt a twinge of jealousy toward Maisie. While Perrie watched August, she knew if he wasn't already hot for Maisie, he would be now.

He never looked at Maisie that way, though. Even that night, it was only like a friend, and Perrie had felt relieved. Then she'd wanted to slap herself for that moment of jealousy, not knowing why she should care if August liked Maisie.

August wore a black suit with a green tie, and it made his eyes stand out, drawing her into them more than ever that night.

When they'd sat down, August went to get them drinks and that was when she'd spotted Neven. He'd come in with some of the guys from the basketball team. Most of them with dates, but Neven and David didn't have one.

As soon as Perrie saw them, she examined her fingernails to pretend she was doing something.

David approached her table, and Perrie glanced up when she heard him talking to her cousin. "Maisie, you look interesting tonight. Do you want to dance?"

Perrie gave him the biggest what-the-hell look. That was the best he could come up with? *Interesting*? He'd been trying to get with Maisie forever, and his lines hadn't gotten any better.

Maisie told him okay, but she'd said yes to anyone who asked her to dance that night. She even asked the guys who were alone to dance since they'd been standing by themselves. That was what Perrie loved best about her cousin—the fact she didn't care what anyone thought, and just wanted to see everyone happy.

After Maisie left with David to dance, Perrie was done playing the examining nails game, so she glanced up and just happened to lock eyes with Neven. He looked so pitiful, and at that moment, she felt bad for him, then got mad at herself for feeling bad.

Neven got up and started to walk to her table. Thinking back, she didn't know if she would've talked to him if he'd tried. She probably wouldn't have and would've gotten mad like she always did for what he'd done.

He never made it to her table, though. August had come back with the drinks just in time.

"Do you want to dance?" He looked shy for the first time when he'd asked her, which made her say yes. She would've said yes anyway, though. Perrie had never seen August like this before, and she'd found it adorable.

As they got to the dance floor, Perrie looked back for Neven but he was already gone. The crisis had been averted.

The song playing was slow, which was awkward for her at first since she hadn't danced before. Then August helped her get into it—he knew what he was doing. Perrie laid her head against his shoulder and wrapped her arms around his warm neck.

His hands at her waist had drifted down toward her lower back. A fluttery sensation bloomed inside of her stomach, like more than butterflies. It was a mixture of things: dragonflies, ladybugs, moths, and maybe even hummingbirds.

The whole dance Perrie had kept thinking to herself, *What if I just leaned up and brushed my mouth against his?* Something about the way his hand rubbed against her back told her that she didn't think he would have minded at all, but she wasn't that brave. Not that night.

After the dance, August walked both of them to Maisie's door before taking Perrie to hers. She'd been such a fool—it was another perfect moment. Instead, she rushed in for a hug and squeezed him goodnight, avoiding looking at his face. Before she closed the door, he was smirking at her—a daring one that let her know he'd wanted to kiss her. Leaning her back against the door after shutting it, she'd sighed but smiled so big that her face had to have been outlined in cracks.

Half asleep, half dazed, Perrie rolled over to August. He was lying on his back, and she lifted herself, then pressed her lips to his, a spark igniting in her—his mouth was soft and perfect. She wasn't sure if he was asleep, but his arm wrapped around her, and she leaned over to his ear and whispered, "Good night, August."

"Good night, Perrie," he whispered back. So, he *was* awake.

Perrie left his ear and placed a gentle kiss against the side of his warm neck. He inhaled shakily, and her body wanted to do more—*she* wanted to do more.

As if hearing her thoughts, August pulled her on top of him, his hands drifting down to her waist. She lifted her dress and her breathing hitched at the feel of his strong body beneath hers. And then his hands began to move with her while she slowly rolled her hips forward, feeling every single inch of him. Her lips found his once more, and this time their mouths parted, their tongues danced as she licked and nipped. His hands drifted under her dress to her backside, gripping her soft flesh. She ground her hips into him, harder, faster, eager for the blissful feeling to wash over her.

It would be so easy for her hands to lift his shirt, then drift down to the button of his pants, and have him inside her. But she didn't. Instead, this was what she wanted for now.

A rush of warmth spread through her until it exploded into a thousand shattered pieces. She moaned in pleasure against his beautiful mouth.

As her blissful moment came to a spectacular end, Perrie continued her pace so August could hit that same crescendo. But then his hands halted her movement.

She frowned, confused. "Don't you want—"

"Another time, doll face. I just wanted you to feel good tonight," he murmured, bringing his mouth to hers again. Although it was the lightest of kisses, one like no other, it seared her straight to her marrow.

With a smile, her legs like jelly, she peeled herself from him and rested her head on his chest. She inhaled his comforting scent as he pulled her body closer to him, and in this moment, the escape had been perfect.

In the morning, Perrie still lay comfortably in August's arms. She risked glancing up and he was already awake, staring down at her. The night before she may have been bold, but right then, her cheeks heated at the wonderful memory.

"Finally awake, sleepy head?" He smiled.

"Why didn't you wake me?" As she sat up, a cold brush of air hit her after leaving August's warm arms.

"Why? So I can bring you out of your lovely dream back to this hellhole?" He maneuvered himself to an upward position next to her, then twisted his body so he was sitting on the bed with his feet flat on the floor. August already had his shoes on and placed the top hat on his head.

"Thanks, I appreciate that." She leaned over and slipped hers on, guessing that neither of them was going to discuss the night before. But she still felt the ghost of his hands on her, the way he'd made her feel.

Downstairs, everyone was eating breakfast and socializing with each other. Perrie spotted Fannie, and they shuffled over and sat in front of her at a table. The young woman poured a little whiskey into her tea from a tiny, silver flask.

"I need something a little stronger than sugar in my tea this morning." Fannie answered Perrie's unspoken question.

"I completely understand," Perrie said. She wouldn't be surprised if these women drank all the time.

Fannie leaned back in her chair and shifted her attention to August. "So, I see you are still here?"

"I have her for the entire week and not only at night either." August stared at her, pointedly.

"A knight in shining armor, I see." Her eyes widened as she sipped some of her *special* tea. "As long as you don't have someone waiting for you at home like most of these men do."

"What? It isn't like that," he rushed on.

"We will have to see about that, now won't we?" Fannie clucked her tongue, her sarcasm thick as honey.

Laughing, Fannie offered them something to eat. Perrie thanked her and accepted the small portion of food and the *un-special* tea since she needed to keep a clear head. Fannie seemed sweet and incredibly smart. It wasn't her business, but Perrie wanted to ask her why she worked at a brothel.

"How did you end up here, Fannie? I don't think I've ever asked you that." Perrie hoped from whatever false memories she had of her that she hadn't.

Relaxing back in her seat, Fannie appeared to consider the question with a great deal of thought. Perrie wondered how many other people had asked her the same question, or rather, cared to ask.

"I lost my parents when I was fourteen, and I had no other family to take me in and nowhere else to go. My parents didn't have a lot of money. When they passed, I had nothing and had to live on the streets for a long time. I was just a street rat, taking food from what I could scavenge out of the trash. Eventually, I ran into two women who told me about this place. They took me in, and now here I am." She waved one hand in the air.

Perrie's face must've looked stricken because she rushed on, "Don't worry about me. This may not be the Queen's palace, but it has treated me better than I was ever treated on the streets. The ones who work the streets have it the hardest." She peered down at her tea, staring at it for a moment before lifting it up and drinking it again.

"Mary!" A loud shout interrupted Perrie's thoughts.

She only turned around because the voice had been so loud. Then she remembered *she* was Mary, and that crazy bastard from the day before was sauntering to their table.

"What do you need, sir?" August pushed out of his seat and stood in front of Perrie. She rose out of her chair and stepped next to August. Two were always better than one.

"I came to apologize for last night." He gazed dreamily up at the ceiling then back toward Perrie. "Thank you so much for everything. I know you did that so I would go and see Irene, and she fulfilled every single fantasy I have ever dreamed about."

Did I just vomit a little bit in my mouth? I believe I did.

"Irene can certainly work her magic," Perrie replied.

"I will be spending my time with her from now on. Please know our time together is something I will always cherish." If the earth opened up at that particular moment, she would kick him into the gaping hole.

"Mm-hmm." Her lips were sealed tight.

Smiling, he left with a final, "Good day."

"Wow," Perrie drawled to August.

"Well, he shouldn't be bothering you anymore," August said.

"I'm glad to say I have never had Thomas in my bed," Fannie piped in.

Ah, so the fucker has a name.

They spent the rest of their time finishing up breakfast. Everyone discussed Elizabeth Stride's death, but no one mentioned a second murder. Two well-dressed men threw out their thoughts on the situation, that it was the woman's fault. Perrie wasn't certain if the time-frame of the murders was the same here.

Brushing the crumbs off her dress, she prepared herself to explore the city, and hoped to find a damn portal leading to Maisie.

SIXTEEN

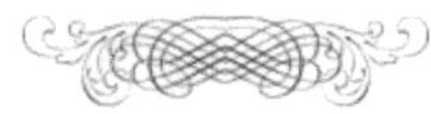

The door squeaked open as Perrie and August took their first steps out of the brothel. She was desperate to find the portal out of here that would lead them to her cousin—whether home or the next display.

But what if we don't find one? The little demon of misery knocked at her brain, and she flicked it away.

Tall stone buildings, with numerous windows, lined the street. The old street had only two directions, left or right.

"Where should we start?" Perrie asked.

August arched a brow. "Let's try left."

Left it was. The sun shone in the sky and the weather didn't have a single chill in the air. No people bustled about in the city, only them. Even the buildings appeared to be closed with no life within. And she wondered why.

Perrie walked to the closest building, green vines running up its length, and peered inside. Nothing except for a few dining tables and two settees.

"Where is everyone?" She glanced at August, then back toward the window.

August shrugged. "I don't even know. That seems to be the go-to answer these days."

"That it does." She sighed.

They set out down the graveled street again, reaching the end of the row of buildings where an intersecting street appeared. Before she reached it, the barrier knocked her back. August caught Perrie and helped right her on her feet again. It was the same as before—she could push against it, but she couldn't penetrate it.

"You take the right, I'll take the left," he said.

Perrie headed for the left row of buildings, with triangular roofs and tall chimneys, while he went right to the other set. She patted the barrier down like she'd done in Sleepy Hollow. They both did this until they were forced to turn where the barrier wasn't letting up. The route to the backside of the buildings remained inaccessible, even though she could see stone streets and other structures past them.

Chest heaving, Perrie met August back in the middle of the street. "Okay, so this seems to be like last time. I bet if we go to the opposite end, the remainder of the barrier will be there, forming a perfect rectangle."

"Agreed. That means the barrier should open up the same as in Sleepy Hollow since this side won't. Let's go." August didn't seem surprised by her logic. An idiot could've guessed the same thing.

Adrenaline took over while running to the other side with August. Everything remained a blur as she passed. She ignored the buildings and stayed focused on her goal, her heart thundering in her chest.

As they inched closer, a small village of houses slid into view up ahead. Thick smoke poured out of the chimneys of several.

Perrie smacked into something and realized they'd reached the end of the barrier. It launched her backward and she fell straight to the ground on her ass, scathing her right arm in the process of catching herself. August wasn't able to stop himself either and landed right beside her.

"Well, fuck." He shook his head, and his top hat slid off. Clenching his jaw, he stood up and kicked it. "That feels good."

In that moment, Perrie was just amazed that he'd been able to keep his hat atop his head while running.

Annoyance and confusion stirred within her—she didn't understand why the portal was still closed.

August clasped her hand to help pull her off the ground. She then brought her arm up and cradled it. His mood changed to one of concern, and he tenderly held her arm, inspecting it. "Are you all right?"

"Yeah, it's just a scrape. It'll heal."

Perrie's gaze flicked to the barrier. Scuffing her feet toward it, she pressed her palm against the rubber-like texture, thinking it might pull them through this time. But it didn't.

One name screamed inside her head. *Maisie*. What if Perrie didn't see her again because they were trapped here?

As she rubbed her palm against her face, a thought formed. "Maybe it only opens up at a certain time of the day or something."

"In Sleepy Hollow it was morning," August pointed out.

She cocked her head and angled her eyes toward the blue sky. "It's early now."

"Then how about we try nightfall?"

"What do we have to lose, right?" *Only Jack the Ripper may come out to play.*

On the way back to the brothel, they passed one of the tall gray buildings, a long crack running up the side. Vines and flowers with brilliant blues, yellows, and pinks covered a balcony on another. Underneath was a shoe-shining station sitting outside of a cobbler's shop. Not a single soul was around to have their shoes shined—its purpose defeated. Everything continued to stay quiet in this hellish town.

Once inside the brothel, Perrie's hope slipped, but she would maintain her grasp and hold onto it until nightfall. She hadn't had time to think about how her dad must be feeling with her gone. She didn't want him to feel abandoned like when her mom had left. But he was safe, so she pushed her thoughts of him away.

August took a seat at the small table they sat at this morning.

Resting her elbows on the scratched wood, Perrie placed her chin on her palms. "Now what do we do?"

August studied the bar. "Hungry?"

"Really? You can still think about eating?" She let out a small laugh.

"All the time." He stood and walked over to the counter, finding two bowls of stew, then headed back to grab them some tea. Apparently, money wasn't an issue downstairs at the pub portion. *Strange.* Perrie continued to stare at the swirling liquid.

"You're going to have to force yourself to eat whenever you can. Who knows when or if we'll be able to eat or drink anything again."

She ate a few bites from the bowl. "There, happy?"

"Thrilled." He smiled and waggled his eyebrows.

Unintentionally, her gaze traveled down each of his features to his mouth, the mouth she'd kissed the night before. He still hadn't said a word. There was nothing she could say, yet so much she wanted to. Her eyes drifted up to his cute and messy hair, wondering what it would feel like to have her fingers tangled in it. She should've done that last night when he'd sent her over the edge in pleasure.

Blowing out a breath, she ignored that matter for now and managed to finish half the bowl of stew. At least the monster in her belly was satisfied at the moment.

Perrie broke the silence and pointed at his head with her spoon. "I see you forgot your hat back there."

Pressing his hair down, he groaned, "Fuck that hat."

Before she could say anything else, the door flew open.

Fannie barreled in and screamed, "She's dead. The Ripper has done it again. Catherine Eddowes has been murdered."

Jolting up, Perrie rushed over to her. "Where is she?"

"She's down the street." Perrie tried to run past her, and Fannie took hold of her arm. "You aren't going to want to see this one. How could he do this to my friend?"

In an instant, August was beside her, heading straight for the door.

"I'll be right back," Perrie told her.

She stepped outside into the darkness and halted at the sudden change of lighting.

"How is it dark this early?" August asked. "We were just out here."

They hadn't slept late, and they weren't gone that long when looking for the barrier. It should've been nowhere near nightfall.

"Things aren't making sense any more than they have been," Perrie mumbled.

To her left, not far from where they stood, was a body with no one around it. No lookers, no help, no police officers.

"Are you sure you want to see? It isn't going to help anything." August pulled her back. She clenched the skirt of her dress, fingernails biting in deeply. No one, including her, wanted to see a dead body, but this was too important. Her theory needed to be confirmed—she had to know if she was next.

"I know, but I need to see for myself." She wouldn't back down from this. "Are you sure *you* want to look?"

"I'm going to be real honest here. Not really, but there's no way I'm going to let you walk over there by yourself," he said quietly.

With quick strides, they headed toward the limp body on the ground. August reached the victim right before Perrie did. A woman wearing a canary-yellow dress lay in a pool of blood. Perrie's vision blurred and the stew in her belly wanted to resurface. Red by her legs, red by her head, and red by her arms. Red, red, red. It was *everywhere.*

Perrie covered her mouth with both hands as August leaned down to check the woman's pulse, but there wasn't a point. The part of her face that Perrie could see was a mutilated mess. No one would be able to survive that brutal savagery. She couldn't look at the rest of her, but something in the woman's expression drew Perrie in for a closer inspection. The left side of the woman's face was undamaged for the most part. Long, silky black hair sprawled about her oval-shaped face.

Impossible... She recognized the victim. She'd spoken with her twice now.

"August, I know her," Perrie whispered.

He whirled to face her. "What are you talking about?"

"This woman, I *know* her." Hands shaking, she stared into his eyes.

"I've never seen her before in my life." He chewed on his bottom lip and shook his head.

"You haven't, but I have." She backed away a few steps from the body. "This is Officer Rodriguez."

August's left eyebrow slid up as far as it would go, like a flag being pulled to the top of a pole. "Well, how did she get here?"

"I don't know, genius. I suppose the same way we got here."

Lifting his finger, he pointed it up at the night sky and waved it like a sword. "Touché. Now keep going."

Gripping her hair, Perrie stumbled backward into a wall. "She was investigating both Neven and Maisie's disappearances. I told her about the Glass Vault and she said she would check it out later. My assumption is that she got sucked into this demonic prison like we did."

"But I thought you said the Glass Vault vanished?"

"I did!" she whisper-shouted. "But maybe it chooses when to disappear and reappear."

August rubbed his chin and asked, "So, Officer Rodriguez went out to inspect it, assuming she was alone, and the Glass Vault just . . . reappeared?"

"Maybe. You saw how even the photos on your phone didn't stay. Plus it reappeared for us." It was a little hard to believe, but it was what it was.

Perrie took another look at the unmarred side of Officer Rodriguez's strong, pretty face. If a well-trained officer couldn't escape Jack the Ripper, then how are they supposed to?

"We have to go back, it's not safe for us to stay out here any longer than we need to. Especially you." Because in this place *she* was Mary Kelly.

Latching onto his hand, she hurried with him back to the brothel. Her mind buzzed with a thousand different questions. How did Officer Rodriguez get here? Did the Glass Vault really just reappear when it wanted? If that was the case, then maybe Maisie was here after all. It had to be more than assuming. Unfortunately, she couldn't ask about Maisie now with Officer Rodriguez lying in her own blood.

Inside the pub, Fannie sat alone at a table with her head in her hands.

"Are you going to be all right?" Of course she wasn't, but Perrie tried to be sympathetic anyway. She couldn't tell her Catherine was really Officer Rodriguez. She couldn't even tell her that her friend, the real Catherine Eddowes, wasn't here. Fannie would look at her like she was crazy.

"No, Mary, I'm not. He's going to pick us all off until we are nothing. I don't want to be left worse off than being a street rat."

"You're not a street rat," August said robotically. Perrie almost rolled her eyes at how awkward he'd sounded.

"Not at all," Perrie chimed in.

"I know I'm not. But all men want to do is *use* us. Jack wants to use our bodies for his own sick purposes." Fannie tucked a red curl that had fallen loose from her bun behind her ear. "He's out there. He looks like a regular gentleman, too, with a top hat and cloak to match his suit and boots—all black. Be careful is all I ask."

"You too, Fannie." If Fannie had made herself known, then she would've most likely been killed and lying in her own puddle of blood in that old alleyway, too. Perrie knew how she felt. She didn't want to be like the other women, either.

August nudged her with his elbow and whispered into her ear, "Do you want to go to the room?"

"Yes." She glanced once more at Fannie, her expression distant, then they ascended the stairs back to the room. She had so damn much to think about. No matter what they did, it was all trial and error—no definite explanation. It was as if this place was a riddle without an answer, an experiment without a solution, or a lock without a key.

After entering the bedroom, Perrie collapsed against the foot of the bed, defeated. August slid down beside her and pressed his strong body next to hers, before leaning his cheek against the top of her head.

"Don't even think about it, Perrie."

She played with the hem of her skirt. "How can I not think about it, August? I'm going to be next."

SEVENTEEN

Perrie couldn't help knowing she would be next. Mary Kelly's death had followed Catherine's murder. She didn't like the idea of a torturous death, especially not her own.

August frowned so deeply it might actually stay that way. "I'm not going to let that happen to you."

"That's easy for you to say. You aren't Mary Kelly. You're not going to be hunted down and murdered by some sick fuck," Perrie said between clenched teeth.

"Well, you aren't Mary Kelly. You're Perrie Madeline, and *we* are leaving here just like we left Sleepy Hollow. Yes, we may enter a new hell, but then we'll get out of there together because that's what we do. We have been a team— we will always be a team. Hell, we were a team even when you hated me."

Rolling her eyes, she palmed her forehead. "Even then I don't think I actually disliked you—I was just mad."

"Oh no, you definitely hated me, doll face. That was loathing at its finest." He knocked his shoulder with hers. She leaned her head against him and tightened her arms around his waist to soak in his warmth.

"Okay, maybe just a little bit." She laughed. "I'm truly

sorry about judging you before I got to know such fine character in another human being."

"I'll take that answer." He snorted.

Perrie loosened her arms from around his waist. "So what if we can't get the barrier open?"

"Maybe it has something to do with not having seen Jack the Ripper yet."

"What do you mean?"

"When we went through the barrier last time, 'the Headless Horseman'"—he used air quotes to emphasize—"was chasing after us, so maybe Jack has to make some kind of entrance before we can make our exit."

It was hard not to laugh, but she kept her cool. She wouldn't want to interrupt his terribly important thought process.

"That has to be the least appealing thing you could've come up with. I, for one, do not have any intentions of coming face-to-face with one of the most notorious serial killers in our history."

August pursed his lips and blinked. Was he really considering this? Accurate or not, she didn't like the idea of facing off against Jack the Ripper before she could make an escape.

"So, you're fine and dandy with hunting up and down the street, calling out Jack's name to lure him from the shadows?" Perrie stared at him hard.

"Better than Jeffrey Dahmer, Ed Gein, and Charles Manson." He shrugged.

"One, those were nowhere near close to Jack, and two, Charles Manson didn't physically commit the crime. Also, who's to say Jack won't come barging into the room either?" She immediately wanted to take that back.

Perrie honestly didn't even consider that as a possibility until the words had flown out of her mouth. She just assumed people would have to be out walking the streets for Jack to hunt them down. It wasn't like anyone knew who he was. He could be a number of people. In fact, he could walk right into the pub and ask to have *her* for the night. No one would know his real purpose.

August toyed with his lower lip. "What if he was already here? What if Jack is Thomas?"

It made complete sense that Thomas was Jack—the sick bastard.

"You know what?" she started. "I think you might be right. It's already nightfall, earlier than expected, but I say we go ahead and try for the barrier. Maybe find a few weapons before we go."

"I'm all for weapons but be prepared to run like hell."

A gun would've been the ideal weapon, if they could find one.

They searched the room to see if they could find anything worth using. She located nothing that was suitable as a weapon, besides a stash of beads. Throwing beads at a full-grown man like it was Mardi Gras was a horrible idea.

"Maybe I should hunt down Thomas and steal his wooden cane from him while he's here undercover," August mumbled while searching under the mattress and coming away with nothing except air.

"Yeah, I don't know about that. He was a master with that cane. Who knows what other sick shit he does with it." If she saw him again, she would shove his cane so far up his ass that he wouldn't know what was happening. "But for all we know, Thomas could be anywhere."

"Good point. By the way, thanks for putting those cane images in my head." He knelt and searched below the bed, coming away with nothing yet again. "I admit defeat. This search is pointless. Let's grab something to use from downstairs."

First, there were heads sprinkled like dessert in the graveyard, then the lunatic in the bedroom who was most likely Jack, followed by graphic murders. It was pure insanity—horror movie style.

Perrie was the one who'd told the officer about Quinsey Wolfe's Glass Vault, and now felt partially responsible. She wasn't the one who'd murdered her, but there were so many "what ifs." What if she had never seen the Glass Vault that day? What if Maisie had never stopped, and they'd never gotten out of the car? What if she'd been honest and told Maisie she didn't want her to go to the museum?

If Perrie had been honest from the beginning, then none of this would be happening. Maisie wouldn't be missing, Officer Rodriguez wouldn't be dead, and she wouldn't be worried about saving her own neck.

She needed a knife. *Now.*

Giving up on the room, they moved on to their next best option, the kitchen. Downstairs, a few people sat around tables, but most of them must've been in rooms having sex or doing other business. Perrie and August easily snuck past them all. Unfortunately, the only weapons around were some semi-sharp knives and forks as backup. A knife was a knife, and she would take what she could get.

Exiting the pub, they walked outside into the night. The darkness curtained itself around the city, and a touch of wind folded and bended its way around her. Lanterns along the road lit up the street, guiding her in whichever direction she chose to follow.

Perrie clenched the utensils in her grip. "Okay, we're outside, and no one's here. So, do we just stand around out here and wait for Jack, or should we head right for the barrier?"

"I think we should try for the barrier—maybe we don't really need him there to pass through. It's only a theory," he said, and she hoped it was only a theory.

Not bothering to take their time, they hung a right and ran for what would hopefully lead them out of the Jack the Ripper display. As they crept up close to the barrier, Perrie slowed.

She took a couple of steps and hit the rubber-like surface—not passing through.

"Fuck. Fuck. Fuck." August gritted his teeth as he pressed his hand against it and nothing happened.

"Are we stuck here?" Perrie asked the invisible wall. Of course it didn't answer back. "As much as I hate to say it, we're going to have to try our next theory."

"Jackie boy, here we come." August held up his fork and knife, appearing more like a guy ready to eat than a guy ready to fight for his life.

She still smiled, but her stomach was sinking into a never-ending black hole. Maisie, Neven, and home. Those were the three things she needed right now. Perrie repeated them over in her head like a mantra as they turned back.

Once they reached the pub, August grabbed her elbow and his eyebrows flew up.

Her gaze followed his, and her mouth fell open. "August, where's the body?"

Was it gone when we left?

"Maybe someone moved her? Or maybe Jack came back to collect his trophy."

"Not the best time for jokes."

"I'm actually pretty serious on this one."

"You're right," she decided. "I'm sure some weird shit went down."

In the spot where Officer Rodriguez's mutilated body once was, now lay nothing but a stone walkway. No body, no blood, no nothing. It was as clear as day.

"I don't think someone cleaned up the blood that fast," August said, clenching his jaw.

"I agree." She doubted someone would be able to scrub all that blood away anyway. Besides, they hadn't even seen one person out on the street to hint at a cleanup crew.

A ticking sound stirred, and Perrie's spine tensed. "August, press your back to mine. Weapons ready."

"The poorly-made utensils are prepared," he said, his back firmly against hers.

"Did you hear that ticking sound?" Perrie cocked her head to the right and listened. Not a single peep that time. She scanned the front area while August did the opposite.

"What ticking sound?"

"Like a clock." She took a deep breath. "And it smells really bad over here." Not like a dead body but something else foul.

August inhaled and gagged a little. "I shouldn't have taken that deep of a breath. It smells like rotten piss."

"Can piss smell rotten?"

"This piss can. It's probably years built up of people coming out here and going on the side of the building."

"That's gross." Her shoulders relaxed. It must've been her imagination. "I'm feeling antsy."

August scratched his bicep with his fork. "Is your ADHD kicking in now?"

"August, you know I don't have ADHD," she huffed.

"Really? You could have fooled me."

A scratching noise filled the air. Their connected bodies stiffened at the same time as if they were conjoined.

"I know you heard it this time," Perrie whispered with knives ready in both hands.

"I wish I hadn't."

A ticking came from her right, but she couldn't see anything. Then another scratching noise erupted from her left. A long screech, a hundred times worse than nails against a chalkboard. She gripped her knives harder, and a couple of forks were ready in the sides of her shoes. Neither she or August uttered a single word.

Low, then higher and higher, a loud, slow creak, like that of a rusty door hinge, sounded. Perrie still couldn't see through the darkness resting in every corner. She wasn't dumb enough to actively seek out the source of disturbance, especially given her special circumstance.

"August," Perrie whispered.

"Yes?"

"Please tell me you've taken karate or something like that."

"No, but I can punch someone in the face." His head whipped as far around as it could go. "Well, we'll see if I can anyway. Have you?"

"No! All I took was ballet when I was like four," she groaned.

"Good, then you should be extra light on your feet."

Another creaking noise, followed by a sharp cracking, echoed. Then a *clack, clack, clack*, like running feet against the ground. Perrie didn't see anyone in the direction she thought it was coming from. Then it all occurred at once. A black shadow popped into her peripheral vision, and she pushed back against August. She shoved him out of the way, but she was too slow.

The shadow was really a person dressed all in black and wearing a dark cloak. The person—Jack—lunged forward and swung at them. Jack spun around and around, flashes of silver darting out like shooting stars in the sky. For a split second, Perrie thought of a magician at a magic show, then a stinging sensation throbbed against her arm. The knife in that hand clanked to the ground. Her hand clasped her forearm and the dark figure retreated in the other direction.

Warm blood coated her palm as it came away from her stinging arm. August refocused his attention on her and her damn arm instead of the murderer.

"We've seen Jack," she grunted. "Let's try for the barrier."

The adrenaline pumped through her veins, giving her momentum. August led the way as they headed back toward the barrier.

When they approached the brothel, which took only a minute, a woman stood outside. Not just any woman either, but Officer Rodriguez—intact. She was wearing the exact same yellow dress Perrie had just seen her lying in. Only, it was clean, not a speck of blood on it. Not a single mark marred her flawless face, both sides matching equally.

"Hey, Mary," she called, "How about you lend your gentlemen over to me for the night."

"Officer Rodriguez?" Perrie's jaw dropped, her brow furrowing.

"I'll even lower the price for the night, love." Her gaze settled on August, ignoring Perrie completely.

"Officer Rodriguez! It's me, Perrie Madeline." She jumped in front of August, both hysterical and relieved. "Don't you recognize me?"

She didn't.

"Mary, you know bloody well my name is Catherine. Don't act dense because you don't want to share."

What the fuck? "I don't have time for this. Come on, let's go." Perrie tugged Officer Rodriguez's arm, but she yanked it out of her grasp.

"We've got to go," August said quickly.

I tried, right? Perrie couldn't let herself feel guilty at the moment, not while they were under attack. She took off on a hard sprint with August again. They were only a few buildings away from the barrier when they were stopped in their tracks.

Jack the Ripper rose from the darkness to block their way. The collar of his cloak was propped high, and a black scarf was wrapped around his face, shadowing his features. He was smaller than she'd imagined he would be. Not that she'd put too much thought into his height.

Jack jolted at Perrie first, and she whirled out of the way at the last second. Her wounded arm throbbed to its own tune, and she tried to ignore the pain.

August lunged at him with one of his knives, and Jack somehow managed to knock them out of both of his hands. Jack dove to the ground and pulled August's legs out from underneath him. It happened so fast that she didn't have time to warn August until she saw him lying on the gravel.

Rushing forward, Perrie pulled on Jack's cloak with all her strength. She leveraged her weight against Jack, yanking harder, and he let out a small choking sound. August hurried to get up.

The Ripper's knife crashed to the ground as Perrie gave his cape one more good pull. August took advantage of the Ripper's momentary disadvantage, knocking the top hat from Jack's head to the ground. He grabbed the scarf and quickly unwound it, leaving her speechless. Wild red curls unraveled from the fabric, curtaining a familiar yet unfriendly face. Perrie's eyes widened to the size of full moons, but she didn't dare release her hold.

August stepped back, his head cocked, his voice low. "Definitely not Thomas."

Not Jack the Ripper, but Jackie *the Ripper.*

For a moment, Perrie was both shocked and stunned—she should've put it together. Fannie was the only person they'd ever seen who went outside, besides the dead body of Officer Rodriguez, and then her reanimated living body. Fannie hadn't seemed unhappy. In fact, her story was almost admirable. Why would she kill her friends?

Her head filled with so many questions that would never be answered—there wasn't time.

Grabbing hold of Fannie, August twisted her arms behind her back. She thrashed like wildfire.

"I am going to destroy you, Mary, from the inside out," Fannie spat.

Ignoring her, Perrie asked August, "What do we do now? Just throw her down and run?"

"Grab the knife first," he agreed.

Perrie picked up the long blade from the ground while August threw Fannie to the side like a sack of potatoes. They then hauled ass to the barrier.

A loud screeching erupted from all around them, but she couldn't let herself look back. She focused on leaving, finding Maisie, and getting the hell out of the Glass Vault. The darkness swallowed her view up ahead, but she knew she was close.

Then Fannie somehow appeared, blocking their way, twirling what looked to be a scalpel in her right hand.

They stopped dead in their tracks.

"Perrie, I'm going to distract her," August whispered. "You head to where you think the barrier might start and see if you can get through. I'll be right behind you."

"Don't be ridiculous!"

"Don't be stubborn!" August barked.

"Fine!" she yelled.

"Good!" August yelled back. He had his mind set on doing what he wanted, and she wasn't going to argue.

"Run left," he said softly.

Perrie took off as if she was heading straight for Fannie, but at the last minute, she moved to the left. Fannie was ready for it, and she turned to run toward Perrie. August yanked Fannie from behind by the cloak, but it snapped off.

With not enough air in her lungs, Perrie arrived at the barrier, and for a split second nothing happened. Then a suction tugged at her, pulling her forward again. The strong wind from the barrier blew her hair every which way. August made a desperate dive toward her and managed to wrap his arms around her waist.

The last thing Perrie saw before being uprooted was Fannie hitting the barrier and bouncing back.

EIGHTEEN

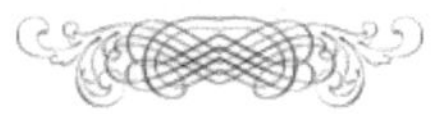

The ride through the barrier was all a big blur. It tossed Perrie out, throwing her in a field of grass with August's arms still wrapped around her. They hit the ground hard, knocking the wind right out of her, and broke apart.

"It looks like we moved on to a new display." She stood and dusted herself off, taking in their new surroundings.

August blinked and peered around. "Yep, circular vacation of death. This one may not be as bad as the last, but with the track record we've had so far . . ."

Relief crashed over her in waves. They were out of that hellish place—no Ripper. She should've paid more attention, shouldn't have trusted so easily. Perrie was so set on Jack the Ripper being a man that she hadn't even thought it was possible. She wanted to believe there was some good in this place, that Fannie was like Katrina, but she'd been wrong. If only she could've done more to save Officer Rodriguez.

"Hey, check out your arm," August said in awe.

She examined the wound on her flesh, but there wasn't one. "It's gone!" With wide eyes, she shoved it in his face.

"Thank fuck for that." He laughed.

"And I'm finally out of that dress." Once again, they were

wearing different clothing—there seemed to be a pattern here. Perrie was trying to be optimistic, given that her arm was newly healed and they were safely out of the Ripper's way.

"Technically, you're still in a dress." He motioned a finger up and down at the length of her body.

Yes, I'm still in a dress… But this one was much easier to manipulate and move in. The olive green blended in with her surroundings, and the material was cotton, possibly combined with another material, hitting right at her ankles. Her sleeves flowed slightly, until the ends cuffed at her wrists—a brown belt with a peculiar tribal design wrapped around her waist. The flat slip-on brown shoes she wore matched the same pattern of the belt at the front where her toes were. Perrie's braid lay right above her waist, and she grabbed it.

"This isn't exactly jeans and a shirt, but it works better than thirty layers of material for a suit." August studied himself and pulled at the end of his tunic.

The length of his hair came to about his chin, and she reached up, running her fingers through it before tugging at a lock.

"You rock the long hair." She let her hand drift away from his curls when he caught it, drawing her closer. Her chest tightened, remembering their moment in bed, him bringing her to bliss, even while still wearing her clothing.

"Do I?" August brushed a calloused thumb against her skin, her fingers, shifting even closer. With a smile, he reached around her waist and tugged the end of her braid. "I like yours too." He brought his hand to cup her cheek, his lips millimeters from touching hers. "Don't think I've forgotten about what happened between us. We need to go, but I just had to do this first." Then his lips were on hers in a searing kiss, the movements of his mouth fueling her to match his pace, demanding more. August's tongue flicked Perrie's and he nipped at her bottom lip, his fingertips trailing down her spine until they were at her backside, pulling her closer. All of his hardness was against her softness, teasing them both.

Too soon, he left her. But they didn't have time for anything else right then, even though she wanted more. His phantom touches still lingered, though.

Grinning, Perrie checked out the rest of him—tight brown pants, dark-brown boots and a green tunic covered his lean muscles. They almost matched, except for when she noticed a sword belted at his side.

"Hey, why do you get a weapon and I don't?"

August unsheathed the long sword and rotated it around and around as if he'd just won the lottery. The light caught and flashed across the silver surface, nearly blinding her.

While still holding the sword, he walked over and pulled out something tucked into the belt at her back.

"You do." He handed her a small dagger encrusted with red rubies.

"This isn't even close to being as good of a weapon as yours." She frowned. "I would have to be fairly close to what I'm attacking. It isn't like I can throw it since, you know, I haven't been trained in throwing daggers."

"Better than nothing." He smirked.

"True. Why do you think we didn't have weapons before?" She studied the dagger, turning it over. Better than being equipped with forks and dinner knives this time. Although a fork could do some damage, she much preferred this tiny dagger. She tucked it back into her belt and patted it several times.

"Again, I'm going to be real honest here, Perrie, and I'm willing to bet this world is worse than the last, based on our track record. So, you'll have to excuse me if I seem a little too excited about this sword." August carefully sheathed his blade.

This place seemed similar to Sleepy Hollow with its lush forest, minus the dense fog. They did the usual routine and checked the barrier. It wouldn't open or give way, so their only option was forward.

"It's déjà vu all over again." August shook his head with an annoyed sigh.

"Maybe we'll find Maisie in this one." *I hope.* "But now I don't know how many displays there are. She could be in any one."

"We'll see. I'm not sure how many of these we're going to have to get through to find her."

"Hopefully not as many as there were in the Glass Vault." But doubt after doubt washed over her.

Taking quiet steps, they trekked their way through the forest's rich land filled with skyscraping trees and bright green shrubbery. It was eerily silent, though. In the trees, a few scattered small birds nestled there, but not a single chirp or caw escaped their beaks. As if they were too scared...

They wandered a little farther until sunlight broke through the tall and narrow trees, guiding their way to a large opening leading out of the forest.

Once they stepped away from the last tree, a row of large gray boulders twice her height came into view. They stopped in front of the first one, and Perrie studied their odd lined arrangement. It almost looked as though they'd purposely been placed there like this. But, who could've moved boulders this big without some sort of machine?

The ground quaked beneath her feet, as if to answer her question. The intensity of the shaking rattled her bones and muscles, seeming to clack them against one another.

Perrie searched for cover, but there wasn't any. The trees weren't wide enough to hide behind, and with how fragile they appeared, she wasn't sure if the trunks would be standing after this. Perrie and August were exposed, and it was basically an open invitation to be attacked.

"Go to those boulders!" August pointed up ahead.

They tried to run, but the debilitating shaking made them stumble too many times before they caught themselves against a boulder.

Perrie dove down first behind a large boulder covered in green moss and dirt, cradling her knees to her chest. She had no fucking idea what was causing this, but then it stopped as fast as it had started. Above the ringing in her ears, booming voices echoed. Someone was speaking … or more like rumbling in another language.

For the moment, they were hidden enough behind the line of ten or so boulders. That was, until lurking danger decided to come searching for them… A large gap rested between each boulder, big enough for her to crawl past. August shimmied up to the open space and peeked through.

"What do you see? Maisie?" she whispered. He didn't seem to hear her, so she tugged on his shirt to get his attention. "August?"

He shook his head, placed one finger to his lips and slid over to the next boulder, motioning for her to follow. She lowered herself to where he once was, then pressed her hands to the boulder and peered out.

Perrie sucked in a sharp breath as she stared out at a huge bridge, built with white rocks and a wide stone pathway, sitting in the middle of a meadow, dividing the luscious green landscape. All in all, the structure was beautiful. The one thing missing was water beneath the bridge—only a sparse patch of dirt rested underneath.

Her heart pounded furiously in her chest as she took notice of what was there. It wasn't Maisie.

Three tall trolls stalked beneath the bridge, their skin sallow and dark brown in certain places along their bodies. It almost appeared like rotten flesh draped their skeletal bodies. These trolls—boney with sharp-looking features—were nothing like what she would've imagined one to look like—not that children's toys were good examples.

Stringy, dark hair caked in dry mud and dirt covered the heads of two of them. Perrie guessed those were the females, judging by their well-endowed breasts and the curls between their thighs. The other turned around, clearly male, his hanging length one of the largest she'd ever seen. Dirt and grime concealed most of their flesh, and from the looks of it, these creatures had never bathed a day in their entire lives. With lazy movements, they lumbered about until something caught their attention, the male pointing upward.

A *clack-clack-clackity-clack-clack* echoed.

Perrie's gaze traveled to the top of the bridge to where a little white goat walked. As it seemed to have a bounce in its step, the goat was one of the happiest things she'd seen since they'd fallen through. A sense of dread filled her as she now watched the goat, her eyes darting back and forth between its snowflake-colored fur and the trolls.

One of the females rumbled something to the others before slapping at her chest. The male nodded, and the other female retreated to the shadows, visibly enraged when she sank down to the ground, no doubt to pout about her loss.

The first female troll licked her thin lips with a long green tongue the color of the vomit that the little girl in *The Exorcist* spewed from her mouth. Perrie couldn't imagine the stench of what the troll's breath must smell like. The female crept to the edge of the bridge and pressed her palms against the stone, waiting now for the moment when the goat was close enough to snatch.

By now, the goat had reached the middle of the bridge. Its leisurely pace and beautiful surroundings appeared to distract the goat from the real sense of the lurking danger below the bridge.

Please run. Please run. Please run! Perrie chanted over and over in her head. But her attempt at mind control failed.

The female troll moved as quickly as a spider, skittering up the bridge, and snatched the goat in her hand with one swipe. An ugly cry tore from the goat's throat seconds before she snapped its neck.

The troll jumped down from the bridge and back to the pit.

From the ease of her movements, Perrie bet the troll had done it a million times before. With a loud thump, the female hit the earth hard and the ground rumbled. The quakes from earlier were the trolls—another mystery solved.

A ruckus stirred beneath the bridge as the female with the goat raised her prize and dangled its body proudly. The other sulking female troll hobbled over to her companion and spoke, loud enough for Perrie to hear clearly, but it didn't matter since she couldn't understand a fucking word.

Then the sulky female attempted to grab the dead animal from the Goat Killer. The male stood and shoved the female down, while the one holding the goat cackled so loudly Perrie's ears ached.

The sulky troll hit the ground with her fists—one struck right after the other, making the ground shake again. She stopped after the others ignored her tantrum and moved back to sit, her lips pulled back into a sneer. Perrie *almost* felt bad for her.

The Goat Killer took her dead prey in her hand and pounded it against the ground, blood spraying. Perrie gasped, so jarred by the action of it that she scooted back and covered her mouth. She watched in horror as the female ripped off one of the goat's legs with a loud splitting snap. At least she'd killed it first before doing that… The troll brought the tiny bloody leg to her mouth, biting and chewing like she was testing it out.

A true smile of satisfaction spread across her crimson-stained lips. The rest of the goat was gone in three bites, not even taking time to chew before swallowing the pieces whole.

Blood mixed with thick drool dribbled down her chin, and Perrie couldn't watch anymore. She whirled toward August, who was still watching the trolls, his disgust mirroring her own.

"Well, Perrie"—he sucked in a breath—"this just went from bad to worse."

ΠΙΠΕΤΕΕΠ

Perrie rested against a boulder, done with troll watching. "Is this what we're in for, August? Are these displays going to get worse the farther we go? This is more than *Three Billy Goats Gruff*. It's Bloody Fucking Troll's Gruff."

"What now?" August asked. He slid beside her and propped himself against another boulder, pulling his legs up and resting his forearms on top of his knees.

As if in response, her stomach growled.

"Really, Perrie?" August shot her "the look" and pointed his thumb back at the troll area. "After seeing that sick shit?"

It was poor timing, she knew. But like called to like, and perhaps monsters did the same since the one in her stomach was ravenous. A few feet from them sat a berry bush, and she nodded at them. "What about those? Do you think they're poisonous?"

He crawled forward to the bush. "They look okay to me."

"How positive are you about that *exactly*?" Perrie joined him and he plucked one blue berry. He inspected the berry, rotating it in between his thumb and index finger. Her fingers fidgeted with a blade of grass as he cut the berry in half with his fingernail and examined the juice dripping out.

"I'm going to say fifty percent sure." August grinned and popped the berry into his mouth before she could snatch it back. He chewed away at it as if he hadn't just risked his life.

"You idiot!" she hissed. It was her turn to give him the "what the fuck" look. "I could have given you that same percentage myself. Fifty percent chance leads to death, or fifty percent chance leads to staying alive."

"What can I say? I'm a daredevil."

"Yeah, well you're no Matt Murdock," Perrie teased. *But, what the hell?* She grabbed a berry and tossed it into her mouth.

About two minutes passed and they'd both eaten a few more berries. She didn't feel sick, but who knew how long poison took to kill someone. She was too hungry to care, so she gathered as many berries as she could in the folds of her dress, then crawled back to the boulders to eat.

They finished up the berries and oddly enough, they were still alive—for the time being. August and Perrie peeped through the hole to find the trolls sitting around. One of them threw a tantrum for no reason and pounded the ground, making it vibrate *again*.

She and August tried going back to the barrier where they'd come through, just to double check if maybe they could make an exit that way. The villains of this exhibit had been seen, more than she would've liked, so she thought that maybe the barrier would open. It didn't. Perrie punched the invisible wall over and over again with her frustration. They then came back through the woods and settled behind the boulders, and she knew their only option was to get across the bridge.

While waiting, two more goats attempted to pass over the bridge, and more blood was spilled. The two remaining trolls had taken their turns, the sulky female being the most vicious of them all, ripping the goat apart piece by bloody piece.

"I think the way out will be through the opening under the bridge. It's just a guess, but since the shape of the barrier is a rectangle again, and we fell through back there—" She pointed behind them.

"Then that means the way out could be straight ahead, right past troll territory, like in Sleepy Hollow," August finished.

"Precisely. Now the question is, how long will it take for them to fall asleep?"

The option she preferred was to attempt to go over the bridge and just hop off the side, but that wouldn't work because the bridge was too high. An issue that dampened another plan was the starting point seemed to curve right by the sidewall of the barrier, preventing them from being able to walk around to the other side of it. Somehow goats kept on appearing, though, the same size and shape. *But a goat's a goat, right*?

August busied himself with his nails, picking at them with a stick he'd found on the ground while they waited for the trolls—hopefully all of them—to fall asleep at once. Perrie remained vigilant, despite her exhaustion, and kept a trained eye on the bridge. She could feel her eyes fighting against the need for sleep as her lids grew heavy. Every few seconds she nodded off, when suddenly, her body straightened, her eyes fully open. A young guy appeared, walking across the bridge, no goats in sight.

"Where did he come from?" The guy was tall with the lightest white hair she'd ever seen, and his complexion was just as pale. He looked like a normal person from a regular village, dressed in a similar fashion to August.

"Who?" August dropped the stick on the ground and turned back to the hole. "Oh wait, I see."

As the trolls came to attention, perking up and listening intently to his footsteps above them, Perrie's heart raced. She fought the urge to run to him, to shout and warn the guy about the trolls. But, she was too afraid to tempt fate, and she wouldn't risk the possibility of saving her cousin.

"Doesn't he know about the trolls?" she whispered.

"Don't think so," August breathed.

They watched the trolls as they determined whose turn it was now. It appeared to be the first Goat Killer's turn again as she geared up to do her spider crawl.

Perrie glanced back at the guy crossing the bridge, recognition hitting her this time. It was clear to her now what was so familiar about him. His hair, that unique shade of white—she would've taken him for any random person if it were a different color. *He* was one of the missing people—she'd seen several pictures of him right after it was announced, after Maisie had told her about him a couple days ago.

"That's Ben Johnston."

August's brows lowered in confusion. "Who?"

"Ben Johnston. You know, that college guy who went missing? It was right before Neven."

He squinted his eyes at Ben a little harder, then he blinked several times in recognition. "I wouldn't have guessed, except for that hair."

"That's exactly what I thought!"

"His chances of making it back home now are slim," August said, his lips forming a thin line.

Perrie waited, hoping this troll was going to do something different this time, but the female slunk low like a spider and crawled. Ben inched closer, then she hopped over the side of the bridge, landing directly in front of him.

Not a single scream tore from his throat, nor did he fight back or run. *Why doesn't he do something?* Instead, he just stayed there, lingering like a fucking moron while staring at the troll.

The troll stood idle, studying her prey with hungry eyes, a smile spreading across her horrid face. Something wasn't right. She held out her gigantic hand to Ben, and he took it in his own. It was as if he was mesmerized by her and under her spell.

"August, what's he doing? No one in his or her right mind would willingly go to a creature that looked like that."

August wrinkled his nose. "Is he even in his right mind? How long has he been missing?"

"A week or maybe less."

The troll yanked Ben to her harshly, pulled him to her chest, then leapt off the bridge, landing roughly on the ground—causing it to ripple. He still didn't scream, only smiled while in her arms. It made zero sense.

The moment was short-lived as the troll tossed Ben to the ground like a toy.

"You're so beautiful!" he cried, his words echoing out from under the bridge.

"There's something wrong here. He has to be under some type of influence," August muttered.

"I agree. Maybe she's somehow enchanting Ben by locking eyes with him," she guessed.

The male troll stumbled toward Ben and picked him up off the ground with little effort. Then, like a whip, he slapped Ben against the side of the bridge, cracking his head wide open. Blood oozed out from the wound as the male beat him against the dirt.

Not once did Ben scream as his body was tossed ragged at the ground. There would never be any un-seeing this. The sounds of his body ripping, cracking, and tearing, reverberated throughout the forest. They wouldn't stop until he'd been taken apart, piece by piece, just like the goats. Blood covered Ben's broken body from head to toe, leaving no life in him.

August pulled Perrie to him, and she shakily pressed her head into his shoulder, holding him tightly. No one deserved this. She hadn't known Ben, but seeing him become their plaything would haunt her for the rest of her life.

"I really wish I knew what time it was," she mumbled. Wearing a watch didn't seem all that awful of an idea, considering how long they'd been here. *Although, who's to say it wouldn't have vanished with our phones?* Her necklace had.

After the incident with Ben, not even a single of his bones lingering, one of the females lay down to rest. Three more goats had followed after Ben's death, and the trolls continued taking their turns.

"Do you think we should try running for it? Maybe sneak up to the edge and run through?" Perrie monitored the situation, her gaze following the length of the bridge and halting. "Wait. *What the hell?"*

Grasping August's arm, she tugged him to the hole. He arched a brow, appearing skeptical at first, but once his gaze landed on what she'd found, he didn't look away. "No way. A reanimated corpse made from thin air."

As sure as her name was Perrie Madeline, she watched Ben Johnston cross the bridge again. Same as before—white hair, pale complexion, and clothing. Everything was in one piece. No broken bones, no missing limbs.

"Can't be a zombie if he was in the trolls' bellies," she said. "This whole place is making less sense than ever."

They chose not to watch any of what happened, not after the last time.

"Let me put my thinking cap on." August placed his hands against his head. After several moments, he looked up.

"What do you have?" She anxiously leaned forward.

He studied the trees for a brief period of silence and then, finally, opened his mouth to speak. "I've got nothing."

With a grunt, her body dropped back to the boulder. What made this world the same as the last? What were they missing?

She thought back to the other two displays they'd experienced. Like lightning, it all struck her at once.

"In the display with Jack the Ripper, AKA Jackie, we found Officer Rodriguez dead at first, right?"

"Right, and then we saw her magically appear alive. What's that got to do with anything?" August asked.

"So, she was dead and then she wasn't. We saw her after that, alive!"

His eyes widened, seeming to catch on.

"It's the same thing here," she continued, "except we didn't see Officer Rodriguez die again, but maybe if we'd stayed longer, it would've happened. The only two people we've seen die have come back to life."

"Okay, sounds fair"—he rubbed his chin—"but what about Sleepy Hollow? We didn't see any dead bodies come back to life."

"What if Katrina already died once before and we just missed it? Maybe we got there right as she came back to life." Perrie knew she was onto something big, something that could help them piece this place together.

August quit rubbing at his chin and rested his hand on his knee. "It's possible."

"Let's assume for the moment then. Now, what do they all have in common?"

"Ben and Officer Rodriguez went missing," he said absently. "Did Katrina look familiar to you?"

Perrie nodded. "A little. I thought I had seen her before."

August's eyes shifted from one side to the other, like a ticking clock. "I think I saw her on one of the flyers, but she may have had really short blonde hair, like a pixie cut."

"Oh. Oh!" Perrie snapped her fingers. "Josselyn Shaw. I remember seeing that flyer, but the picture was grainy. Those flyers were everywhere. She didn't really look like her photo at first, but I can see it now."

"That means each display we've been to contains a

missing person within it. The question left is, why?"

TWENTY

Somehow, there were missing people inside the Glass Vault. *Why? How did they get here?* If it was true, then Neven and Maisie must for sure be in here somewhere. Perrie still wanted to get out of this nightmare, but they were going to have to find Maisie and Neven first.

"I think we'd have to find Quinsey Wolfe to answer all of our questions, but I'm sure he's nowhere inside his own scenes of horror," Perrie whispered. But she didn't know if Quinsey Wolfe even existed. "More importantly, we now know Maisie and Neven both are in a display somewhere."

August was peering through the hole when he said, "The trolls might be going to sleep now. Let's get past them and see if we can find Maisie or Neven in the next display."

One of the female trolls was already lying down, making grunting and choking noises like she had something stuck in her throat. It was probably *only* a human or goat bone.

With light movements, the sulky troll patted the hard dirt, as if softening up a feathered-down mattress. *Ridiculous*. Even if she sat there and patted and smacked at the ground for an hour, it wasn't going to get much softer. Finally, she lay down on her side in her freshly patted dirt bed, dragging her legs up to her chest like a small baby. Her matted hair fell over her face, and Perrie couldn't really tell, but she thought the troll closed her eyes.

"Okay, we need a plan now," she said to August. He sat back and tapped the tips of his fingers together like a villain in an old cartoon.

"Ah yes, the plan." He paused for effect. "We'll go as far as we can to the left side of the bridge, get to the edge of the hole underneath, and dash through it like madmen."

"Great minds think alike. That was my plan, too. Now, what do we do if the trolls wake up?" She sighed.

"This would be a whole lot easier if there was only one troll," he groaned, crossing his arms.

"I know, right? Isn't it supposed to be one troll to each bridge? I've never seen multiple trolls sharing bridges. Not that I've seen a troll until now, besides in the actual nursery rhyme. And in that story, all the goats got across. That didn't happen here," Perrie huffed.

"The trolls are spaced pretty well apart. We walk as quietly as we can, and if one moves, we start running."

"Are you ready to do this?" Her hand shook unsteadily as she freed the small dagger at her waist. Perrie had zero experience using one, but she would swing it like fucking crazy if she had to find a way to her cousin.

"Better than dying behind a boulder." He unsheathed his sword.

They avoided any twigs that might snap or any leaves that could crunch. The sun's light was lessening as it started its descent, and Perrie hoped it stayed lit long enough to see as they passed through. August took his first step into a lush field with tiny pink flowers blooming everywhere. The place was beautiful, but the hidden ugliness gave nothing a real chance to live here. She wondered if the displays in the museum were real. And if they were, how were they transporting them to places like this? She couldn't focus on that now.

Perrie and August made their way to the bridge with no way of seeing the trolls ahead of them. Her hands had stopped shaking, but her heart pounded fast—so fast she couldn't believe she wasn't having a heart attack. She squeezed her dagger harder.

As August reached the rustic stone bridge, he stopped and listened. Only snoring sounded, so she advanced and joined him. While stopped, she took a few deep breaths.

August whistled quietly, signaling for her to move ahead of him before they continued. As they approached the opening under the bridge, the grass started to thin out. No more small flowers existed in this part of the grass. Then, there was no grass at all, only soft dirt that became hard earth.

Slowing down, she tiptoed quietly to the hole, and plastered her body so close to the wall that she imagined she was one with it.

Carefully, Perrie peered around the edge of the opening. *So far, so good.* The trolls still snored and gurgled in their slumber. Body odor and rot invaded her nostrils as she stretched a little farther around the corner. She gagged on the thick stench of it, grateful for their snoring to mask her disgust.

Beneath the bridge the lighting was dim, but enough rays seeped inside so she could see everything clearly. Long fissures marred the high ceiling, and she assumed it was from each time the trolls' heavy bodies scaled up it, causing its damage.

The sulky troll lingered in her fetal position, a huge puddle of drool running from her mouth to the ground, her matted hair soaking in it.

The second female rested on her back with her mouth wide open, and every single one of her sharp teeth on display. Black, green, brown, and yellow teeth all crooked and decayed. The urge to brush her own teeth had never been stronger.

The male twitched and his stomach gurgled. He shifted around on the floor until he appeared comfortable again. Perrie didn't dare move. *Yet*.

Aside from the overwhelming smell of the trolls' domain, they were clear to keep moving. Perrie signaled to August with a wave of her hand. As she started walking, August pulled her back and shook his head, pointing to himself, then at the troll nest. He wanted to go first, and she didn't waste time arguing. He grasped her hand and rubbed it softly with his thumb, as if to silently reassure her that everything would be fine.

Their steps were so quiet, calculated, that even a mouse wouldn't hear them coming.

Clack-clack-clackity-clack-clack.

They froze. Something was on top of the bridge, and from the sound of its steps, it was one of those *fucking* goats.

August's gaze widened at Perrie, telling her to run. Just as they moved, one of the trolls opened its eyes. Red. There were no dark pupils or whites outside the irises—it was as if blood had swallowed those colors.

The troll settled those orbs of blood on Perrie and August and barreled for them. They'd made it halfway to the end when August was thrown back. Whirling around, Perrie found a female troll's hands tightened around him.

She didn't have time to think—she ran with her dagger and stabbed the bitch's hand repeatedly. Red liquid spewed from the wounds. The troll released him and cried a monstrous noise, causing the bridge above to rumble.

August rebounded quickly, just in time, and darted forward with sword in hand. Another troll jolted for them. August maneuvered to the side and sliced the tendon right above one of the troll's rotten feet.

"Go," he yelled.

Perrie sprinted to the other side of the bridge, legs and arms pumping as hard as she could. August reached the barrier right before she did—the force of it pulling at him the second he came close. She didn't make it. A large, dirt-covered hand wrapped around her waist and yanked her back.

"August!" she screamed.

"Perrie!" He looked back in horror, pushing against the draw of the barrier. It was too late, though—and he vanished into thin air. Nothing was left except a field on the other side.

Perrie screamed again, unable to stop, gripping the dagger with such force for fear she might drop it. She wiggled and writhed to free her arm with the dagger, but it was trapped.

The troll tightened her fist. Lucky for Perrie though, the female switched her hold and freed Perrie's arm with the dagger. Then the troll lifted Perrie to her face, each getting a proper look at one another. *Fuck.* Perrie was in the hands of the one troll who seemed the most vicious of all. And the troll was *pissed*.

No time to waste. Perrie used what was left of her adrenaline and thrust the dagger right in the center of the troll's left eye. The female roared, the sound piercing Perrie's ears as the bitch stumbled back and dropped her. Perrie didn't hesitate when her body hit the hard dirt. She ran.

The ground vibrated, making her tilt sideways. Her body ached, but she had to keep going. The barrier was right ahead.

Please take me, she silently repeated inside her head. As soon as she reached the barrier and struck it, the wind swept her up and dragged her forward. The last sounds she heard were the wild screechings of the ravenous trolls.

Perrie's feet landed on solid ground. Falling forward, she caught herself with her forearms and hands, right before her face collided with the grass below.

She rolled over to glance behind her, making sure none of the trolls had made it through the barrier. Relieved to find not a single monstrous beast, she lay there and let herself breathe, hard and rapid, until she could think clearly. The pain from her fall to the ground in the troll display was gone, just like the cut to her arm from Fannie had simply disappeared. It seemed if someone was hurt in a single display, then moved to the next, the individual would be magically healed.

That answer she could deal with.

Laughter bubbled up her throat and she slapped the ground. Maybe she was losing her mind being in here too long, but she almost felt invincible in that moment. This world was completely fucked.

Finally, she sat up and looked around. More trees, this time pine and oak, enveloped her, and August was nowhere in sight. He'd gone in before her, so he had to have landed somewhere else, just like in the Jack the Ripper display. Even though she knew he had to be here somewhere, worry filled her.

Pulling herself up to stand, Perrie brushed the dirt from her dress. This time the bodice was dark red while the skirt was a darker brown, like the color of tree bark. Matching brown flats covered her feet and no weapons in sight. *Whatever, I'll use a tree branch for a weapon if I need to.*

Perrie turned around and touched along the barrier to see how wide it went. She yanked her hand away, afraid it would suck her back through. She had no intention of being chased by trolls again.

Taking a deep swallow, she took the path laid out before her and ditched the trolls. She hadn't walked very far from where she'd landed when she spied a cottage in the distance. *There's a cottage in the middle of a heavily wooded area? Why does that sound familiar?*

Gray smoke curled upward into the bright blue sky from the chimney on the roof. She wasn't even sure if she *wanted* to know who or what was in that damn cottage, but someone was home.

The trees in the surrounding area seemed tall and wide enough to climb. She glanced at the cottage and back up at the trees, then one more time toward the cottage. Shaking her head, she postponed the cottage and would attempt to climb a tree to see how far the forest reached. Perrie padded over to the nearest one where clusters of large beetles trailed its trunk. She'd seen much, *much* worse in the last couple of displays.

A branch dangled right above her head, and Perrie grabbed hold of it. She started to climb up the tree, but her feet caught on her dress and she slipped. *This is why I hate dresses.* Hiking up the skirt to the middle of her thighs, she knotted the excess fabric between her legs.

Perfect.

Again, she reached for the branch and managed to lodge her foot into the bark and swing herself up. Perrie climbed a few more branches, her new curls brushing her shoulders as they fought with the breeze. When she stretched for the next branch, she couldn't grasp it, and her hand connected with the barrier. She guessed that proved the barrier was more like a rectangular box. There were limitations, even when her feet weren't touching the ground in this prison.

Stepping down a branch, she surveyed the area and found no sign of human life coming from anywhere—except the cottage.

Could August be in there? What about Maisie or Neven? The cottage was the only other option she had.

A soft scratching sounded from below her, and she stilled. Before she could do anything else, a small furry thing scurried past her, and she almost lost her balance. Perrie risked glancing up and found the furry thing was only a squirrel. She breathed a deep sigh of relief.

As she carefully climbed back down, leaves crunched somewhere nearby. She gripped the branch tighter, when a small deer zoomed by beneath her—this place seemed to have more animal life than the other displays.

Perrie lowered herself to the ground and was proud of herself for not breaking her neck in the process. She untied the fabric of the dress, freeing it back to her ankles, and looked ahead. Something about the cottage had changed—a light illuminated from inside the glass windows. Someone was definitely home. She wondered if maybe it *was* August who could've been using the smoke to signal her. It was worth a look inside. Then again, what if he wasn't even in this display… What if he'd landed somewhere else?

Perrie thanked every tree around here that the cottage wasn't covered in sugary treats and frosting. She really didn't want to have to deal with a damn witch at the moment. Although, it was possible that a smart witch would leave her house unfrosted to better lure in her victims who didn't know about *Hansel and Gretel*.

"One thing at a time, Perrie," she told herself.

When she and Maisie were younger, *Hansel and Gretel* was their favorite fairy tale. Perrie was never afraid of it back then, even though the story itself could be disturbing for children. When she looked back, she was always so intrigued about a cottage made of desserts and sweets, regardless that the witch would eat the children's cooked flesh for meals.

They'd always played in Maisie's backyard. Maisie would grab a loaf of bread and tear up slices for crumbs, pretending their fake stepmother had abandoned them in the woods. Back then, Perrie didn't think it would be her real mom who would eventually abandon her.

Birds were never around to peck at the bread for them to pretend to lose their way, so they had to use Maisie's dog, Roosevelt. He wasn't alive now, but he'd gobbled the pieces of bread up just as well as any bird.

Maisie and Perrie would argue over who would be Gretel and who would be Hansel. Perrie would usually give in and be Hansel most of the time. Her cousin was persistent, always had been.

In Maisie's backyard under the trees, Uncle Jaron had built a small cottage for them to play in. It had been so much better than those cheap plastic ones.

One day, while they'd been pretending to be Hansel and Gretel, they decided to *decorate* the small "cottage". They'd snuck inside Maisie's house and grabbed anything they could find to make it look like a cottage of candy. They'd used just about everything, from condiments to potato chips. To draw the designs, they'd used ketchup and mustard, which were the brightest colors they could find.

They'd wanted to make it vibrant.

She and Maisie didn't go unpunished. Her aunt had made them clean the house up as best they could and help Uncle Jaron repaint it. Perrie wouldn't really have called it a punishment because it had been fun getting to redecorate it again. That time, they'd chosen the colors, and they made sure the house was brighter than before.

The little hammer inside Perrie's head knocked the memory away. *God, I miss Maisie.*

Using caution, she walked toward the cottage. The roof wasn't covered in candy. A normal roof sat on top of a normal green cottage. *Thank the display for this one common courtesy.* The house was a regular storybook home, complete with pretty flowers and lush green shrubbery.

Perrie attempted to peer inside the windows, but too much grime covered the glass to see anything. Swallowing her fear, she found her inner courage, which was buried very, *very* deeply at that moment. She marched to the front door and lifted a shaky hand to knock, rapping against the door three times, and each time it reverberated around the cottage. In case someone, or something, monstrous answered the door, she took a few steps back. The distance gave her a chance to take off running if need be.

No one answered, so she tried again and did the same thing, except this time she gave the door an extra knock before stepping back. She realized then that no one was going to answer.

"Guess I'll just let myself in then," Perrie mumbled. Grabbing the unlocked doorknob, she shakily opened it and stepped inside.

TWENTY-ONE

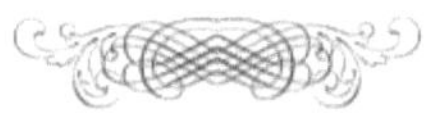

Once inside the cottage, the smell of death permeated the air.

The odor was so pungent and heavy that Perrie's stomach churned with nausea. She covered both her nose and mouth, hesitant to keep going. But she did, and turned the corner of the small foyer. A comfortable warmth enveloped her body inside the cottage, and she stepped into a large living area. Perrie stopped dead in her tracks.

A rocking chair sat in front of a fireplace, and a girl occupied it. Perrie couldn't see what the girl was doing with her hands exactly, but it looked like she was sewing or knitting something.

"Excuse me." Perrie balled her hands into fists, prepared to use them, or run if this went awry.

The girl didn't turn around. Instead, she continued to rock herself back and forth. Each slow creak of the chair echoed in Perrie's bones.

"Hello," she said even louder.

Nothing. The girl didn't even flinch. Heart pounding, Perrie inched closer to the girl and reached one hand out toward her shoulder.

Her eyes widened in recognition. "Maisie!" she gasped,

inhaling the thick scent of smoke and decay. The rocking stilled for a moment, but her cousin didn't look up.

Perrie bit her nails into her palms to calm her initial shock. Kneeling beside Maisie, she scanned her soft features. Her cousin appeared fine, changed even. Maisie's normally straight, black hair rested just below her chin in loose ringlets, making her look a lot younger than her almost eighteen years. She wore a remarkably similar dress to Perrie's, and her feet were bare.

"Maisie? What are you doing?" Perrie asked, her attention drawn to Maisie's hand where she continued her methodical stitching. It wasn't cloth she was holding, but looked to be some sort of animal skin, possibly deer.

Maisie stopped then, slowly lifting her head and focusing on Perrie with the strangest look on her face. "Who is Maisie?"

A solid blue patch that matched her dress covered one of her eyes. Although, there was nothing vibrant about it like her usual patches.

"You're Maisie." Perrie grabbed her hands, desperate for her cousin to recognize her. Maisie gently removed Perrie's hands from hers.

"Aren't you just the silliest? My name is Snow." Maisie giggled.

Perrie's eyebrows shot straight up, and she nearly toppled over. "Uh, as in Snow White?"

"Yes," she said sweetly, giggling an octave higher than before. "How did you know that?"

"Lucky guess." Perrie cringed.

Something was fucking wrong with her cousin. Her smile was too wide, her voice too sweet, and there was an overly dreamy expression on her face that made Perrie shiver. She took a careful look around the room, tuning herself into her surroundings now. All over the floor, piled up in one of the corners were dead animal carcasses, blood pooled beneath them.

Next to the animals, pushed into the shadows, rested seven little beds in a row. Seven beds meant seven damn dwarves. Perrie stood shakily and walked closer for a better look. Seven little men lay in their beds with the sheets pulled clear up to their chins. At first glance, one might think them asleep, but the blood on their slashed faces proved otherwise. The light red sheets on their beds were drenched in blood. She'd been too focused on Maisie to notice any of this sick shit.

She whirled back to Maisie, horrified. *"What is that?"*

"Those little men weren't very kind to me." Maisie shook her finger in the air. "Now they won't be mean to me anymore."

Tossing her head back, Maisie laughed hysterically. Perrie's chest tightened as she became more and more disturbed by her cousin's behavior. Maisie lifted the animal fur to flip it over and Perrie squeaked. Ruby blood, from where the underside of the fur had been laying, caked her cousin's dress.

"Um, Maisie?" Perrie rasped.

"You mean Snow." Maisie tilted her head to the side, grinning wide.

"Right, I mean Snow." She pressed her lips together and nodded. "You do realize you're getting your dress a little messy. Maybe you should put that down and find something else to wear. Do you have another dress?"

Perrie wanted to take the animal fur and toss it into the lit fireplace, but the burning smell would make the odor of the room even worse than it already was. So instead, she reached for the fur to set it on the floor, but Maisie moved it away from her hands. Maisie's brows drew together in a hard line, then she hopped up from her seat.

"Yes. I believe I do!" Maisie softly set the fur on the floor, as if it was fragile enough to break. She then skipped over to a wardrobe.

Hesitantly, Perrie followed Maisie, moving her hand

gently to her cousin's arm. "Snow," she started, "do you recognize me?"

At first, Maisie didn't look at her, she was too busy tossing out dwarf-sized clothing from the wardrobe.

"Snow!" Maisie looked at Perrie then, staring hard, as if this was the first time she was *seeing* her. "Do you remember the name Perrie? That's me. What about August or Neven? Does that ring a bell?"

"Perrie." Maisie sounded out her name like it was a new word she was learning for the first time. Perrie thought there might be recognition starting to form, but then her eyes lost focus.

"Let's clean," Maisie said with a wild grin, forgetting all about the dress.

"Let's not."

Her cousin seemed to not like that particular answer as her face contorted into a childlike pout.

"You know"—Maisie gazed over toward the beds—"they did an awful thing to me, and I taught them."

Perrie avoided staring at the massacred men. *Do I even want to know*? But yes, she had to know, even if she didn't like what Maisie was insinuating.

"What did they do to you?"

"When I first arrived, I didn't know there were people who lived here. I fell asleep in one of the beds and when I woke up to whispering, my wrists were tied together."

"Then what did they do?" Perrie's fear shifted to fire as anger coursed through her. She was certain she wasn't going to like the direction this story was taking.

Maisie reached for her eye patch and lifted it back. Perrie's hands flew to her mouth as a loud gasp escaped her lips, her knees weak. There'd been no time for her to prepare herself for the ghastly sight. She'd been beyond wrong and now she thought she was going to be sick.

"They took out a knife and removed my eye."

Her eye was gone. Maisie's beautiful whole fucking eye was missing, and in its place was a gaping hole. They'd mutilated her face. A mixture of emotions stirred within Perrie—rage, despair, fear. If those little men weren't lying there already dead, she would've slaughtered them herself.

"Don't worry"—Maisie giggled, pulling her eye patch back down—"after they fell asleep, I was able to free myself and get them all back. You see that bucket over there?" She pointed at the corner with a bloody bucket beside the pile of animal carcasses.

"Yes, I see the bucket." But that didn't mean she wanted to know what was in it.

"Take a look inside," Maisie said anxiously.

"I think I'm going to pass on that."

Ignoring her response, Maisie lifted her hands to cover her one remaining eye and patch. "Now they see no evil." Then she moved her hands and covered her ears tightly. "They can hear no evil." Finally, she drifted her hands in front of her mouth, and her solo eye opened wide. "And now they will forever speak no evil."

"Uh-huh." Perrie's lips remained parted in shock. What the fuck was she supposed to even say to that?

Maisie pointed furiously at the men and giggled with pure excitement. "Here, I'll show you my collection."

Clapping frantically, Maisie dashed for the bucket, tugging Perrie along with her. Before she had time to protest, the bucket was in front of her. Her hand fisted her mouth as she dry heaved and stumbled backward. Bloody eyeballs, severed tongues, and ears filled the bucket. This was… This was… *Insanity*. Maisie had gone insane. And being here had made her this way.

"They wouldn't sit still, so I had to put them to bed first," Maisie said, pointing directly at her heart. "I used the same knife they used to cut out my eye."

After seeing her cousin's wound, Perrie knew she

would've had to defend herself. But the way she was acting, and the way she went about it, wasn't like her at all. Perrie needed to snap her out of this trance. There wasn't much time to think, so she came up with the first thing she could.

"Snow, look at me." She approached her cousin and gently placed her hands on the sides of her face. "Do you want me to tell you a story?"

Maisie clasped her hands together at her chest and made it seem like Perrie had just given her the best birthday present in the entire world.

"I love stories!" Maisie steadily shook her clasped hands.

"Then you'll love this one, I promise." Perrie walked her cousin back to the rocking chair and helped her sit, kicking the bloody fur out of the way before Maisie tried to drag it onto her lap again. Once her cousin was settled and content, Perrie took her place in front of the fire and began.

"Once upon a time, three good friends traveled far and wide to attend the great carnival. They were—"

"What were their names?" Maisie interrupted her. "These three good friends."

Shit. "They were called—uh—Mais, Nev, and Posie."

Maisie nodded her approval and Perrie continued, "So, like I was saying, these three good friends—Mais, Nev, and Posie—traveled far to attend the great carnival. All Mais wanted to do was eat a funnel cake before going on their favorite ride, the Zipper.

"The three good friends ate their tasty pastry and took turns riding their favorite ride. Nev and Posie, when riding together, would watch as Mais rode with the new friends she made. Mais was a silly girl, but silly in every good way."

This wasn't only a story—it was a memory. Maisie had dragged Neven and Perrie to the carnival one summer for a fun night. They'd taken turns riding the Zipper with each other, and Maisie would ask some random person to hop on with her so she could keep going.

"Eventually, Mais wasn't feeling up for another ride. Nev and Posie asked if she was all right, but Mais ran off and lost her pastry. Never one to quit, Mais went on and on again, until she felt sick. Nev and Posie suggested she take a break and play some carnival games!

"Posie was not very good at these games, but because she loved her cousin, Mais, she tried to win her something anyway. She picked a game, the hardest one in all the carnival, and tried her best to cheer up Mais. When the game was done, Posie won the smallest baby dragon and gave it to Mais, who suddenly felt much better that day."

The stuffed dragon Perrie had won for Maisie was still proudly displayed in her cousin's room.

"Every now and then, Maisie, you talk about how that was one of the greatest days of your life." Perrie waited patiently, congratulating herself for a job well done. Her English teacher would be proud that she'd managed to sneak in a couple of rhymes, too.

Maisie pressed her fingers to her cheeks as if she had dimples there and laughed. "That wasn't a story at all. There weren't any animals or castles or anything."

Perrie dropped her chin to her chest and mumbled sarcastically, "There was a stuffed dragon."

"Do you have any better stories?" Her cousin's eye widened with enthusiasm and a glazed shine.

"No." Clenching her jaw in frustration, she tried to come up with another. "Okay, I have one." Perrie then told her the story about Hansel and Gretel, about the ketchup on the house, and Aunt Krista's reaction. After that, she went on about high school, the Halloween party where they'd dressed up as Hansel and Gretel. It was the same year they'd tricked Neven into dressing as the witch.

"You have to remember that, Maisie," she urged her frantically. "That was our sophomore year—it was the best Halloween of all time. You even said so."

The fog in her eyes cleared for the slightest moment, and then it was gone. Maisie jumped out of her seat and clasped her hands together once again, and Perrie waited to hear what she'd been hoping for. But then she yelled maniacally, "I love dessert!"

That was it. That was the last straw. Perrie couldn't keep this charade up anymore. She dragged Maisie out of the chair by both arms and shook her hard.

"Damn it, Maisie. I don't know what the fuck is going on here, but we're done with this shit. I can't sit here anymore and play these games with you like we aren't in some demonic house. This house is filled with the dead bodies of people you say that you slaughtered. Then there are the skinned animals." She pointed at the bloody furs in the corner. "Not to mention, the stench in here reeks of a thousand deaths. If I have to slap you repeatedly to get you to remember, I will. Snap out of it, Maisie!"

Perrie released her cousin's arms and raised her hand, ready to smack the crazy out of her.

Then Maisie's one good eye widened. "Perrie?"

TWENTY-TWO

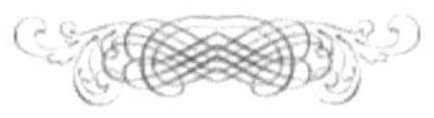

Perrie had done it. She didn't know how, but she'd done it. Her cousin was back.

"Maisie!" Perrie rushed forward, practically crying as she wrapped her arms around her, and squeezed her tighter than she had ever before.

"How did you get here?" Maisie blinked, appearing a little disoriented.

Perrie explained to her how she and August went to the Glass Vault to search for her, but instead got magically sucked into the hellish displays. Maisie stayed focused as Perrie told her about the previous places—Sleepy Hollow, Jack the Ripper, and Billy Goats Gruff—about what she and August had gone through—how they'd discovered the mystery of the missing people.

"Between Ben, Officer Rodriguez, and Josselyn, none of them recognized themselves either," Perrie said.

Maisie considered the information, furrowing her brow, as if trying to puzzle the pieces together. "Where's August, then?" she finally asked.

"I don't know." Perrie sighed, her chest heavy with regret. "What about you? What happened? Do you remember everything?”

Maisie pushed her hair behind her ears. “I remember most of it. I think? I left your house and arrived at the Glass Vault, but when I came inside there was no one there.”

“Did you meet Quinsey?”

She shook her head. “No. I didn’t see anyone in the museum. It was like what you saw. I wandered down a bunch of halls and wound up in the exhibit. I waited for a little bit, figuring that he was either late or somewhere on the premises.”

Leaning her back against the wall, Maisie slid to the floor. Perrie sat on the wood floor with her legs crossed, facing Maisie.

“While I was waiting, I walked around and looked at the displays. I remember stopping in front of Snow White.” She closed her eye. “The seven dwarves were lying asleep in their beds and someone was peering in through their window. Then it felt like something was sucking me in, and suddenly I was in a forest, a little further away from this cottage.” She pointed in the direction Perrie had come from, which was interesting since Maisie hadn’t encountered the trolls.

“Is that all you remember?”

“I remember more, but a lot of it is a blur.” She toyed with the skirt of her dress, observing the red still covering it. Perrie had never seen Maisie so not herself. She almost didn’t want to ask her about her eye, but she had to.

“What about your eye? Do you remember that at all?”

“I do, but I don’t. It was like I was possessed by something. It’s as if the person who was speaking to you wasn’t me, yet was me at the same time.” She paused. “I know how it sounds, but you have to believe me.”

“I do believe you, I promise. Trust me when I say that August and I have seen some seriously fucked up things.”

“Okay, so the odd thing is, I was already missing my eye when I got here. I lowered the patch to get a clearer view of my surroundings. That’s when I discovered my eye was gone.”

She traced her fingertips over the blue patch, staying silent for a few moments.

"Maisie, it's part of the display. As soon as we get out of this scene, you'll have your eye back."

She shrugged and smiled. "I'm used to seeing with one eye anyway."

Perrie was sure Maisie was the only person on the entire planet who wouldn't be freaking out just a little bit over a missing eyeball. If it were Perrie, she would have lost her shit.

"What about the dwarves? They didn't attack you?"

"No. I came to the cottage as soon as I saw it. The men were already dead—their ears, eyes, and tongues were already missing, and in that bucket over there." She tilted her head in the direction of the bloody pieces.

"I didn't see the Snow-White display," Perrie said. "However, this earlier version of you that was here before the real you came back said she'd murdered the dwarves after they ripped her eye out. This could be the story of the Snow-White display that had already happened, and by you coming here, it's the continuation of the story."

"That does sound plausible. By the way, I like how you said *she* instead of you." She smiled a genuine Maisie smile.

"You may remember all the crazy stuff this person said, but that wasn't you talking. Quirky and crazy isn't the same thing."

"Why thank you, Perrie, I'm glad to know you enjoy my presence."

"You're one of a kind." She laughed. "What else happened after you came into the cottage, or have you just been here the entire time?"

Maisie bit her thumbnail and chewed on it. "There's something else, and it's too much of a blur. I remember having a semi-meltdown after finding the dead bodies and the animal carcasses in the corner with the pail of body memorabilia. It had me panicked, and I ran out of the house. Outside, I screamed and kicked a couple of trees to cool myself down."

Perrie's stomach dropped, and anger boiled within her for what Maisie had to face. When Perrie had come through the first display, she was with August. She didn't know what she would've done if she'd been alone. Even when she'd been alone with that Thomas asshole, she already had experience with this place because of Sleepy Hollow. Maisie had gone to the Glass Vault by herself, got sucked in by herself, found all these dead bodies by herself, and she was missing an entire fucking eyeball.

"After moaning and groaning for a bit, I gathered my wits and set sail through the woods, away from the cottage in my pretend escape ship. Then I remember seeing a man."

"What man?" Perrie asked, wrinkling her nose.

"I have no idea. He had dark, brown hair that fell to his shoulders. That's all I can remember. Then somehow I ended up back at the cottage."

"He wasn't a giant or a troll, right? Someone who can lift you up with one hand?" Perrie tapped the middle of her palm several times for emphasis.

Maisie squinted her one eye. "I'm going to go with smaller than a giant, but I mostly remember a well-structured face and hair blowing around."

"From your detailed account, there's a model running around somewhere in the woods."

"That would be a strong possibility," she said, pointing a finger in the air.

"And you haven't seen anyone else pass through here?"

She shook her head.

It made sense. Perrie had only seen one missing person in each of the displays. This wasn't including August or her, though. Finding Maisie was checked off her list. Now August was gone, and they still had to find Neven.

"We got separated once before, but we both wound up in the same display. I'm sure he's here somewhere. Nev will probably be in another scene, so we can work on him next." A new rush of confidence flowed through her. "Let's turn this plan into pure action and find the guys."

Inside the lone bedroom, Maisie discovered a dresser filled with rows of the same shoes, eye patches, undergarments, and dresses. Not much variety there.

Maisie tore off the bloody dress, then threw on a clean one and a pair of shoes in record time. "There, I feel a little cleaner."

On the way out, Maisie picked up a bloodied knife and wiped it semi-clean using the sheets on one of the dwarf's beds. Then Perrie grabbed them each a pickaxe propped against the wall near the dwarves. *This is definitely better than forks or knives.*

Once outside, they trudged through the trees beneath the overcast gray sky. Animals darted in and out of the woods, seeming to dance happily around them. With Maisie being Snow White and all, she must be attracting these creatures. *Weird.*

"It's like we're at a zoo with all the different animals we're seeing, minus the whole locked-up-in-cages thing," Maisie said in astonishment.

"A zoo without cages," Perrie agreed.

Maisie had been against zoos since she was small. She would never go near the cages, preferring to sit around and watch the nature wildlife shows, where those animals had some freedom.

When they were nine, Aunt Krista had taken them to the zoo, but Maisie wasn't having it. When they approached the bald eagle, it was in a smaller area than an armadillo had—her little nine-year-old self almost blew a fuse. After that particular visit, she started a petition and went around the neighborhood asking people to sign it. Perrie went along with her to show her support.

Maisie was quite proud of herself after getting fifty

signatures.

Aunt Krista had then taken them to turn the list in at the zoo. Needless to say, the bald eagle still remained inside of the same small cage, and all they'd received from the zoo was a sucker and a sticker.

Maisie hadn't been back since. She must've had an impact on Perrie, though, because she couldn't look at the zoo the same way anymore.

A rustling stirred from up ahead, interrupting Perrie's thoughts … and animal gazing.

"What is that?" Maisie turned in the direction of the noise. Perrie strained to listen and another sound, like someone struggling, making desperate grunts, came.

"Whatever it is, it doesn't sound good."

Maisie and Perrie exchanged a glance, pulling their pickaxes up over their shoulders and hurried in the direction of the sound. The grunting continued, growing louder as they ventured nearer.

A large pink flowering bush blocked whatever was behind it, so Perrie used her weapon to maneuver the branches back.

The source of the grunting was a face Perrie was *very* familiar with. "August!"

His eyes flickered with relief, despite the gag in his mouth. She raced to him and removed the black cloth, pulling it down to rest around his neck.

August breathed in the fresh air, his chest heaving as leaned back against the tree where his hands were bound. "Hurry and untie me. We have to get out of here before the guy comes back."

"A guy with long hair blowing around?" Maisie asked.

"Maisie?" August blinked repeatedly, finally acknowledging that she was standing next to Perrie.

"I know you're always too busy ogling Perrie, but come on, August, you had to have noticed the eye patch." She laughed and pointed at her eye.

"Good to see a friendly face," he said, biting his lip while looking about. "Now untie me before he comes back, please. And to answer your previous question, yes, he has long hair."

Perrie took Maisie's knife from its hiding place and cut the rope binding August's hands. He winced when he was freed and rubbed at his wrists.

"What happened to you?" Perrie tucked the knife into the sash of her dress.

"Not much. I landed somewhere over there." He pointed to the left of where they'd come from. "Next thing I know, I'm hit with something hard from behind and tied to a tree."

"Did you get a good look at the guy?" Maisie asked.

"Sort of? Big guy, too. Arms the size of bowling balls." He flexed his arms, which weren't near the size she was imagining of his attacker. Although, his arms were quite nice to look at, and strong when they'd held her. "He kept asking me about Snow. At first, I thought he was curious about, you know, the white stuff that falls from the sky. But then he kept asking me where the girl is."

Maisie's eye widened. The guy must've been the one Maisie had mentioned earlier. Only two men come to mind who would be searching for Snow White—either the Huntsman or the Prince. She was about ninety-nine percent sure there wasn't any fucking Prince Charming out here.

"Don't worry, guys, I'm totally prepared." Maisie lifted her pickaxe in the air.

Perrie helped August stand, his forehead slicked with sweat. He arched his back and shook his legs and arms out, seeming to try to rid himself of any stiffness. She would be too after sitting in that position for so long. Another person off her checklist—leaving only Neven.

"August, in case you didn't already know, meet Snow White." She waved her hand toward Maisie. Her cousin stepped forward and bowed slightly.

"I'm not surprised," August stated flatly then grinned at

Perrie. "I'd say it's a step up from working at a brothel, though."

Maisie's eye crinkled as she gave her a mischievous look.

Perrie sighed. "Seriously, don't even ask."

Twigs and branches snapped, one after another, interrupting what Maisie was going to say. The sound continued, as if an animal was running through the woods. It wasn't an animal, though. The pounding of feet against the earth matched the beating of her heart.

Maisie grabbed the pickaxe Perrie had left on the ground and handed it over to August. He shifted his weight and prepared his weapon for the strike. Perrie didn't want to stay here one second longer. They could look for the barrier later.

"Let's go," Perrie said sharply.

August and Maisie didn't argue. They made it a few feet, when something powerful yanked Perrie to the side, and she screamed as she dropped her blade, her only weapon for defense. She didn't understand. The noise she'd heard—she thought it was far enough away, coming from the other direction.

"Where is she?" A booming voice with hot breath pressed against her ear.

"Fuck," August ground out, turning around with Maisie right behind him. Perrie mouthed for them to run—neither one of them listened.

A strong hand pulled her face to meet his, and she couldn't see August or Maisie anymore.

His eyes were liquid gold, molten and rich in color, and his face square but strong. Most people would find him ruggedly handsome. Apparently, she was right when she'd guessed a male model from Maisie's earlier description.

"Do I have to ask again? Where. Is. The. Girl?"

"I'm a girl," Perrie answered stupidly, but it was a way to distract him from Maisie. She wouldn't let him have her.

"Don't play games with me. I saw you with Snow just

moments ago," he rasped.

"Let her go!" August shouted.

The man tore his eyes away from her and spotted August. "Either you're a wizard and freed yourself, you little rat, or perhaps this little tart here helped you escape." He squeezed her tighter.

"Sorry, not a fan of bondage," August said as he raised his pickaxe. "At least not with you. Now, let her go."

Her jaw ached with the pressure of the man's hand on her face. She scratched at his arms and kicked her feet, but it didn't affect him. He just gave her a shake hard enough to jar her neck. She looked around and realized that August was alone. *Where is Maisie?*

"When I have Snow White's heart in my hand, then you can have the little mousey," he growled. *Okay, definitely the Huntsman.* "Now, where is she?"

"August, go!" Perrie would rather die right here and now than let him lay one single finger on Maisie or her loving heart.

The Huntsman clamped down on her jaw, holding it in place. "Snow, come out now—I know you're here. I might have to make it so the little mousey will not be able to make a single squeak ever again."

His voice was soft, but dangerous. The threat beneath was subversive, but effective. As he spoke, his fingers slowly stroked her cheek. She wanted to bite them off.

"Here I am." Maisie appeared, leaving the safety of her hiding spot, and struck a warrior pose, complete with the pickaxe. She should've taken the damn opportunity to run away.

"Maisie! Run," Perrie tried to yell, but the Huntsman's hand tightened on her face, so much so that she feared her skull might burst into a bloody pulp.

"Ah. There you are, my little doe. I have been searching everywhere for you. You have made things quite difficult for me, and I don't like things to be troublesome," he drawled.

"I'm here now, so let her go," Maisie insisted. "Once she's safe, I'll come with you."

Oh, hell no, she won't. If he released Perrie, she could grab the knife she'd dropped on the ground and bring it up to stab him.

"How sweet. My little doe thinks she has a choice," he purred in Perrie's ear.

Maisie hadn't lowered her pickaxe. She looked prepared for anything, anything except his lightning quick reflexes. In less than a few seconds, he tossed Perrie to the ground and slid an axe from behind his back faster than she'd landed. He thrust it with one muscular arm and it swung round and round toward its target. The sharp end sliced clean through Maisie's neck perfectly, before slamming into the trunk of a tree at the same time her head tumbled from her shoulders.

Time stopped.

"No!" Perrie howled, her heart disintegrating. Her scream was louder than a thousand screams put together and longer than a thousand echoes. She crawled to Maisie's crumpled body, her hands shaking as she touched her cousin's pale face. There was blood *everywhere*.

While the crimson liquid poured out of her cousin, all Perrie could think was, *Let me put her back together. She'll be fine.* As Perrie lurched forward to try and reattach Maisie's head, two strong hands pulled her from her delusional thoughts. She flailed frantically in his arms, violently tossing herself around to break free. Her fists pounded against muscle that wouldn't give way. She was going to murder the fucker.

"Perrie, it's only me," August said gently, and she halted. "We have to go."

The ringing stopped and the world swung back into full motion.

"But, Maisie . . ." she croaked miserably.

The Huntsman, decked out in the furs of his prey, retrieved the embedded axe from the tree. His back remained turned to them and her knife in the grass gleamed. She could grab it and attack him from behind.

Perrie tried to loosen herself from August's grip, but his hold was like iron. Despite that, she broke away, reached for the blade shining in the grass, and snatched it.

"We have to get out of here now," August said hurriedly.

The Huntsman watched Perrie, smirking as if he was the devil himself. He already knew what she wanted to do to him, how badly she wanted to drive the knife into his heart. His eyes dared her to do it.

"Go on then, little mousey," he shouted, motioning to the cottage. "Before I change my mind and kill you both."

Neither one of them had the skills to throw a pickaxe the way he did, so, for now, they ran.

"I will see you again," the Huntsman called.

She didn't look back.

The run was a blur, the world spinning. Perrie kept seeing Maisie, whole one minute, then head severed the next. As if her brain wouldn't let her forget, she couldn't stop the replay constantly rolling in her mind. She'd always thought the mind would block out traumatic events like that, but she guessed not.

August stopped once to ask her for directions to the cottage, but she couldn't hear her voice as she answered him. She didn't want to go back there, but it was the only place that had water, shelter, and better weapons.

"I need a break." Perrie turned to lean against a tree, even though they weren't far from the cottage.

August slowed and walked back over to her, his face solemn. He pulled her away from the tree and tugged her to him, wrapping his arms around her. She was like a rag doll slumped in his embrace, unable to bring herself to hug him back.

"I'm not going to sit here and tell you everything is going to be okay, but we have to keep going." He stroked her hair.

"Even if we have to go back and stop others from coming into this place, we have to try."

Her heart ached. Maisie was more than her cousin—she was like her sister.

"She's gone." Perrie's voice was barely above a whisper.

Hot tears slid down her cheeks and the loss consumed every fiber of her being. Maisie was a major chess piece in helping Perrie become who she was. She was there for her through everything. The day they moved into the house beside her cousin, Maisie was there with a tray of rainbow cookies and a smile brighter than sunshine. She shared her mom with Perrie when she needed one—she was her best friend.

How could she be gone?

"Look at me, Perrie." August cradled her face, and she lifted her head, their eyes locking. "I cared a great deal about Maisie, too. I know for a fact she would want you to keep going, not just for her, but also for yourself and for your families. Do it for her, do it for me."

More tears poured down her face, and she found the strength to hold him. He rubbed slow circles against her lower back to try and soothe her. After a few silent moments, she was steadier on her feet. She wanted to leave this nightmare and be done with it for good.

"I'm ready." Perrie sniffled with a hollow spot in her chest that would always be there. But she had to push forward.

"I'm right here, doll face." He took her hand, interlacing their fingers and gently squeezed.

They spotted a well a few paces from the cottage, neatly tucked behind some flowers and bushes. August turned the crank—a loud, screeching sound poured out as the rope wound up.

A tiny bluebird darted right above her head—she ducked as it chirped and flew to sit on a windowsill a few feet away. The bucket finally reached the top and August handed it to her. They didn't have the luxury of cups around them, so she drank straight from the bucket. She hadn't realized how thirsty she was until half the water in it was gone.

Perrie passed it to August, and he finished the rest, wiping his mouth with the sleeve of his shirt. Three other bluebirds flew and chirped past them, joining the first one by the window. Their chirping struck her as oddly melodic, harmonious even. *Strange.*

A commotion came from inside the cottage.

It sounded like someone was singing.

TWENTY-THREE

A voice… A singing voice… How could there be a voice coming from inside the cottage?

"You heard that, too, I'm guessing?" August asked.

"Yeah, but I thought for a second I might be imagining it." Perrie focused on the window. The singing grew louder as someone belted out a long high note, lovely and sweet. A melody that could lure anyone in, just like a siren's deadly song.

"No. You definitely weren't hearing things."

Perrie didn't understand. Maisie was murdered right in front of them. There was no way she could just come back to life like the living dead.

No. Not like the living dead—something else. "We have to go in there and look."

"All right," August agreed, "let's go."

Perrie gripped the hilt of the knife to keep from shaking.

When they reached the front door, August didn't hesitate and went right in. Slowly, she followed behind him with her knife raised. The familiar stench of what she now knew to be bloodied animal carcasses and dead little men invaded her nostrils once more.

Perrie trailed August around the corner of the foyer and he paused. She peered over his shoulder, taking a sharp breath. In the wooden rocking chair, moving back and forth, sat Maisie. The same deer fur rested in her lap as she stitched it. It seemed impossible, but it wasn't.

"Maisie?" Perrie whispered, rushing to her. The rocking chair halted. "Maisie, what's going on? How did you get back here?"

She glanced up at Perrie with a big smile on her face. "Maisie? Who is Maisie? My name is Snow."

Perrie's heart withered. Maisie was herself only minutes ago.

"Oh, no. Not this shit again," Perrie hissed, bringing her hand to her forehead, both in relief and frustration.

August knelt beside her cousin, resting his hands on the chair. "Maisie, what's going on?"

"Why are you calling me Maisie? My name is Snow, silly." She giggled.

August stood and took a step back. "We just saw you, Maisie. You were *dead*," he said, brows lowered in confusion.

Maisie lifted her head, acknowledging the both of them with that same too-wide smile. Just when Perrie thought her cousin was going to speak, she instead burst into a spell of giggles. It went on for an uncomfortable amount of time. Then, as if the joke was no longer funny, she went quiet.

"You die here, you stay here," Maisie sang.

"What was that?" Perrie barely heard her.

"You die here, you stay here," she sang louder.

August turned back to Perrie and frowned. "This is the same as it was with Ben, isn't it?"

"I think so." Perrie nodded. "I was thinking earlier about why they can't remember who they are, but we can. It's because they died here, and we haven't. It's like they become a part of the story, doomed to repeat it so long as they're stuck here."

August rubbed at his chin. "So, if we die, then the same thing will happen to us."

"Mystery solved. Now what do we do?" Maisie still wasn't herself and the Huntsman was out there somewhere, waiting for them … or Maisie again.

"First things first," August started. "What's wrong with Maisie? How do we fix this?"

"It will take some *convincing*."

"What did you do last time?" He smirked.

"I yelled at her." She left out the part about nearly smacking her senseless, though. "But I don't know if it will work a second time."

"Won't know until we try, right?" August suggested.

Sighing, Perrie attempted to muster the same amount of frustration as last time and yanked her cousin out of her seat. Gripping her shoulders, she shook her as hard as she could. If they were lucky, maybe the jarring sensation would be enough to wake her up.

"Maisie, snap out of it!" Perrie yelled.

Maisie's lashes fluttered and her lips parted in surprise, but there was no trace of her cousin in her dreamy gaze.

Perrie whistled their birdy signal to no avail. "Help me," she pleaded to August.

He scratched the side of his head, seeming to not know what else to do either. There had to be a better way to get through to her.

"Look at me." Perrie locked her eyes with Maisie's. "I'm not going to waste my time here telling you stories about how we know each other. We tried that already and it didn't help."

Maisie excitedly clasped her hands together. "Oh, I love stories! Will you tell me one?"

"I just said I'm not going to tell you a story. Now listen, try to remember, we were in the forest and we were attacked by the Huntsman from the story of Snow White."

"What story? I am Snow White, you silly little thing." She

broke out of Perrie's grasp and took a seat back in her rocking chair. Perrie was about to unleash a loaded sentence of fury when August beat her to it.

"Maisie, knock this fucking shit off and come out of there already. Perrie had to listen to this bullshit once today. She doesn't need to deal with it anymore." His voice sounded deeper than ever from his anger. "I was tied to a tree for who knows how long, and I'm tired as hell of this place. If it isn't a prostitute killing other prostitutes, it's the Headless Horseman or a Huntsman chopping off heads! I don't want to hear the ramblings of a crazy person for another second. Wake the hell up!"

"Don't forget the trolls," Perrie added.

"That shit, too." He sighed heavily.

"Wow." Maisie gazed up at August in wonder, blinking several times and rubbing her temples. "Give me a second here. I've never seen you so angry before. I'm willing to bet Perrie enjoyed seeing this new side of you."

Perrie laughed, even though tears pricked her eyes again, but this time because of relief. It was true. That was one of the few times she'd ever seen August mad, not that she was complaining. Perrie never thought she would find anger so down right sexy.

"Maisie, you're the only person I know who could make this day interesting. Thank God you're back." Perrie launched her arms around her, not wanting to let her go, especially after watching her cousin die in front of her. "What do you remember?"

"Everything, mostly. I know the Huntsman was chasing us, and I think something bad happened." She stroked her neck with both hands. "He got me, didn't he?"

August and Perrie stayed silent. Maisie already knew the answer.

"Anyway, I remember everything with the exception of how I end up back here every time."

Every time? Does that mean this has happened more than once? At this point, she couldn't keep herself from grabbing her own throat. She couldn't begin to imagine how it would feel to lose one's own head like that more than once. *When the Queen of Hearts says off with your head, that's normally it— but that's a different story, I guess.*

"How many times?" August asked.

"I think this makes seven." She rubbed her eye. "Sometimes it takes me longer to pull myself together. I don't understand how Crazy Maisie takes over."

"Crazy Maisie won't take over again—we won't let it come to that." Perrie wanted to be as reassuring as she could, but based on what they knew, Maisie might be trapped here like the rest.

"Perrie, I'm not afraid. I've been putting the pieces together, even the missing ones." Maisie's conviction unsettled her. "This time it was an axe, before that it was a knife to my heart, then a knife at my throat, once it was my own pickaxe, and the list goes on. After I die, I come right back to this house and it starts all over again."

Maisie was too calm, too collected for someone who had died and come back to life multiple times. It didn't surprise Perrie, though. Her cousin adjusted her eye patch, and Perrie cringed a little inside about her missing eye.

August gripped the back of his neck. "Have you tried to leave?"

"A couple times, yeah. It was around my fourth 'death day' when I found the barrier. I had the pickaxe with me and managed to duck low and hit the Huntsman in the thigh. I didn't get much farther than that, though. I slammed right into the barrier and bounced back. Again, I tried, but it knocked me off my feet. Then the Huntsman was there with my pickaxe and the rest is pretty obvious." Maisie was not as phased by the repetition of death in this world as Perrie was. But not a hint of sadness lingered in her cousin's eye.

Maisie turned to August. "He didn't murder you, did he?"

"From what I remember . . . just the whole tied-up-to-the-tree situation. That about sums it up on my end."

She breathed a sigh of relief.

"That's good. Perrie told me earlier you guys have been able to pass through each barrier safely." Perrie already didn't like where she was going with this.

"Safely is an understatement." August's words made her think of her personal incident with Thomas.

"If I'm right, if I can't slip through, then all I can do is help you two get past the Huntsman. Hopefully, he doesn't take the only eye I have left this time," she said with finality.

"Are you insane?" August shouted.

"What are you thinking?" Perrie cried.

"I know I'm not going to get through. If you two can manage to get home, you might be able to figure out what's going on here. Not to be all gloom and doom, but if dying here is real, then I'm already gone." Maisie shrugged, as if it was really not that complicated or hard to understand.

Perrie's heart sank and sank. "What if you're wrong and you're not really dead?" She grabbed her cousin's forearm and squeezed it. "You don't *feel* like a ghost, and you're warm. You'll be here by yourself with that maniac on the loose. I can't watch you die again, Maisie."

Maisie seemed to fight to hide the grin on her face. "Have you ever even seen or felt a ghost, Perrie?"

"It's not the time, Maisie!" Perrie snapped.

"I'm willing to sacrifice myself to get you two out of here. Take it or take it. There's no leaving it."

"But—"

She shook her head. "But nothing. You're going to have to warn people, especially Mom, Dad, and Uncle James."

"That's going to go over really well. They'll probably lock me up in a mental institution." Perrie's shoulders slumped.

Maisie waved a dismissive hand at her and refocused her

efforts on August. "You know I'm right."

He didn't even *try* to argue.

"I need you to get yourself and Perrie out of here. Try and find Neven, maybe he's safe like you two. I'll go as far as I can to help you distract the Huntsman. When we get to the barrier, you'll both go through it without me. Once you make it out of here, and if I'm not really a ghost, then you can find out how to save me."

Perrie folded her arms. "I refuse to agree to this plan. I'll stay right here. I want to try and find Neven, but I won't leave you here."

August reached for her, his expression sympathetic, and she knew what he was going to say. She didn't want to hear it.

"I don't want to do this either, but Maisie is right. If we can get out of here, maybe we can find a way to release everyone from these prisons. We can't save anyone by staying inside the displays." He uncrossed her arms and took both of her hands. Tears stung the corners of her eyes.

"We're all they've got," he murmured. She didn't want to argue anymore—it would be pointless. Maisie would never give in.

Perrie was beginning to see the bigger picture, but she wasn't a superhero or anything otherworldly and neither was August. They were two regular people fighting for their survival against something supernatural. Yet, if there was a slight chance they could get out of here and find a way to rescue Maisie and everyone else, she was going to take that chance.

Perrie grabbed August's hand and Maisie's in the other.

"Okay then, let's do this."

TWENTY-FOUR

Perrie inhaled the outdoor air, the crispness and freshness slowly erasing the stench of decay.

Sliding out her knife, Perrie handed it to Maisie, who needed more protection since the Huntsman was after Snow White. Each of them had also collected a pickaxe before leaving the house of death.

To her credit, Maisie didn't look the least bit nervous. Her determination to get out of this place was aligned with Perrie's. But Perrie just hoped that when the time came Maisie would try to pass through the barrier, too.

Overhead, birds chirped loudly, flitting carelessly from one perch to another. Perrie and the others kept their steps quiet, careful as they trekked through the forest. The Huntsman could be lurking anywhere.

God, this fucking thing is heavy! Perrie switched the pickaxe to a different shoulder, taking turns to rub her sweaty palms against her dress.

August glanced back at her, giving her a steady, wide smile. Perrie wanted to bottle up that smile, tuck it into the deepest depths of her heart as she grinned in return.

Maisie didn't miss the exchange and leaned over to

whisper in her ear. "I know this isn't the time or the place, but he's a good guy, Perrie. He's good for you."

"I know," Perrie said. She'd known this for a while now. And she remembered his perfect mouth on hers, his strong hands on her body. Perrie wanted to tell her cousin more of what had happened between them, but there might never be a time to do so.

Maisie opened her mouth to say something when heavy footsteps snapping twigs interrupted. Her cousin quickened her pace ahead of them, readying her knife.

"He doesn't even try to conceal himself." Maisie chewed on her thumbnail and shrugged.

"Get ready to run," August said.

Perrie was getting tired of running—that was all they seemed to be doing these days. If they made it home, she would avoid it for probably ever.

A flash of movement came to their right, so they broke left and ran for it. Perrie had once heard somewhere to avoid being shot, that one should move in a zigzag pattern so the person couldn't get a proper aim on the target. But would that work when the attacker was using an axe? As something heavy struck her shoulder from behind, she wouldn't have time to find out. A sharp pain shot up her entire arm, feeling like she'd been hit with a baseball bat. Perrie stumbled, losing her balance and dropping the pickaxe. As she fell forward, she caught August, bringing him down with her and landing on the ground in a heap of tangled limbs.

Where the handle of the axe struck, her shoulder was on fire, pain radiating. Body trembling in panic, Perrie could barely hold back a scream as she pulled herself to her knees.

"Jesus." Perrie fumbled to August's side and helped him to stand. Blood oozed from his nose, but other than that, he was still intact, his pickaxe beside him and, at least, not *through* him.

"You are a lucky little mousey. The end of my axe only

grazed you," a loud voice boomed, closer than she wanted, like lightning crashing through the sky.

The Huntsman emerged in all his bravado from the thick brush. "I could have taken you down easily, making you bleed if you were who I was after. Now, *where is she?*"

Perrie searched around the forest and through the trees for Maisie. But she had no clue where she'd disappeared. Her cousin was apparently sneakier than the Huntsman.

"I have no idea." Perrie only had her fists and legs at the moment. Her weapon was on the ground, and he was already twirling another axe in his hand like a baton.

"Snow? Come out, little doe. I don't want to harm your pets, but I will if I must." To prove his point, he closed in and Perrie and August stepped back. Perrie was prepared to bolt as she examined the location of her and August's pickaxes on the ground. They couldn't reach them in time.

The Huntsman raised his axe, ready to swing, when Maisie leapt from a tree and crashed onto him. He released a loud grunt, the force of her attack knocking him to the ground with her landing on top of him. Maisie's fierce expression remained on her face and she didn't hesitate. Lifting her knife high above the Huntsman, she brought it down, slamming it directly into his heart with a sickening squelch. She ripped it out, his body jerking, and she pierced him again. Again and again. Maisie continued stabbing him until his body remained still, no longer moving. Dead.

Perrie watched with wide eyes, not knowing Maisie had it in her, but after being murdered seven times, one could only take so much.

"Run!" Maisie screamed, still holding the bloodied knife, the entire front of her dress splattered in scarlet.

Together, they took off running through the forest, carelessly snapping every twig, branch, and leaf within an inch of their path.

They just *ran*.

Perrie hit the barrier first and bounced back to the ground. August stopped before he smashed into it. He reached out his hands, feeling for the barrier, but no breeze of wind stirred.

Maisie joined them within seconds and pushed on it. "This is what happened when I made it here last time."

Rustling echoed through the bushes. It couldn't be.... The Huntsman, who seconds ago was lying in his own blood, now loomed before them. Completely untouched, as if his clothes and entire body went and had a magical bath.

"There's no way . . ." Perrie panted.

August ground his teeth. *"What the hell?"*

"Try it again, August," Maisie said in a soft voice, seeming not at all surprised.

"Enough of this," the Huntsman growled. "Are you going to come to me, little doe, or do I have to come for all three of you?"

"Try it again," she repeated, sterner this time.

August reached for the barrier, and it flexed, responding. A strong gust of wind pulled at him, whipping his curls around his face.

Its strength then tugged at Perrie. "Maisie, it's working. Hurry!"

Maisie stretched for the barrier, but her hand was pushed back by it. "Until we meet again," she said, meeting Perrie's gaze and giving a final salute.

Perrie thrashed against the pull of the barrier, fighting it, desperate to get Maisie back, but it was too forceful. August shouted Perrie's name and when she swiped for him, the wind yanked him through. She couldn't escape its powerful pull— it was too late. Maisie winked at her with her uncovered eye before, almost gleefully, darting away from the Huntsman.

Then Perrie was ripped away without Maisie.

Perrie landed on top of a bed, bouncing from the force and colliding with the floor. Darkness covered her face and she screamed. She thrashed her hands, pushing away layers of her own golden hair from her face until she could see. Using the edge of the bed, she pulled herself up.

"August?" Perrie shouted. "Are you here?" No reply.

A light shone from an open window on the far side of the stone-walled room. She hurried toward it and tripped, catching herself against the bedpost. A pile of hair had been the cause of her tripping.

Her gaze fell to the bed where gold hair lay, *her* gold hair. She followed its path across the floor, sprawled against the wall—it was *everywhere*. And all connected to her scalp.

Fuck.

Perrie toed a path in spaces where there wasn't hair to get to the oval window—the only actual source of light in the room. The space was large enough for a person to fit through. When she made it without tripping, she placed her hands against its light gray stone edges and peered out.

Her heart accelerated and a woozy feeling rushed through her. She wasn't in a house, but a stone tower wrapped in thick green vines covered in thorns and vibrant orange flowers, like the color of the setting sun. But while being so dangerously high above the ground, she couldn't focus on their beauty.

"I must be Rapunzel," she murmured. Perrie knew that story like the back of her hand.

For the moment, she was trapped in a tower with long, unruly hair, and of course, no escape. Not a single door was in sight. Perrie searched the floor for the possibility of a hidden exit, but only a cool stone floor and two ornate rugs were there.

As she focused on the bed, then to the table stocked with

fresh fruit and a pitcher full of water, it was as if the Glass Vault was preparing her for a long stay.

Snatching an apple, she rolled it around in her hand, examining the sensuous redness. Then she set it back down beside a banana and an orange.

"I'm going to lose my mind in here," Perrie said to herself.

Plopping down on the bed, she wrapped herself in a scratchy wool blanket and pulled her feet up. *Surprise, surprise—I have on a different dress.* Although, considering the rips and holes along the skirt, it wasn't much of a dress anymore. *How perfect. Here I am, all alone in a tower, warming myself up with an old blanket in rags fit for a rat.*

Everything hit her—*all* of it. Tears pricked at her eyes before raining down her cheeks, a storm all its own. Her checklist was back to zero—no Maisie, no August, and no Neven. Perrie lay back on the bed, helpless. She couldn't save Maisie, Officer Rodriguez, or Josselyn, and she couldn't save herself. Everyone trapped here would continue to suffer, and she felt responsible.

Perrie wondered if August had landed outside the tower, and if so, where? What about Maisie? Was she still out in the forest, running for her life, or was she back in the cottage fighting for her sanity? Were Josselyn, Officer Rodriguez, and Ben still battling their obstacles, or did these things only happen if someone else was in the display? Would she ever find Neven? There were so many displays at the museum—it would take forever to travel through all of them, and that was if she didn't die along the way. It was a never-ending nightmare they wouldn't wake up from—that *she* may not wake from.

"We're all they've got." August's words rang loudly in her ears. He was right.

Abandoning her pity party, a new determination filling her, Perrie returned to the window with her long hair in tow. The hair wasn't very heavy, but it was sturdy, strong. She leaned out and studied the bright greenery which hid the tower away. Rows and rows of trees swayed in the breeze under the shimmering sunshine. She'd always wanted to be surrounded by nature, but after this… *Hell no.*

"August!" Perrie shouted out the window. It might've been an ignorant move but there weren't many other options.

Nothing. Nothing except the flapping of blackbirds' wings around the trees.

Guess that means it's time for Plan B. There had to be another way out of there. With all this hair, she wondered if there was a way she could actually use it to climb down. She stared at the ceiling, around the walls, but there was no real place to put her hair. Maybe she could tie it to the bed, like in the movies when they'd used a sheet. Only, once she was on the ground, how would she cut her hair off?

There had to be another way… But her other options weren't looking too good at the moment.

Her stomach grumbled. Despite everything, she had to feed the little monster before trying to venture into the unknown forest in this display.

Perrie snatched an apple from the bowl of fruit, biting into the round suppleness. The sweet, juicy flavor almost made her moan. *Who knew an apple could taste this good?*

"Screw it," she finally said, deciding to drag the bed to the window.

Before she could execute her plan, a commotion sounded from outside. Perrie rushed to the window, nearly tripping over her hair again.

"Perrie! Perrie, are you up there?" At the sound of August's distressed voice, she could jump right out the window.

"August, I'm here! I'm in the tower," she shouted back.

From the shadows of the trees, August stumbled forward in a full-out sprint. Perrie grabbed for her hair and fished it down like a rope, just as Rapunzel had in her story. He bounded toward the side of the tower, faster than he broke through the tree line.

But, he wasn't alone.

TWENTY-FIVE

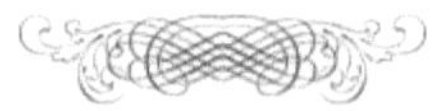

The blackbirds that were seated on the tops of the trees now formed a frenzy. As they dove at August from all angles, their sounds made a thunderous roar, reminding her of the classic movie *The Birds*. He did his best to fend them off, but they pecked and shrieked frantically.

Someone stood at the edge of the forest shrouded in darkness and hidden behind a black hooded cloak. With their lifted hand moving, it looked like he or she was controlling the birds' madness.

August wildly gazed about, seeming unsure of what to do with Perrie's hair dangling in front of him.

"Climb!" she yelled desperately.

As soon as his hands touched her hair, the birds darted back to the forest. The cloaked figure remained, watching them from where they stood. At least, she thought the person, or *creature*, was watching them. She couldn't make out a face from this high up.

"What do you mean, climb your hair? How will that possibly work?" He hesitated, giving her hair a few tugs. Perrie's head moved like a bobble head toy.

"Well, it's not going to fucking work with you pulling on

it like that. Just hurry and climb up before they come back."

Perrie braced herself against the wall, praying with everything in her that August wouldn't drag her out the window. She didn't intend to find out what it was like to smack onto the dirt below.

"Are you ready?" he asked.

"Yes. Please don't slip and fall!"

A light pressure pulled at her head, but it was nowhere near what she'd been expecting. If she tried this at home, she was sure most of her hair would've been ripped out. She couldn't even tell he was climbing it—she only knew it was working by the sound of his boots scraping against the stone structure.

"You know, I wasn't even thinking about that until you said it. So, thanks for putting that image in my mind," he grunted.

"You're welcome." Perrie didn't dare move her head to look down the tower. The only place she was able to stare was to the side, toward the forest, where the blackbirds again rested peacefully in the treetops. Their squawks had quieted, and the cloaked figure was gone.

Perrie's heart wouldn't stop its desperate beating. "How far up are you? I'm getting nervous."

"*You're* getting nervous? I'm about halfway."

An eternity seemed to pass before August's hand clasped the edge of the window, then his other one. The top of his head slid into view, and she grabbed his arms, helping him lift his body up onto the ledge.

He fell softly to the floor with a light, "Oof."

"Please, no more of this fucking insanity." He lay his whole body flat against the ground, and brought his hands to his chest, breathing deeply. He turned to face the window and shouted, "I'm serious!"

Perrie hauled her hair back up swiftly. All the while, her heart was still beating beat by frantic beat. After all her hair had been recovered, she collapsed beside August. She grabbed his arm and closed her eyes, practically meditating.

"What's wrong? Did I hurt you?" August studied her.

"No, no!" Perrie tried to catch her breath. "I didn't even feel anything. I'm just overwhelmed."

"What's with all the hair? I know Rapunzel supposedly had a lot of hair, but this is extreme." He lifted a lock of it in his hand, twisting it and pulling the strands apart. His surprise made her want to laugh.

Perrie stopped herself when she noticed specks of blood on his neck and cheek. She sat up and scanned his whole body, shocked by the number of holes in his shirt and pants.

"You're hurt!" Perrie wiped away a trickle of blood on his cheek. The cut on the side of his neck was bleeding, too.

"I'm okay, doll face. It barely stings. It looked worse out there than it really was." He pulled himself up slowly, moving her hand away from his neck and holding it in his lap.

"Really? You sounded pretty terrified." She examined other parts of his clothing—several holes were in his shirtsleeve where the birds had nicked his arm. There were other holes in the shirt from where they'd pecked, but thankfully hadn't drawn blood.

"I was mostly terrified because I didn't know where you were." His legs had a few shallow nicks, but his pants and tunic were made of a thicker material. It seemed to have protected him for the most part. The worst spots were his cheek and neck, but even then, he was lucky the birds didn't do more damage than they had.

Perrie walked to the table where the fruit was and poured a little of the water from the pitcher into the cup. Then she grabbed a pillow from the bed and removed the pillowcase, taking both to August. He was leaning his back against the wall of the tower, watching her.

"What are you doing?" he asked.

"What does it look like I'm doing? I'm not going to let you sit here with blood all over your face and neck."

Dabbing the water with the corner of the pillowcase, she raised it to his cheek and pressed it against his cuts. He sucked in a breath when she wiped away the drying blood. The cuts actually weren't that bad once the blood was removed.

The next spot Perrie drifted to was his neck, swiping away the small streak of blood streaming down to the collar of his tunic. She stared at the exposed skin a little longer than she should've, her stomach fluttering. August seemed to be watching her with the same burning intensity.

"So, what happened when you got here?" she asked, averting her eyes and instead busying herself with his arm. Rolling up his sleeve, she wiped an area on his arm that clearly didn't need cleaning.

"The portal spit me out into a tiny house somewhere in the middle of the forest. I waited around to see if you were going to show up. When you didn't, I went searching for you." He readjusted himself against the wall.

Perrie moved to his legs next, spying the hilt of a sword tucked beneath his thigh. "Looks like you got lucky. You've got a sword and all I've got is long hair for a weapon."

"Luckily I did have it," he said. "I just forgot to use the damn thing."

"What happened?" She set the cup of water and the pillowcase down beside her.

"I couldn't find you, so I went back to where I'd started. Next thing I knew I was surrounded by birds." He rubbed his neck and cheek absently. "They were everywhere. Seriously *everywhere*. Sitting in the tops of trees, sprawled across the branches, trickled over the ground, and resting on the rooftop of the house. As I walked through the forest, the birds didn't budge. You know how normally when you walk too close they'll fly off?"

Perrie nodded.

"Well, not these birds." Hiking his thumb up, he pointed it back toward the oval window.

"What about your cloaked stalker? Did you see who it was?" Perrie knew there was a witch in the story. She'd kidnapped Rapunzel and raised her like her own. But if it wasn't the witch, she wondered if the cloaked figure was another missing person.

"I couldn't see anything underneath the hood. It was . . . just darkness." August folded his hands beneath his chin and rested his elbows on his knees. His blond hair slid forward, delicately caressing his eyebrows.

She reached up and brushed it aside. "How did you find me?"

"We are in these rectangle boxes," he said, and she rolled her eyes. "I wandered around until I saw a tower poking up from the tops of the trees, practically calling for me to come. The second I saw it, I knew that's where you were." He paused. "Then there was a loud crackling behind me, and when I turned, the cloaked figure was there."

"That's it?" she pressed.

"Well, no. That isn't it. I stood there like an idiot, and she lifted her willowy hand with long pointed fingernails—it was definitely a woman's hand. Then she snapped her fingers a few times and the birds went from cool to fucking crazy. I mean, their heads all turned at the same time as if her snapping made them obey her."

Perrie smacked the ground with both of her hands. "And you didn't run away?"

"Fuck yes I did! She pretty much had me cornered. I didn't want to agitate the birds, so I didn't run away at first. Big mistake. She snapped again, and all those birds turned to look at me. Slowly too. Perrie, it was the craziest thing I've seen." He took a deep breath. "And then I took off running like there was no tomorrow. I heard one more snap and those blackbirds collapsed into sheer pandemonium. That's when I started calling for you."

"First, I think you should be a storyteller." Goosebumps

covered her arms. "Second, that creeped the shit out of me."

He whistled lowly. "You and me both, doll face. You and me both."

"Now what do we do?" she asked after a long silence.

"I think we should stay here for the night." August took her hands and warmed them in his lap. "Now, the real question is, what are we going to do with this hair?"

He left her hands and lifted a knotted mess of gold from the floor.

She couldn't help but laugh and agree. "I would've cut it off earlier, but there's absolutely nothing of use here, least of all scissors."

"Do you want me to?" August stroked the sword resting against his hip.

"Yes, please!" If Maisie were here, she would've been blowing into one of those little party horns.

August chuckled and raised his sword, shearing away the golden locks right at her shoulders. When he was finished, an uneven mess fell around her face, but it was so much lighter and freer.

"When we decide to leave," August started, "we'll just tie the hair to something and travel down."

TWENTY-SIX

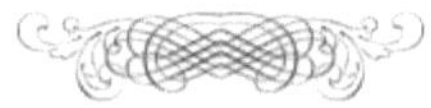

Perrie and August placed the hair in a neat pile in the corner of the room, making sure it stayed untangled so it would be easier to shimmy down. He'd agreed to her original plan, that the only thing stable enough to anchor their weight would be the bed. More than anything, she was relieved her head wouldn't have to be attached to the hair when they shuffled down it.

"Are you hungry? There's fruit in here. No poison apples, thankfully. I would know—*I tried one.*"

August arched a brow, a question dancing in his eyes.

Perrie shrugged. "Sorry, you can't be the only risk-taker to do the job first. Remember the berries?"

He grinned while lazily plucking up a banana. "Fine, I'll give you that."

They sat beside each other, comfortable in their silence as he finished his last bite. Perrie leaned into his shoulder, inhaling the scent of pine and soap. If they weren't in the middle of nowhere, inside a magical glass display, this would be romantic. Yet, it still felt it was…

"So, how are you doing? I mean, *really* doing." August's green irises settled on her. Perrie knew he was asking about

Maisie.

"I don't really know." But she did. The horrible twist of guilt took up space in her chest, an ache there that wouldn't go away until Maisie was safe.

"If anyone can be 'all right' here, it's her. She's tougher than nails." He wasn't wrong. If anyone were able to survive this place, Maisie could.

"What if Neven is like Maisie?" A brutal image sliding in her mind of an axe slicing off his head, the way the Huntsman's had done to Maisie. There would be no more crying. Now, it was about *surviving*.

"I thought about that, too. I for one want to assume he isn't. I mean, he could kick my ass in a fight any day."

"He is tall." She smiled. If she and August were still here alive, then Nev might have found a way to do the same thing.

August changed the subject, and she was grateful for the distraction. Between getting home and the possibility of rabid birds pecking away at her eyes and flesh, his rambling on about nonsense was a relief.

"What's the first thing you want to do when we get home?" Perrie asked.

August slipped off his boots and placed them under the side table. "Eat a whole cake."

"A cake?" She laughed. "After we save everyone from this place?"

He tugged a lock of her newly-cut hair. "Yep. If we're still alive after that, you and me"—he pointed between the two of them—"we're going to have a slumber party and sleep for days. Of course clothing is an option."

Grinning, she tugged one of his curls back. "Slumber party, huh?"

"That's what I said, doll face."

"Then we have to load up on cake first. A big cake, with a lot of frosting. Frosting is my jam." If only Perrie could dive into a swimming pool of cream cheese icing right then, she would be happy for a little while.

"I wish you wouldn't have said that." He chuckled. "I'm going to have frosting on my mind until I can get my hands on some."

"Okay, only about this much frosting then." Perrie held out her hands in front of her about a ruler length apart.

"No, no, that won't do." He grabbed both her wrists and spread her arms all the way open. She couldn't hold her position and toppled backward, bringing August along with her.

All of him pressed against her. Their faces were practically touching, and they stayed perfectly still. Perrie's eyes fell to his mouth, just as his did to hers.

"Maybe you should get some sleep," she suggested with no backing behind her words.

"What if I don't want to sleep?" He propped himself up on his forearms, caging her in.

With August, things had always been easy, even when she was a mess. Besides Maisie, he'd been her best friend, even when she didn't think she had room for anyone else. After what had happened with Neven, she refused to see August as anything but a friend. Following their right out at the prom, though, she started having glimpses of endless possibilities.

Perrie was so incredibly weak with this. If something were to happen and destroy her friendship with him, the way it had with Neven, she didn't know what she would do. She hadn't worn her heart on her sleeve in a long time. She'd wanted to focus on the future, on where her life led, and then maybe she could have the extras.

Her mom was someone who always depended on men—she never worked one single day of her life. Her dad worked hard to support her mom, and in the end, he and Perrie weren't enough for her—they never were, and they never could be.

Love wasn't money or material things. She wasn't sure if her mom ever truly loved either one of them. *I mean, how could she*? If she left Perrie's dad for another man with more money, and he made her dreams come true, couldn't Perrie still be part of that dream? Instead, she left both of them behind and never looked back.

Perrie couldn't do that. There was no way she would end up like her, a parasite that fed off the people who loved her most. She would go to college and find a good job where she could support herself. Then she wondered, *Is there room for someone else*? Could she be in a relationship with someone and still be better than her mom?

"What if I don't either?" she finally said, her voice husky.

"Yeah?" August pressed his forehead against hers.

"Yeah," Perrie whispered back, answering more than just his question. She knew she could be better than her mom.

He was here, wasn't he? He'd even engraved it on a necklace, the same one that the Glass Vault had stolen away. But she didn't need the possession to know how he felt, how *she* felt. August already had a hold on her heart in its entirety, and right now, she didn't think she could ever take it back from him.

"So, you remember the night we kissed, when you pulled me into your lap?" she asked, any nerves she had dissipating. A golden hue shone in his green eyes from where the sunlight struck them through the window.

"How could I forget?"

His mouth was mere centimeters from hers when she said, "I want to continue where we left off."

"What's stopping you, then?" August was close, but she wanted him closer.

"Nothing." Perrie broke out from his "cage" and flipped him to his back. It felt like a true moment of strength when she positioned her legs around his waist and straddled him, like she had the other night.

In this light, August was ethereal. Perrie remembered where they were, and if they were in any other display at the moment, it would be the Rumpelstiltskin one. August's blond hair was like pure gold, and it reminded her of the straw the maiden in that particular story had spun to gold. This wasn't the time or place to be thinking something strange like that, although it kind of was.

As August leaned forward to sit up and draw her closer, Perrie pushed the story away and ran her hands up the back of his neck and into his hair—the curled tips brushing against her fingers, soft as feathers. His breathing quickened at her touch and her confidence grew bolder. She pressed her lips gently against his, tracing his bottom lip with her tongue, tasting the saltiness of his skin. It was cruel to tease them both like this, but she wanted to savor the moment.

August gripped her thighs, deepening the kiss. A volcano erupted inside Perrie's chest and hot lava flowed and spread until her entire body was cocooned in the warmth. Everything felt right, and it was as if the world suddenly made sense. August made sense.

She pushed lightly against his chest, their kiss growing fiercer with the need to be closer. Her heart pounded, the rush of blood racing against her body's adrenaline.

Perrie didn't know if they were going to make it out of Quinsey Wolfe's Glass Vault, and even if they did make it out alive, then what? They would move on to another display, and then another, and another after that?

If something happened to one of them, if they lost each other along the way, then she didn't want to have any regrets. She wasn't going to waste time today, tomorrow, or any other day she had with him.

"August, I love you," Perrie murmured the words against his mouth.

His lips curved into a smile against her kiss, and that was all the answer she needed.

She fumbled with the strings at his chest, loosening the tunic, then hauled it over his head and dropped it onto the floor. He went to help her take off her dress next, but it stuck a few times as he tried. They both laughed and tempted fate once again, letting the fabric pool to the floor.

He then flipped her over, and she unbuttoned his pants, sliding them off and throwing those on the floor, too.

Perrie reached down and grasped his hardened length, loving the feel of it in her hand, and how it would fit perfectly inside her. While she stroked, his chin dropped to his chest, a deep groan escaping his perfect mouth.

When she released him, his weight pressed back down on her as he trailed kisses from her shoulder, up the length of her neck and along her jaw. Then his mouth molded to hers, and he ran his tongue across the seam of her lips before parting them. They kissed again and again, their tongues growing more and more demanding, until there were no other thoughts.

"Are you sure about this? We can slow down," he rasped.

"I'm sure. Are *you*?" She laughed.

"Perrie, I've been sure about you since the day you pressed your cello bow to my chest."

"Really?" She laughed again. "That didn't run you a hundred miles in the opposite direction?"

"No. It left me *intrigued*."

Perrie hadn't felt that way since then, though. He had waited for her to meet him halfway for a while now, and she was finally there.

Their remaining clothing was tossed to the floor, and his skin was against hers, deliciously warm, hard and soft all at once. August's lips tasted like nectar, and she never wanted to stop kissing them, but then he was leaving a path of sparks from her neck to her breasts. Perrie's knees melted as he took a hardened nipple in between his lips, sucking, and turning her bones to rubber. And she couldn't breathe as his hands took over, leaving those heavenly lips free to travel lower, lower, until they were between her thighs, licking, caressing. She moaned, throwing her head back, helpless. Useless. In bliss.

He slid back up to her, kissing her lips once more, his tongue dancing with hers as his hips rocked harder between her thighs.

He pulled back and hovered above her for a moment, taking it all in, their closeness and her. Finally, August pressed inside her with one swift stroke, filling her with everything he had, and it all made sense, even in this nonsensical world because together they could do anything. It was possible perfection did exist.

Performing a gentle rhythm at first, he moved inside her. Perrie dragged his face back to hers, gripping his hair and kissing him, then kissing him fiercer. He seemed to know exactly what to do as he took charge. With each thrust, each touch, she wanted to devour the moment. This was more than she could've ever imagined as emotions roared through her, and her entire body quaked when he tore her world apart.

"Perrie," he shouted, her name echoing off the walls, his slick body collapsing on hers. She wrapped her arms around him, holding him tight, her chest heaving. No words. No words at all.

They were legs and arms braided together for several long moments before he rolled off her. Perrie curled into his side, and shut her eyes, easily falling asleep in his embrace.

She dreamed a dream with no twists, turns, or running for her life.

It started with a normal morning at the breakfast table. Her dad had already left for work and the remnants of her cereal swam in warm milk.

Maisie came to the door in one of her newly-designed eye patches. A giant peach—with the words, *Everything is peachy* sewn across the fabric. Her cousin was excited about starting a new job at a resale-clothing store. She rambled on about her half-price discount and all the possibilities the clothing would supply for materials toward her designs.

Maisie drove them to school, as usual. It was such a

beautiful day. At school they spotted Neven and he waved, joining them and talking about how he'd gotten a basketball scholarship. She and Maisie both congratulated him, and her cousin gave him a high five. August strolled through the doors, his presence causing Perrie's stomach to swarm with butterflies. Neven patted him on the back like they were the best of friends.

August wrapped Perrie up in his arms, dipped her back just like in the old films, and kissed her long and slow. She should've been embarrassed about kissing him in front of everyone, but she wasn't. He brought her back up, and Maisie and Neven were smiling.

"You two need to get a room." Neven laughed. Maisie just stood there, shaking her head.

Perrie left their faces behind, as she slowly woke to the feeling of warmth pressed against her skin. She was definitely not dreaming anymore. *What a strange dream.* To think she and Neven could be friends like that again someday felt right.

Draping her arm across August's stomach, she rolled her head to the side and smiled at him.

"I was wondering if you would ever wake up." He grinned at her, the smile reaching all the way to his eyes.

She pecked his cheek and snuggled against his shoulder. "I was having such a good dream."

"Oh? Were you dreaming about me?"

Perrie arched a brow. "What do you think?"

"I hope so, because it will be the last good dream you'll have for a while."

She didn't have time to think about what he'd said. August swiftly flipped her onto her back and hovered above her, the look on his face devious. His head dropped to the side of hers, swaying lazily, as his mouth tickled her ear.

"Thanks for the fuck."

TWENTY-SEVEN

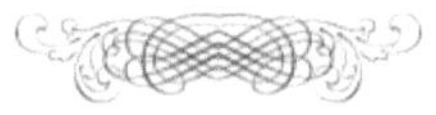

Perrie's body stilled. Everything within her did. *What the fuck did he just say?*

"August?" Her mouth hung partially open, and her breathing increased.

"I have to admit. Out of everyone I have ever pleasured, you are at the top." His face was mere inches from hers.

"What are you talking about?" she whispered. Her body had grown cold.

"I mean, there is one other female who comes close, but not quite. I cannot recall her true name," he said, tapping the side of his head, "but I do remember the red hair. About six months ago . . . at Neven's."

He knocked the wind right out of her. Perrie's mind was spinning, and so was the room. What was he talking about? She'd seen *Neven* having sex with that woman, clear as day.

"That's right. You thought it was Neven, didn't you?" The sides of his lips tugged down, and he moved a lock of hair from her forehead. "Oops."

"August, what's going on?" She jerked forward, but he already had her pinned by the shoulders.

"August," he said the name like it wasn't his own. "That is

the name I am going by at the moment."

Perrie's brows lowered and she couldn't release any words. August, or *not* August, cocked his head and stared at her with a form of humor she didn't understand. He observed her like she was a child, a stupid, foolish child who didn't know the simplest answer.

If that wasn't Neven and it really was August, then she was a fucking idiot. Whoever the hell he was, whatever he claimed to have done, she just had sex with him. Perrie tried to force herself up, but his hold was too strong.

"I will let you in on a little secret. My name isn't August. I am whomever I choose to be, whenever and wherever I want. You have known me as August. Others have known less. I am a name without a face, but you, Perrie, I'll tell you my real name." His voice was almost a laugh. "My real name is Vale."

August wasn't actually August? He preyed on her, screwed his way into her heart, tightening the bolt as hard as he could with a screwdriver. She wanted to scream, to kick and flail, and beat his face.

"Get off of me." She wanted to scream, but it came out as a whisper.

"Does it bother you? I have toyed with you, Perrie, for months and months." He lifted a hand toward the ceiling, as if he was proud of this precious tower. A wicked smile spread across his face. "All this time, only to get you inside the walls of my palace."

What? Nausea churned in her stomach and she thought she was going to be sick.

"That's right. This is all mine. Every display, every person you have encountered, they are all part of a very big plan." Vale stood, and though Perrie was free, she couldn't scrounge up the strength to move. "Inside this place they cannot wither away. They are immortal now. I brought them here, to live inside the displays, where they will become the perfect creatures for destruction."

"How?" Perrie asked, her voice weak.

"How? I *chose* who I wanted to see my vault. It is all part of a grand plan that I have concocted to take humanity, and *you*, my darling Perrie, are going to help me lead it."

Perrie took a deep swallow. She had to get away from this bastard.

Before she had a chance to run, he snatched her by the hair and yanked her off the bed. Her scalp burned and she cried out in agony. Each and every single one of the tiny hair follicles was on fire, thumping in sync with the beat of her heart. Perrie screeched as loudly as she could, and the sound of her own scream was even worse than the squeal of squeaky brakes.

"We need to hurry so we are not late to meet your friend," Vale sang as he dragged her across the floor. Then he stopped. "Before I forget. Do you remember the redhead from Neven's room? I recall you mentioning something about recognizing her hair anywhere. Did you?"

Perrie thought back. How had she not noticed it before? She had stood right in front of Perrie in a display.

"Fannie," she whispered.

"That's right. That's right. That is the name she uses now, yet that is not her true name. I never cared to ask. If I need her, I let her come out and play. A small reward for being trapped below with me, after all." Perrie struggled to break from his hold, but his grip only tightened. "Like I said, nowhere near as good as you, though."

Again, with a hard yank, Vale dragged her behind him, making the pain sharper than it was before. He hummed to himself, to her, to both of them, or maybe to no one.

What have I done? I trusted this monster.

Cement scratched at her bare back as she was pulled along. She didn't care about the throbbing of her back, though, she needed him to let go of her fucking hair. *Now.*

The tower became a distant memory as Vale somehow walked through the wall on the opposite end. They passed down a darkened, narrow hallway. She screamed the entire way, right up until he tossed her onto another cement floor like a sack of trash. The pain at her scalp lessened only a fraction, but she could breathe again. Before she could push herself up, something clicked into place—Vale had locked her in a cage.

"I will give you two a few minutes," he purred, before sauntering away.

Give you two a few minutes? Perrie's hands shook, half afraid to see what he was talking about, but she needed to know.

In the corner behind her, someone was sitting against the bars with his head hanging down, pushed as far from the cage door as possible. She knew that shaggy black hair.

"Neven?" *Shit.* Tears flowed from her eyes, and she ran over to him, lifting his face. An iron ring circled his neck, like a collar, with no visible way to remove it. A short chain connected it to a bar that held him back, so he couldn't even curl up on the floor if he wanted to instead.

"Perrie? Am I dreaming or are you really here?" He blinked, his words coming out in a slur.

"I'm here," Perrie sobbed.

"Where are your clothes?" he groaned.

Of course, that's the first thing he asked. She was so relieved about him being alive that she laughed while wrapping her arms around herself as best she could.

"Don't worry about it—not right now," Perrie insisted. "What happened to you?"

Nev looked the same, but not. Scarred lines ran along his arms, neck, and face, as if he'd been torn apart and stitched back together. She inhaled sharply as she *remembered* a particular exhibit.

He was Frankenstein's Monster, the one she'd seen in the museum.

"After I left your house, I wanted to go to the museum again since you had seen it, too. August was there when I pulled up. I thought he was there for the same reason as me." Nev rested his arms on his knees, leaning the back of his head on the metal bars. "We went inside, wandered through the halls and wound up in the display room. Everything was literally made of glass—strange shit. After that, it's kind of been a blur. Somehow I ended up in the Frankenstein's Monster display."

"You don't remember anything after that?" Perrie covered her mouth and shook her head, wanting to rip the chain off the cell to free him.

"Oh, I do. You know that August isn't *August*, right?" Nev said softly.

"Yeah, I know. Go on, I'll be fine."

"He strapped me down to a table, saying he was really Vale and some weird shit about needing immortal souls to become stronger. He went on like that for a while, cutting into me with all these fucked up tools as he *chatted*. I passed out during the process and wound up in this cell. Been chained here ever since."

Perrie hunched forward, tears raining down her cheeks. It was so stupid, but she'd just been so happy, and now, it was a true hellish nightmare. Neven was just like Maisie, like the others.

"This is insane," Perrie said. "He also told me his name is Vale, he said he tricked me, that he was the one with the redhead. He wore your face, Neven." She covered her own face, humiliated. "I don't know how that's even possible."

"I told you, I can make myself into anyone at any time, anywhere." Vale's voice reverberated around the room. She looked back at the door where Vale now hovered.

He wore black slacks and a white long-sleeve shirt that buttoned at the ends. The neck was a collarless V-neck with ruffles that Perrie wanted to rip off and use to strangle him.

With repeated motions, he ran a silver nail file across his fingernails as he examined her. "I have been hidden away for too long, and it is my time to rise and take over. We will bring destruction to everyone. I made this place and filled it one by one with my creations to help carry out my deeds. They may look like glass on the outside now, but after this, they won't anymore. You are to be my last."

"I don't understand," she shouted. "Why me? Why go through all of this? You could have tossed me into one of the displays like everyone else. Why make me—" She couldn't even say the damn words. *Why make me fall in love with you?*

"Why? *Why*? I would not have noticed you at first, Perrie. When you approached me as if you were a queen with that bow in your hand, I felt the light in you, that electrifying energy with a subtle potential for darkness. The minute you walked out of that room with Neven at your side, I knew I wanted you. It didn't matter how long it took for you to give yourself to me, because I could wait. Now that I have you, the time is right." Vale tucked the silver file away into his pocket.

"What the hell is this asshole talking about, Perrie?" Nev sounded drained but fury was there too. She was too ashamed to answer.

"That's right, Neven. As you were sitting here chained to the cell, I had her in ways you can't even begin to imagine."

Nev gripped the bars, pushing hard against them to free himself in his anger. The ring around his throat prevented him from going anywhere, and his face was flushed so red that he might pass out.

"Leave her alone," he roared.

Perrie couldn't even look at Neven's face anymore. Her self-loathing had already taken root—that must've been what Vale had wanted.

Vale unlocked the cage and moved at an inhuman speed, yanking her up by her hair once more.

"What are you?" Perrie seethed.

"To you? A demon, a monster, your worst nightmare. As I told you before, I can be anything."

Perrie could only see half of Vale's face and the gray ceiling above her. With her neck straining at this angle, she couldn't even spit at his face—that perfect skin she desperately wanted to claw off.

"Your soul is mine." Vale stroked her cheek. Then with his inhuman speed, he brushed something sharp against her throat and sliced across.

Pain. Searing pain.

It all happened so fast.

Her hands flew up to her throbbing neck, instantly covered in a warm, sticky liquid—her own blood. Neven's frantic yelling echoed.

She couldn't make the bleeding stop. She couldn't sew the wound shut. There was too much blood. Her body grew weaker with each passing second as a numbness settled. No part of her life flashed before her eyes like she'd heard it did when one dies. Only the desperate urge to live lingered.

Perrie's hands fell limply to her sides, and no other part of her could move. Not even to blink. She waited for all of it to go away, to let the darkness take her.

Vale must've been dragging her. If he was doing it by her hair again, she couldn't feel it. All she could see was the ceiling and part of Vale's black pants. She could hear every detailed sound, like the tapping of his shoes on the hard floor. It was as if the universe wanted her to sit inside of this body longer just to watch her suffer.

"You know, Maisie was right about one thing." Vale lifted her body and set it back down on something solid, then his face hovered over hers. "When you die here, you stay here. She is smart but not smart enough to piece it all together. You do die here and stay here, but only until I am ready to release you. You, my darling, are going to transcend your humanity. When I am done, all that hate in you will continue to grow and gather and lead to true carnage. You will be like the others, like Maisie and Neven. When I bring you back to life, the old

Perrie will be gone. You will be made new. And my Bride will rise."

He brushed his lips against hers. Perrie didn't feel a thing, or she would've bitten his lip clean off. Finally, Vale closed her eyes, and the escape into darkness she'd been waiting for took her.

Epilogue

Vale stared down at the Bride, admiring his new creation in all of her glory. She truly was the most exquisite creation he had altered.

Perrie had told Vale she loved him. He didn't know what love was. He still didn't, but she was his. All he had known was satisfaction and ruination.

His heart was darker than midnight, and he liked it that way. The wound at her throat was stitched, the skin healed over, a clean cut with a clean mend. Greater care had been taken to preserve his Bride, as she was the culmination of all his efforts. Like all the mortals inside the Glass Vault, she was no longer human—they were fiends, prepared to feed upon the earth. Their thoughts now matched his.

Vale reached for a lever and fed his Bride the electricity she needed, until the sparks crackled and ceased.

Her eyes burst open with a wickedness that had him giddy with glee.

One by one, sculptures once made of glass, all rose from their cold displays. They were like the living dead thawing out of hibernation, digging through the dirt to reach their destination.

Vale opened the door to Quinsey Wolfe's Glass Vault. The Bride was the first to exit, and they all followed her into the night at the witching hour. The palms of her hands popped and cracked with electricity.

She was ready to strike.

End of Book One

Did you enjoy Vault of Glass?

Authors always appreciate reviews, whether long or short.

Want more of Perrie and Vale? Be sure to check out Bride of Glass, Book Two, for the final epic installment in the Wicked Souls Duology!

He brought her to life. She is destruction. Together, they will take over the world.

Perrie Madeline failed to escape Quinsey Wolfe's Glass Vault, and she became trapped in her enemy's clutches. No longer the master of her own mind, Perrie serves a new purpose as the Bride. She is now bent on destroying the world with her demon lover—Vale.

Maisie Jaser is determined to save her cousin, even if it means forming an alliance with an old friend, one who makes her feel things she would rather forget. But as they embark on the journey through a trail of carnage left by the immortals, they soon realize that finding Perrie is more difficult than Maisie ever imagined.

With the world crumbling around them, and time running out, if Perrie doesn't break free from the Bride's hold over her, they will all face the consequences of Vale's triumph: annihilation.

Want another addicting dark fantasy romance? Try Clouded By Envy.

He only ever wanted to be human. She only ever wanted to save him. Sometimes the very thing you wish for, is your undoing...

Brenik has always been envious of his twin sister, Bray. Everything always came naturally to Bray, even after crossing through a portal from their fae world, while Brenik spent his time in her shadow. So, when Brenik discovers a way to get what he has always desired—to become human—he takes it. However, the gift turns out to be a curse that alters him in ways he never saw coming.

Bray can't help but be concerned for her brother, more so when he vanishes. While waiting for Brenik to return, she meets two brothers who realize she isn't human. Her dark bat-like wings are proof of that. But somehow, an aching bond forms between Bray and the hot older brother, Wes.

When Bray reunites with Brenik, she finds he has an overpowering need for blood stirring within him. If Bray doesn't help Brenik put an end to his curse, it will not only damage those who get close to him, but it could also destroy the steamy romance blooming between her and Wes.

Subscribe to Candace's Awesome Newsletter for the latest news and giveaways!

Join Candace's Facebook Group: Candace's Pretty Monsters

Check out Candace's books!

Wicked Souls Duology
Vault of Glass
Bride of Glass

Marked by Magic
The Bone Valley
Merciless Stars

Cruel Curses Trilogy
Clouded By Envy
Veiled By Desire
Shadowed By Despair

Faeries of Oz Series
Lion (Short Story Prequel)
Tin
Crow
Ozma
Tik-Tok

Cursed Hearts Duology
Lyrics & Curses
Music & Mirrors

Immortal Letters Duology
Dearest Clementine: Dark and Romantic Monstrous Tales
Dearest Dorin: A Romantic Ghostly Tale

Campfire Fantasy Tales Series
Lullaby of Flames
A Layer Hidden
The Celebration Game
Mirror, Mirror

These Vicious Thorns: Tales of the Lovely Grim
Between the Quiet
Hearts Are Like Balloons
Bacon Pie
Avocado Bliss

Vampires in Wonderland Series
Rav (Short Story Prequel)
Maddie
Chess
Knave

Demons of Frosteria Series
Frost Mate (Prequel Novella)
Frost Claim

Once Upon A Wicked Villain Series
Spindle of Sin

Acknowledgments

First, I would like to thank the readers who decided to pick up and read my book. A book is not an easy thing to do, so thank you for your support!

Next, I would like to thank my family. My husband for being supportive and letting me live out my dream. My daughter with her encouragement at such an early age. My parents for always being there for me.

To Amber H. for helping me so many times with this book! To Elle, Donna, Didi, Christis, Jenny, Patricia, Victoria, and Amber R. for being such amazing people.

Lastly, my history on growing up with horror movies, fairy tales, and real-life unsolved mysteries. I love a lot of retellings and wanted to combine the love of what I had for these things while growing up.

About the Author

Candace Robinson spends her days consumed by words and hoping to one day find her own DeLorean time machine. Her life consists of avoiding migraines, admiring Bonsai trees, watching classic movies, and living with her husband and daughter in Texas—where it can be forty degrees one day and eighty the next.

Connect with Candace:

Website: https://authorcandacerobinson.wordpress.com/
Facebook: https://www.facebook.com/literarydust
Twitter: https://twitter.com/literarydust
Instagram:
https://www.instagram.com/candacerobinsonbooks/
Goodreads:
https://www.goodreads.com/author/show/16541001.Candace
_Robinson or ignore that and just try searching for Candace Robinson!